I0762126

The Tandoori Box

David Powers

THE TANDOORI BOX

First Edition - March 2017
Second Edition - May 2026

This book is a work of fiction. Names, characters, places, and incidents are either a product of the author's imagination, or are used fictitiously. Any resemblance to actual persons, living or dead, business establishments, events, or locales is entirely coincidental.

Library of Congress Cataloging-in-Publication Data
Powers, David.
The tandoori box/David Powers.
269 p. 22 cm.

978-0-9914248-9-4 (hardcover)
978-0-9985447-0-0 (paperback)
978-0-9985447-1-7 (ebook)
979-8-9925863-4-3 (audiobook)

1. Science fiction. 2. Mystery fiction. 3. Fantasy fiction.
I. Title.

Library of Congress Control Number: 2017902070
Printed in the United States of America

Eerie Forest
www.eerieforest.com

For Edith and Hale Powers

ALSO BY DAVID POWERS

UNBURIED MEMORIES
TIDINGS FROM THE ABYSS
THE MAN FROM BUZZARD ROOST
PROTECT THE FLOCK
KIN AND CLAN
THE ARMAGEDDON DIARIES - ALICE AND JULIE

AFORE HOMO SAPIENS ROAMED PLANET EARTH, on the rugged highlands of what is now the East African country of Ethiopia, a troop of seventy baboons encircled a shining disk. The top-ranking member of their social hierarchy, a brutish, silver-white male known to his descendants as Cain, bared fearsome canine teeth and roared. As the Old World monkey knuckle-walked to the humming mass of extraterrestrial metal, he shook a sun-bleached antelope's thigh bone over his maned head in a threatening spectacle of masculine dominance. His harem vocalized displeasure by jumping high and smacking their lips. A few of the shrewdest females even presented their bright-pink rumps as a distraction. The baboons' guttural babbling—eerily humanlike in nature—did not forestall their savage leader from beating upon the ship's chromium skin with his crude club. Infuriated by the strangers invading his territory, Cain swatted aside his younger brother, Abel, who, ever the diplomat, tried to stop the escalating levels of aggression. Recessed in the sleek, curved side of the spacecraft, a mechanical iris glistened in the baking sunlight. The finely machined iridium blades winked open. Cain, lured by the intoxicating aromas of cooked meat and grain alcohol, dragged the antelope leg into the shadowy portal. Several moons later, he emerged from the interstellar ark on two feet and swinging a leather sack stuffed full of troubles. The man, hairless, tailless, and very conscious of his own superiority, now wielded an improved weapon—a sharpened spear. Here, in this cradle of humanity, he stood erect before his worshiping tribe. Cain raised a fist and shouted to any gods that would listen, "Hear me now, for I am here!"

Chapter One

ON WEDNESDAY MORNING, KENYA ALAN WATSON TUCKED the green Woodward Supermarkets reusable jute shopping bag under his elbow. He headed toward the main conference room in the east wing of Delphic Industrial Sciences' corporate offices. From the side and from a distance, the junior software engineer could pass for the famous actor Will Smith. Not the hunky, kick-ass mutant killer in the movie *I Am Legend*, but more in line with the tall, bony kid from *The Fresh Prince of Bel-Air* TV show. In the lengthy, industrial-carpeted corridor, he said hello to Joyce Benning. The director of Human Resources returned a friendly nod. He checked his digital wristwatch: 11:40 a.m. Kenya, always punctual, was twenty minutes early to his company's annual holiday party. In preceding years, the brass held the soiree crosstown at the swanky Radisson. This season, because of budget cuts (a direct result of executive management's exorbitant salary bumps and the seven-figure pay packages doled out to the greedy board of directors), the shindig was taking place in-house. No spouses or significant others were allowed. Without a "plus-one" to accompany him to the luncheon, or anywhere else, this new, restrictive stipulation imposed no personal impact.

Watson went into the breakroom, excusing himself as he wedged between a gaggle of clamorous mothers one-upping each other with exaggerated stories about their mischievous offspring. He tugged the refrigerator door open and inhaled the ghostly emanations of a thousand forgotten leftover lunches. After Kenya rummaged among the Styrofoam containers—some clown had relegated his potluck dish to the lower shelf—he shoved the tray of frozen Swedish meatballs into the tomato paste-splattered microwave oven. He set the timer for eight minutes on high. As the sizzling meat rotated on the glass platter, Watson contemplated the item he had purchased for this year's White Elephant gift. He hoped that whoever won his present would cherish it forever.

The Amazon Prime cardboard mailer had arrived at his apartment's doorstep two days ago. Kenya had sliced the sealing tape, opened the box, and popped the inflatable air pillows. He'd perused the comical image on the colorful package. Plastic blue jeans, no longer suspended by the unbuckled, shiny black belt, sagged below the pink cheeks of a perfectly rounded pair of androgynous buttocks. A cartoon gas cloud encapsulated the squiggly letters *PFFFFFTTTTT!* In the photo, a female hand model—the gender was easily determined by the long piano fingers and red nail polish—inserted George Washington's minted head into the simulated anus.

Watson had stumbled upon the Tushie Fun Farting Coin Drop Bank in the Toys & Games department on Amazon. The product description had stated: "Guaranteed to be hilarious" and "an excellent tool for teaching our youth how to save for the future." And what's more, the ass-shaped coin bank had scored four out of five stars with six hundred and seventy-eight mostly positive customer reviews (one disgruntled mom had alleged that her boy, Skyler, had started using his own fanny as a piggy bank). A comedian in the question section had inquired whether the device farted in Cambodian. Kong Thary, the helpful answerer, had written: "LOL! Don't you know farting is a universal language?" At $11.45, with AA batteries and free shipping included, the total price was close enough to the fifteen-dollar limit set for the White Elephant game.

The microwave's beeping brought him back to reality. Kenya withdrew the three-pound mix of ground beef and pork and recovered the steaming balls with plastic wrap. As he exited the breakroom, the loudest woman professed—to him, it sounded like bragging—that her daughter, Harper, had fed the family's pet bunny, Bella, to Butch, the neighbor's pit bull.

In the meeting room, coworkers laid out plates of food and placed their White Elephants on the red-and-green tablecloth. He found a prominent location to exhibit his meatballs—a narrow space bookended by a greasy bucket of Kentucky Fried Chicken and an aluminum cooking tray laden with sweating bratwurst. The email blast at the beginning of December had advised party participants to maintain donor anonymity by transporting their White Elephant offerings in bags. Kenya did not think it particularly mattered who submitted the entries. Nevertheless, he deposited his sheathed gift on the countertop and stood aside. Watson, always ill at ease around crowds, yearned to return to the solitude of his cubicle.

As Kenya waited for the festivities to kick off, Sally Green entered the room. The leggy young woman held a bag of baked tortilla chips and a paper sack containing her present. As her emerald eyes inventoried the attendees, he looked away, not wanting to be caught staring.

"Doctor Watson, I presume?" Russell Fisher greeted, smacking Kenya squarely on the shoulders.

"Hey, Russ," Watson responded. Fisher worked with him in the Mobile Applications Group.

Kenya hated being called "Doctor Watson." A bully in the third grade had been the first to nickname him that derogatory epithet, not after Sherlock Holmes' astute sidekick but for one of *The Muppet Show's* shaggy characters: the spectacled Baskerville the Hound. Brianna O'Reilly reveled in inflicting public indignities. Bitter memories of the girl's excruciating purple nurples and shameful atomic wedgies shriveled his testicles.

Kenya, seeing empty hands, asked the stout hardware engineer, "Where's your stuff?"

Russ used his fingers to comb his shock of red hair. "Valeska mixed batter for chocolate cupcakes, but she got tied up with the kids. Danika couldn't keep nothin' down. I mean, split pea soup was squirting out both ends. *Disgusting!* No rest for me and the missus with all the bellyaching going on. I did manage to bring a gift." He walked to the table and lifted a mass of crinkled tinfoil from a bag.

Kenya, curious to know if the misshapen blob hid a balled-up FREE MUSTACHE RIDES T-shirt or fake dog poo, said, "You're not supposed to show me which one is yours."

"Whatever, bro. How 'bout you? What delicacies have you cooked up? Pink tacos?"

Kenya pointed at the Swedish meatballs. The cream sauce had hardened to a crust resembling old saddle leather. He wondered if reheating might revive his dish.

Fisher, laying eyes on a more digestible substance, rubbed his palms and said, "That's Filipino lumpia. Give me a minute." First in line, he loaded his plate, drenching the fried rolls in sweet and sour sauce.

Again, Kenya peeped at Sally Green—smart, pretty, and way out of his league. Two weeks ago, he had initiated a conversation with her at the new Flavia Brewer. She had breezed into the breakroom as he'd endeavored to comprehend the fancy machine's controls. Disconcerted, Watson had dropped a hot chocolate Freshpack on the floor and, when hastily moving out of Sally's way, had stepped on the foil packet. Dove liquor—"Silky Smooth and Indulgent"—had spattered onto her shapely ankle and run into her fashionable pump. As he'd wadded paper towels and jabbered weak apologies, she'd stomped from the room, leaving a trail of brown footprints.

Russ returned, zeroed in on Kenya's focus of enthusiasm, and blurted, "Dude, that girl is smokin' hot! You should go ask her out."

The software engineer blushed and shushed, questioning whether true friendship abided within Russell's nature, or if he, too, had no one else to talk with.

Kenya thought of himself as a loser. It cannot be said that other people viewed him as an outcast. On the contrary, most workers respected his trenchant opinions and simple solutions more than he realized. Still, due to his stifling self-hatred and excessive emotional baggage, Watson projected a standoffish demeanor. It wasn't as if he didn't feel anything. He felt too much. This repressed behavior germinated from a horrific incident he'd experienced as a youth. To evade confronting his title role in this loathsome and reprehensible act, after school and on weekends, Kenya had locked himself in his bedroom. There, alone, he'd spent hours tearing apart transistor radios, video game consoles, and any other electronic equipment he could lay his nimble hands upon. Watson's fascination with understanding what made things tick had evolved into an obsession with computers and ultimately software coding. And since DIS's Information Technology Department brimmed with techies and nerds, nobody paid any mind to his social awkwardness.

Kenya spooned a double portion of his own meatballs and a dollop of macaroni salad onto the Rudolph the Red-Nosed Reindeer paper plate. Together, he and Russ wolfed down free food and guzzled generic soda pop. The cold, fatty, lumpy meatballs left a gamy aftertaste in his mouth. Later, at home, he planned to dig the meat's plastic shrink-wrap out of the garbage can and check the label for the sell-by date.

Sally passed in front of them. She eyed his unpopular dish with disfavor and scoffed, "What do we have here? Donkey balls?" Her friend snickered and snapped a photo of the food with her phone. Mortified that his milky balls were about to be posted on Instagram, Watson elected to ditch the tray and duck out.

As Kenya stood to depart, Pamela Cousins, the administrative assistant who had organized today's affair, crossed to the center of the room and held up her palms for silence. Flustered, he sat and shrouded his uneaten food under a napkin.

In her early sixties, Pamela relished slipping into high heels and short, tight-fitting dresses, all charged on a Forever 21 credit card. Up until three months ago, Cousins had acted as executive assistant to David Hutchings, Delphic's Chief Information Officer. After her humbling demotion (the CIO desired someone much, much younger), she now served as girl Friday for the Mobile Applications Group. On bad days—Monday through Friday, and Sunday afternoons if the New England Patriots lost—Pamela barely contained her resentment. If provoked, those around her might categorize her attitude as somewhat snippy.

But today, despite a persistent migraine and an ulcerated corn on her left baby toe, Pamela slipped on her game face. She trumpeted, "Welcome to the Delphic Industrial Sciences holiday party! Thank you for taking time from your busy schedules to join us in glorifying the birth of Jesus. This has been a trying year for everybody. I am sure that if you're like me, you are glad 2015 is almost at an end." Pamela massaged the hand grenade pulsing in her forehead. "Mr. Hutchings is in Belize on important company business. If David were here, he'd appreciate all your hard work!" She prayed that Sunshine Meadows, the CIO's new executive assistant, who was at this very moment soaking up the Central American heat in her skimpy string bikini, had neglected to pack sunblock—*or contraceptives.*

Many at the gathering peered intently at their smartphones or gazed longingly out the windows at the lunchtime traffic.

Pamela raised her voice a notch. "Now for this month's service award." She unfolded a sheet of notepaper and perched a pair of horn-rimmed bifocals on her aquiline nose. "This person was instrumental in the successful rollout of the Wildfire Project. Russell Fisher, please come forward."

Resentment squeezed Kenya's chest. He had put in the most overtime, knuckling down on this highly visible program. Russ came in late and left early each day, always making outrageous excuses concerning his wife and kids. Furthermore, Fisher took long liquid lunches, often not returning to the office. Watson pasted on a slanted smile and said, "Congratulations."

"Thanks, Doctor Watson!" Russ exclaimed. A big grin stretched across his flat face. "I cannot believe I won this for the second time!"

Pamela presented the Pinnacle Award to Russ, a twelve-inch-tall black obelisk with the words DELPHIC INDUSTRIAL SCIENCES - FOR OUTSTANDING ACHIEVEMENT engraved on the bronze plate. Additionally, he received a $75 gift certificate to Bennigan's and 1,000 shares of company stock (DIS was then valued at only 9 cents per share, but with the recent rumors of an impending IPO, only Warren Buffett could predict its eventual worth).

Kenya got the vibe that their boss, Marisa Lanka, favored Russ over her other team members. Fisher stopped by her office a dozen times a day, sympathetically touching—literally laying a hand upon her shoulder—on the status of her "blessed" autistic child, her "dear" mother's snowballing dementia, and her "darling" husband's endless job hunts. *It's a miracle either of them gets any work done.* Marisa saw Russ as indispensable—her right-hand man.

Pamela asked Marisa if she wished to speak to the department.

The head of the Mobile Applications Group, a pear-shaped woman dressed conservatively in a yellowish pantsuit, squinted at the tiny font on her Apple Watch and said, "Russell, we admire your single-minded efforts. You are consistently willing to go the extra mile. Russ faced numerous obstacles, yet he found innovative ways to overcome them. You are a truly. . . ."

Watson tuned out the accolades. He peeked at Sally. The business analyst was busy texting.

Marisa concluded her long-winded, plagiarized speech.

The strands of Pamela's multi-hued hairdo swept and swirled as she rolled a cart to the whiteboard. A spherical bingo cage filled with ping-pong balls rested on top. Last night, the admin labeled the pearly globes with each employee's name while jeering the dimwitted contestants on *Wheel of Fortune*.

A line of White Elephants paraded along the counter. The bags they arrived in were piled on the floor. Kenya recognized Russ' crinkled mess and, of course, his own contribution concealed in a newspaper, the Tushie Fun Farting Coin Drop Bank. The other entries—a few large, most small—were tastefully wrapped, except for a lone item still in a plastic sack.

"We're going to play a game," Pamela articulated, as if articulating to a shrewdness of apes. This party was one of the rare occasions when the admin retained a modicum of power, and she intended to make the most of the favorable circumstances. "Growing up, we used the terms 'Dirty Santa' or 'Cutthroat Christmas.' You locals may refer to this game as 'Yankee Swap.' Nowadays, they call it the 'White Elephant Gift Exchange.' Listen carefully to the rules."

"Nasty Christmas," Russ whispered to Kenya.

"Nasty what?" Watson questioned.

Fisher made an obscene gesture with his right middle finger and his cupped left palm. "During the holidays, my mom loved to play Nasty Christmas."

Kenya had seen Russ' mother drop off her son before work in a flashy convertible Mercedes. His skin flushed as he remembered the Tareyton 100's cigarette jutting from her pouting lips and the silicone implants ballooning from her too-tight tube top.

Pamela inclined her head at the bingo cage. "The first random individual I select gets to choose and open any of these goodies. Then, the second contestant picks out a wrapped White Elephant or takes the previous person's gift. If yours is 'stolen,' you earn a new turn." She monitored the wall clock. "Since we need to be back at work by one, the same present can only be stolen once."

Harvey Grubman inquired, "Who came up with these rules? At Microsoft, we—"

"These are *my* rules, Harvey," Pamela interrupted. "There are many versions of White Elephant. We don't have time to discuss your tickle-torture sessions with Bill Gates."

Grubman dared to ask again. "How do we know when the game is finished?" He scratched a pimple on his chin and sniffed his fingernails. "I've got an agile software development meeting to prepare for."

"Harv, I was coming to that," Pamela snapped. "It's really easy. When the last contestant is holding the last White Elephant, the game is over. *Finito.* Everyone returns to work." She adjusted her sleeves. "Any more questions?"

Just as Susan Thorpe shyly lifted her hand, Pamela turned a blind eye. The intern self-consciously lowered her arm.

As the admin cranked the shaft, the clacking bingo cage spun on its axis, and the twenty-three plastic orbs poured down the brass ribs. One by one, the little dipper collected each ping-pong ball and dumped it into the ramp running beneath the apparatus.

Kenya felt a nervous pang as Pamela rolled a ball to read the name. He despised being first and making a fool of himself. Watson exhaled when she called out, "Jack Gantz!"

"Handsome Jack"—his pet name around the office—put his plate on the seat and sauntered to the table. The quality assurance manager hefted a couple of the gifts, shaking the packages close to his ear in playful attempts to guess their contents. Pamela twiddled her hoop earrings as Gantz settled upon an elongated piece. He ripped off the paper.

Pamela testily instructed, "Hold it up so we all can see!"

Jack raised a set of six flameless tea lights; the dented, retaped boxes were glaring indications of a re-gift. The curly-haired Apollo boasted, "These babies are safe alternatives to candles!"

Pamela scooped up another ball. "Harvey Grubman!" The pockmarked scrum master snatched Jack's LED candles and scurried out the door.

"Well, I'll be screwed, blued, and tattooed," Pamela said to herself. "Jack, come on up and help yourself to something else."

This opportunity, Gantz freed a cylindrical object. "Two-Buck Chuck!" he announced and pretended to drink from the bottle of wine. "Booyah!"

"Trader Joe's boosted the price!" Milton Mumford declared jovially. "It's now Three-Buck Chuck." Mumford's turn came next. The network architect swiped Jack's 750 milliliters of budget vino.

To the amazement and glee of all the participants in the room, Jack Gantz held high his consequent selection: a SHART SURVIVAL KIT.

The entertainment continued. During the thirty minutes before Kenya got his chance, he witnessed Frank Walker, a senior project manager, pulling a latex Horse Head Mask over his bald dome, Suzy Thorpe opening a bag of Unicorn Farts (Russ' improvised gift of pink cotton candy), Fisher raving about his Big Gulp toilet bowl-shaped ceramic coffee mug, and Pamela Cousins' Naughty Pigs salt and pepper shaker set—this raunchy prize winning the loudest applause. Kenya's entry, the Tushie

Fun Farting Coin Drop Bank, went to Gregory Barnes, who appeared overjoyed. Sally Green—likewise thrilled—picked a $20 Starbucks gift card.

There were two submissions remaining when Pamela pronounced Kenya's name. Aware that time was limited, he rushed to the table. Neither of the unwanted entries looked promising—both were unpretentious and unimaginatively wrapped. The software engineer grabbed the nearest parcel and undid the creased birthday paper. He glumly read the pocket-size package of Emergency Underpants, "Ideal for travel, sauna, and sports. Always ready to use."

Walter Conrad, the newly hired senior software engineer, took one glance at the final gift—a squarish block inside a plastic sack—and bellowed, "Kenya, gimme those doggone panties! That roach-coach breakfast burrito tore me up. Give it here! I need those hip huggers *tout de suite!*"

Drowned out by his coworkers' laughter, Kenya Watson slipped his fingers into the polybag's looped handle. As kismet would have it, the last White Elephant was his.

Chapter Two

A FAINT BUZZING WOKE KENYA. Startled, he thought an intruder had broken into the apartment. Then, he surmised his cellphone was vibrating. Watson, bleary-eyed and with a pounding heart—most nighttime calls were unpleasant news—checked the nightstand. Below the green charging symbol, the iPhone's screen showed only the time and date: 12:01, Thursday, December 17. He gave the rectangular device a shake. The noise had originated from the living room or the kitchen.

Kenya, wearing baggy boxers, scratched his close-cropped dark brown hair. He flipped the light switch and entered the short hallway leading to the kitchen. Watson's abdomen registered the dull soreness of a full bladder, but he could not answer the call of nature without first establishing the genesis of the annoyance.

In the kitchen, under the fluorescent tubes' electric hum, the shifting sound waves made it harder for him to home in on the source. Louder than the hiss of refrigerant pumping through the refrigerator's compressor, the whizzing came nearer in tone and volume to water swooshing in the dishwasher during the rinse cycle or the grinding purr of the microwave's thousand-watt magnetron. He crawled along the linoleum in pursuit of the culprit. The cadence swelled and peaked before floating away into the ether. *It's not coming from any of the kitchen appliances.*

Kenya tilted his head. Now, less mechanical and more animate, the steady drone prompted memories of the hellish week he had spent as a youngster camping with his family in upstate New York. Not one to plan ahead, his father had made the huge blunder of scheduling their vacation on the seventeen-year emergence of the Onondaga Brood of periodical cicadas. Kenya and his younger brother, Edward, snug as bugs in thermal sleeping bags, had risen to the alarming "chorus" of a zillion horny male insects flexing their tymbals. Beyond the shelter of the tent, hordes of voracious nymphs had decimated the park's maple and oak trees. Over the campfire, Mom's asparagus and goat cheese omelet had slid from the iron skillet, "organically seasoned"—Dad's not-so-funny euphemism for locust excrement.

In the living room, Kenya felt the vented lids of the television set and cable box. Both electronics were running in hibernation mode and were cool to the touch. The wall-mounted steam radiator was silent, the portable space heater beside his easy chair was unplugged, and the air-conditioning unit was turned off for the winter.

As Watson raised the double-hung window sash to listen outside, the humming ceased. He turned his cheek from the cold draft and scanned the space. *Was that noise inside my own mind?* Bewildered, he urinated, replenished his digestive tract with a glass of tap water, and went back to sleep.

At work, on the way to concoct his morning cup of hot chocolate, Kenya saw the Tushie Fun Farting Coin Drop Bank on a shelf in Gregory Barnes' cubicle. Since no one was around, he jiggled the plastic rump, pleased to hear the jingle of loose coins. Watson extracted a penny from his pocket and poked the Lincoln head into the rubber orifice. This covert action culminated in a fulfilling eruption of realistic flatulence—a nice, juicy one. He hurried along the hall, giggling into his palm.

The elevator opened, and Sally Green emerged, struggling to keep the laptop bag strap on her shoulder. Kenya synchronized his stride with her arrival at the breakroom. He reached for the door handle.

"Thanks," Sally said. She placed her satchel on the sideboard. "The traffic was bad—fucking ridiculous. It took me an hour and a half to drive here." She consulted her wristwatch and scowled. "My boss will be pissed. Jim wanted me to update the requirements spreadsheet for our meeting with Frank Walker."

"I heard a truckload of soup spilled on the I-95," Kenya mumbled. The semi wreck happened on Maine's major highway, so he surmised that Sally resided in the northern section of Portland—out in the sticks. "On the radio, the state police said a drunkard riding a Harley lost control and lay down his bike in front of the rig. The truck driver tried to swerve, but the cab jackknifed and hit an overpass."

Sally, in remembrance of the gruesome accident, grimaced in revulsion. "Yeah, a god-awful mess. The biker's guts soaked right through the sheet. Not something you want to see before your first cup of coffee." She armed the Flavia machine with a Freshpack and stuck a DO EPIC SHIT! mug underneath the spout. Her French-manicured fingers pressed buttons as if dialing long distance. "Last time we were in here, you destroyed my favorite shoes."

"Sorry," Kenya stammered. The business analyst wore the same pair of black high heels. They looked fine to him. His eyes lingered on her glittering ankle bracelet. "I—"

Sally cut him off. "Don't sweat it." The brewer fizzed and gave a final sputter. His coworker stirred in three half-and-halfs and sprinkled a sunny packet of granulated cancer into the miniature whirlpool. She blew steam from the java's surface. "They weren't actually ruined. The stain wiped away with a little spit and polish." She raised her foot and twisted the slender anklebone up and down. "See? Good as new."

"I'm glad the chocolate washed off," Kenya said, enjoying the show.

"Me too." Sally clutched her bag. "Well, off I go to get reamed out."

He waved goodbye. "The traffic wasn't your fault. Accidents do happen."

She grinned. "Tell that to my lawyer."

"Marisa is such a bitch," Russell Fisher grumbled. "She allocated me to another project."

Fisher loved to complain. Griping was what he did best. Russ grew up in Peoria, Illinois, where, as a rising star on the high school gymnastics team, a gang of older boys cornered him in the locker room. Most people would be appalled to learn how half a pack of Marlboro Lights and a virtually empty Winnie-the-Pooh butane lighter hindered this budding tumbler's cerebral maturation and, as a result, permanently modified his adult personality. He never communicated to anyone what transpired—not even his nana—and it took him many years to bury this hurtful humiliation deep within the layers of his subconscious. At this point in his life and career, as a full-time pessimist and a part-time masochist, only a patient hypnotherapist had any hope of unearthing the root cause of Russ' mental issues.

Despite his multifarious problems, at the very center of Fisher's ethical core, he was a good man. However, and not to his fault, Russ did not know this yet.

Kenya, lacking the intestinal fortitude to enact change, mutely put up with his teammate's carping. He nibbled the dry peanut butter sandwich and remarked, "Being the golden boy has its disadvantages. What did she give you?"

"Sharktank."

"What's that?"

Russ smirked. “If I told you, I’d have to kill you.” He chugged a liter of flat Dr Pepper. “That megalomaniac has me working on twelve assignments at the same time.”

Watson dumped the remains of his flavorless lunch into the trash. He had lost his appetite upon hearing that Marisa had put Fisher on Sharktank, a project that he himself hadn’t been included in, much less briefed on, as part of her team. To end this subject, Kenya said, “The White Elephant gift you received was a riot.”

“What am I going to do with a crapper coffee cup?” Russ inquired. He tugged down his sleeve to hide the unsightly scars of self-harm. “So asinine.”

“You liked the mug before. The toilet is good for a laugh. Give it to your wife.”

“Valeska will strangle me if I bring that gag gift home. Slavs don’t have a sense of humor—anyway, my Slav doesn’t.”

Fisher once informed Watson that he had found his stunning wife in a Belarusian mail-order bride catalog and that his teenage daughters, the even-tempered Danika and Zoria, the powder keg, had been included in the package at no additional charge.

Just when Kenya got up the nerve to ask if he could have the Lilliputian commode, Russ questioned, “And what about your present, that lame box? What in the world is that thing?”

Yesterday, as the holiday party had wound down, Watson removed his gift from the plastic bag, held it aloft, and inquired, “Anybody have any clue what this is?”

Deiter Steuben—habitually politically incorrect—had shouted, “Feel the braille! You’re the proud owner of Helen Keller’s Rubik’s Cube!”

Pamela, wobbling her impressive Technicolor beehive in ethical disapproval, had the German national help her load the cart with the unused plates, utensils, and napkins.

Following the potluck, Kenya returned to his cubicle and examined his reward. Steuben had been right. The square block did approximate a Rubik's Cube in shape, although its dimensions were slightly smaller by several millimeters and decidedly denser—not made of cheap plastic. Unlike the archetype three-dimensional combination puzzle's six colors, this object was black, neither flat nor shiny. A blue glimmer flashing along the box's edge had produced a small shock. *Static electricity?* Watson had rubbed his boots on the rug, unable to duplicate the effect. He felt gypped. *Everybody else walked away with something decent, or at least amusing.* Miffed, Kenya had thrown his gift in the sack and brought it home.

Kenya turned to Fisher. "It's a stupid box. How about I trade you for the toilet bowl?"

"Nah. Not interested." Russ, fishing for meat with the tip of his pinkie, flossed a fingernail between his crooked teeth. He sucked and swallowed. "At least I'm sure what mine is, Doctor Watson."

Once again, buzzing alerted Kenya. He repeated his actions of the prior night by picking up his cellphone and noting the time and date: 12:01, Friday, December 18. Rather than investigating the commotion, he shut his eyelids and plunged into the same dream. This recurring nightmare featured an ex-girlfriend whom he suspected of cheating. Possessed by desire, he begged: *Please take me back. We can make it work. I'll do anything!* Then came the frenzied warnings: *That's it! I can't take it anymore. If you leave me, I'll kill myself!* His screamed rant always regressed into this repetitive mantra: *I want to kill you! I will kill you! I am killing you. . . .* These horror shows always ended with his trembling hands wrapped around her two-timing throat.

Kenya sat on the mattress, grumpily staring out the frosted bedroom window. He daydreamed of pointing a .50 caliber rifle into the sky and firing a projectile—a smart bullet—that could somehow locate and explode his ex-girlfriend's deceitful skull.

The clouds had dispersed. Icicle stalactites sparkled from the rain gutters. Kenya heard the landlord's snowblower on the sidewalk outside the apartment. It was nearly nine o'clock. On normal Saturday mornings, he seldom chose to sleep this late. Unrefreshed, his eyeballs grated in their sockets, and his brow ached as though the thin skin had spent the night clenched in anger.

In the well-lit bathroom, Kenya splashed water on his hollow cheekbones. He put on his Coke-bottle eyeglasses. For an uncomfortable moment, the stooped man appraised his reflection in the mirror. *Haggard.* At thirty-one years of age, he looked beaten. "Ridden hard and put away wet," as his dad often drawled. Watson's pallor emphasized the dark circles—bagfuls of dirty laundry—under his bloodshot brown eyes. Ashamed, he swung away from the glass.

At the kitchen table, Kenya munched a bowl of Froot Loops while reading the back of the cereal box. An anthropomorphic, big-nosed tropical bird roosted in the basket of a boy's red bicycle. The furiously pedaling clean-cut lad beamed at any adults hungering to invest in sugar commodities. Sam, the crafty toucan, aimed to sell carloads of the round, fortified nuggets of tooth decay by offering free Day-Glo SAFETY FIRST stickers. Apathetic and depressed, he knocked over the carton. A peloton of varicolored loops spun off the countertop and rolled beneath the refrigerator.

What shall I do today? Kenya kicked around notions to kill time. *Should I go see a movie?* None of the Marvel or DC Comics action flicks playing seemed worth sitting in a darkened theater with a bunch of complete strangers. *A leisurely drive down the coast to Old Orchard Beach?* That jaunt would necessitate filling the Honda Civic's gas tank. He was short of cash. Moreover, it must have snowed a foot overnight. *I'll get into an accident.* These lackluster brainstorms had slim prospects of happening anytime soon. Watson yawned, anticipating a long nap.

On the beige couch by the bay window, Kenya sorted the mail. He built twin stacks of correspondence: bills and junk. A purple envelope fit neither collection. Hand-addressed to Kenya Watson, the letter had a Portland postmark of the sixteenth of December. He tore off the edge instead of throwing it on the junk heap. The folded notebook paper contained a smudge of yellow sauce and the two scrawled words: *FORGIVE ME.* Watson did not recognize the cramped handwriting. He shredded the ominous message and tossed it into the trash.

A musk redolent of sodden earth, zesty mustard (Grey Poupon?), and burned motor oil tickled Kenya's nostrils. He turned to the windowsill, where he saw his White Elephant. With the heel of his palm, he pushed up the sash to air out the room. The polybag flapped in the brisk breeze, exposing the black box and rousing his curiosity. *What is that?*

Kenya nestled the bag on his lap. The item felt warm, no doubt from lying in the sun. He reached into the sack and saw the words HEAVEN IS WHERE ALL CHEFS ARE INDIAN stamped in purple ink onto the inside of the plastic. Kenya pulled out the baffling cube and set it on the end table.

The interior of the bag preserved the tang of strong spices. Watson, hoping for instructions, shook out three pictures and one crumpled receipt. The takeout order totaled one combo plate of chicken curry and shrimp saag, plus a side of garlic naan. The name of the restaurant, THE TANDOORI HOUSE AND MEAT SHOP, along with the address—some place in the Old Port Exchange district—headed the top of the printed sales slip. He rolled up the paper and threw it at the wastebasket. The ball bounced off the rim.

Kenya lifted the first photograph. It was congruent in size and shape with the instant film designed for Polaroid cameras: a four-sided image surrounded by white borders, with the bottom border wider. His dad had owned an SX-70, the cowhide-clad model that whirred and spat square mysteries out the front. He frequently took snapshots on family holidays or at his children's birthday parties. As a boy, Kenya delighted in watching the murky colors gradually develop into distinguishable forms before his wonder-stricken eyes. This glossy print showed Watson slumped at his desk, a hand propping up his drooping head. *Ha! Who snapped a picture of me nodding off? Russ?*

There can be junctures in a lifetime when a person is unsure whether they are conscious or asleep and dreaming. For this man, the next moment marked a pivotal point in his existence.

Kenya picked up the second photograph. Taken again at the office, this time in the breakroom, Sally Green—as alluring as ever in a blue blouse and short, black skirt—stood at the Flavia Brewer aligning her DO EPIC SHIT! coffee cup beneath the dispenser while selecting options on the menu screen with her free hand. Sally glanced over her shoulder at him, a gleaming smile on her face. His mouth hung open as if he had just cracked an extremely clever quip. He remembered yesterday's scene quite vividly, thinking back on their private encounter, his mind endlessly replaying every word. Kenya recalled Sally's comment about the traffic accident and the grin on her face as she left. But he had no recollection of her appearing remarkably happy while pumping liquid caffeine.

Who shot the photo? Weren't we by ourselves in the breakroom?

Somebody else *must* have been there with a camera or phone. Sally and I were busy gabbing. We simply did not notice them. *Right?*

Wait, a minute. Something is not adding up. I took this bag home on Wednesday night, *after* the party. Sally and I talked in the breakroom on Thursday morning. *How the hell did the pictures get in here?*

Watson unlocked the deadbolt to his apartment and peered into the second-floor hallway—empty, except for the rubbish bin and four green potted plants. At the window, he gazed downward—fifteen feet to the ground. There were no fresh footprints in the snowbank. *Maybe the storm covered them.* One more time, he inspected all the locks, doors, and window frames, finding no marks of forced entry. Not satisfied that he was indeed alone, Kenya plucked a knife from the butcher block and checked inside the closets, behind the shower curtain, and under the bed.

In the living room, Watson seized the third photo. Shot on a day as bright as today, he stood on the end of the Maine State Pier. Kenya identified the Portland Harbor locality by the red-and-orange sign for the Casco Bay Lines Ferry Terminal in the background. In July, he attended a reggae concert at this venue. The photographer's point of view skimmed the water, as though composed while sitting in a kayak or lying upon a paddleboard. Watson studied the expression etched on his lean face. Did he see joy there, or did the relaxed lips indicate relief?

In the image by the bay, Kenya wore an unzipped winter jacket. A red Sea Dogs T-shirt, a free souvenir from one of the city's minor league baseball team's home games, was clearly visible underneath the green Gore-Tex. In the bedroom closet, Watson yanked the lid off the wicker laundry hamper, dug to the dank bottom, and held up the cheesy, cotton giveaway. Last week had been the first time he had worn this pullover. Hawaiian teriyaki sauce splotched the front. And the strangest part? This T-shirt, *his* Sea Dogs T-shirt, *was white, not red.*

Kenya dragged the shirt across the tiles and slumped into his upholstered chair. He looked up, hardly recognizing the glassy-eyed man reflected in the television's blank screen. *How do you know if you are clinically deranged? Is the onset of mental sickness comparable to a squirm of pork tapeworms slowly burrowing into your brain? Or does madness hit you as quick as a grand piano dropped from the thirteenth floor?*

Watson pinched his forearm—hard enough to bruise. Then he slapped his face on both cheeks. Kenya opened his eyes and winced. Either awake or dreaming, he saw that nothing had changed. The goddamned box and the impossible pictures were still with him. *Yes, it is true. I am crazy.*

Chapter Three

KENYA, WARMED BY A GREEN GOOSE-DOWN PARKA (white Sea Dogs T-shirt beneath) and a blue ski cap, jogged to the terminus of the long Maine State Pier. His hand clenched what his intellect now christened but was not ready to utter aloud—the *Tandoori Box.* To anyone watching his actions, the man's stance resembled that of an Olympian hammer thrower. Without thinking twice, Watson held the plastic bag's handles and spun in a tight circle. As his weight shifted from his left to his right leg, he released his fingers. The fluttering sack arced high over the bay. A loud kerplunk, followed by circular ripples, proved the cursed anomaly had been real. *Problem solved.*

Screened from the wind in the indoor garage, Kenya gazed at the bizarre photograph of himself on the wharf. For some curious reason, he had kept the three pictures. *Because Sally Green is in one of them? Did fate, mere coincidence, or my own doing guide me to the same spot overlooking the bay? I could have disposed of the box anywhere. Why didn't I chuck it in the dumpster behind my apartment building? I should've flung the White Elephant out of the car window on the way here. Let a diligent dog owner scoop up the square turd and bring it home.* He regarded himself in the rear-view mirror. *And what made me put on this dirty sports team shirt?*

Watson grinded the transmission into first and floored the little four-banger. The Honda shimmied and shook on the black ice. *No, by god. I am in control of my own destiny.*

The diving barge drifted above the underwater kelp forest. On the rugged coastline, a black-and-white lighthouse perched on the brink of a high cliff. Revolving carbon-arc lamps cast halos of hope across the placid water. Sailors outfitted in greasy overalls hand-cranked the dual wheels of a manual pump. Humid air forced through the coiled hose fogged the glass portholes in Kenya's cumbersome copper and brass helmet. The cigar-smoking divemaster gave the thumbs-up signal to a crane operator. As the boom swiveled Kenya overboard, the crests of the bigger waves wet his lead boots. With great puffs of steam and an abrupt dunk, the squeaking winch lowered him into the indigo ink. Kenya hung limply as the weight belt did the work, towing him down fathom by fathom. A sharp chill penetrated the canvas diving suit's flimsy insulation. Frayed from overuse, the rubberized seams leaked needle-thin jets of seawater. At the mirrored surface, toothy sea creatures circled an oozing bucket of chum. Nearing five hundred meters, a yellow mark on the corroded cable indicated halfway, the definitive point of no return. Far below his dangling ankles, the submarine ridge remained an unimaginable destination. Kenya craned his throat upward, seeing the thick wire diminish into a silken thread. The stiff shoes filled with frigid water as the pressure compressed the khaki twill against his perspiring skin. Unexpectedly, the helmet's tinny headphones crackled with a man's familiar voice. "Son, can you hear me?" Kenya's lips locked shut, afraid his response might come out as a shriek. Outraged, his father accused, "Boy, it's all your fault!" Kenya pleaded into the microphone, "Dad, I didn't mean to. Please forgive me!" An eerie keening preceded the final burst of static. Brown seaweed snagged the unraveling umbilical cord, suspending the diver ten feet above the ocean floor.

Kenya detached the air and communication lines, unhooked the tricky harness, and sank into the soft sand. His oversized gloves fumbled with the waterproof torch. The bright light illuminated a past adventurer's trail of crisp footprints across the undulating seabed. Barnacles pockmarked the shell of a Honda Civic rotting upon the dead coral reef. A bloated shape wearing a cowboy hat was strapped into the driver's seat. "Something is coming to get me!" a hysterical woman—*his mother?*—screeched from the disconnected speakers. Kenya sucked in one last lungful of air before unbolting the round helmet and shrugging off the bulky suit. He joined a school of silvery herrings swimming into a sloping trench. Eons of shipwrecks—their pirated bounties pouring out of riven hulls—littered the fringes of his peripheral vision. The lack of oxygen seared his bronchi and muddied his cerebrum. *Would an impulsive inhalation of saltwater cure my woes forever?* A sunken Russian merchant vessel teetered on the rim of an abyssal plane. Kenya dolphin-kicked into the cavernous hold and up into a large bubble of stale air. Upended cargo containers, crates, and bales were pitched against the concave hull. The nethermost regions of the ship's storage area pulsed with toxic phosphorescence. Surrounded by teeming biodiversity, superheated sulfuric gas bubbled from a mile-long hydrothermal vent. As Earth's groaning tectonic plates separated, every ounce of water drained into the gaping crevice. Kenya, gulping in pure air, kneeled on the bedrock of a vast oceanic basin. His fingers dug into the shifting sediment, dredging up a small black cube.

Kenya awoke on guard and filled with consternation. Goose bumps covered his forearms. The short bristles at the nape of his neck stood up and saluted. Palpable dread permeated the bedroom, the overpowering foreboding that compels a rational being to yank the wool overhead, press their face into the pillow, and beg absolution from their deity of the day. This man was not that sort of believer—not figuratively an atheist, but undeniably an agnostic. Watson put on his eyeglasses, tugged up the elasticized waist of his boxers, grabbed a baseball bat, and charged down the hallway.

Still dressed in the same Sea Dogs T-shirt—bushed, he had gone to bed as soon as he had returned from the bay—Kenya toggled on a light switch. He saw the hour on the thermostat: 12:02 a.m. Electrical fumes congested the living room, a metallic odor reminiscent of the time he'd inadvertently blocked the ventilation slots on the cable box with a pile of magazines. Similar yet not identical, the underlying scent stank of burning hair. Or worse—*flesh.*

Kenya ran straight to the bay window, not altogether shocked to find the sack he had heaved into the harbor yesterday afternoon. Wisps of waxy effluvium spiraled out of the polybag as the infernal buzzing intensified. He spread the plastic handgrips, inverted the bag, and unloaded the contents. A paper receipt fluttered to the carpet as the smoking Tandoori Box bounced on the couch cushion and rolled to a standstill under a pillow. The tan cotton glowed as the fibers ignited.

"Jesus!" Watson shouted, darting to the sink. At the faucet, he stamped his feet, waiting for the spaghetti pot to fill. Flames leaped to the fabric on the curved armrest. In a red haze of panic, Kenya tripped as he flew from the kitchen. His body off-center, the water spray failed to extinguish the blaze with a direct hit. The cube sizzled and steamed as a corner charred the yellow stuffing. He used oven mitts to shove the overheated block back into the polybag and, like a hot potato, tossed it onto the windowsill. Even though the fire was out, the Tandoori Box continued to be a wasp nest of discontent. Watson retreated, his egress impeded by the dining room table. A shapeless substance expanded the sides of the translucent bag. Kenya's eyes widened in terror as the nebulous blob flopped violently—*a fish?*—

and then, its protruding mouth sucking the polyethylene amniotic sac, lay dormant.

Kenya, resolved to crush the alien being, approached the loveseat, brandishing the Louisville Slugger. When he raised the wooden club above his head, the end grazed the popcorn ceiling. Chips of stucco flaked onto his hair and shoulders. Indecision swayed his determination. *The cushions are bouncy. What if I miss?* Watson reversed the bat and, holding his breath, hooked the knob through the polybag's loops.

Kenya mimicked the moves of a rattlesnake handler by carrying the sack on the stick's tip. He opened the front door one-handedly and entered the hallway. The potted houseplants wilted underneath the flickering ceiling lights. *They were okay yesterday.* On the stairwell landing, Watson faltered. *Where am I going? I'm not getting into the car with this thing again. Hurl the cube in the swimming pool or hot tub? They're both drained for winter. Dumpster? The garbageman doesn't come until Friday.* Conceivably, he could bury the square block in the garden or, since the ground was frozen, leave it in the laundry room for one of his neighbors to happen upon.

Pinholes in the plastic's welded seams dribbled inky liquid onto the sidewalk.

Almeta Lampert, an elderly resident on the lower level and an active member of the Neighborhood Watch, peeked out of her doorway. She recognized the lurker and put down the sawed-off shotgun. "Good morning, Kenya."

He tried to hide his prize behind his back. "Hi, Mrs. Lampert. What, may I ask, are you doing up at this hour?"

On the stoop, she massaged her wrinkled elbows. "Myalgia—couldn't sleep a wink. Heard a noise and decided to take a look before dialing 911." The octogenarian clasped the collar of her quilted bathrobe. "Hun, you'll catch your death of cold out there. What have you got in the bag? Is that a dead puppy?"

"No, ma'am. Just taking out the trash."

The woman sniffed. "Well, you're making a mess. Please don't hold it over the walkway. What's that putrid smell?"

"Must be this can of bacon drippings, Mrs. Lampert. The cooking oil turned rancid."

As she went indoors, Almeta advised, "Put on a jacket, and keep away from fried foods. Saturated fat will give you heart disease."

Watson dutifully held the bag above the snow and considered his options. Each solution flashing through his brain involved pulverizing the Tandoori Box.

Along with a well-equipped gym, the Baxter Woods apartment complex provided a half-size basketball court. The green rectangle twinkled under the security spotlight. Kenya laid the sack on a bare section by the free-throw line. He stepped backward and lifted the bat.

Aroused, the thing in the bag hissed.

Watson paused. The cube had practically torched his apartment. He still detected the smoke on his clothes. Was the Tandoori Box angered by his failed attempt to eliminate it? *Ludicrous! It is not cognizant. It's a meaningless White Elephant gift! But then again, as burning alive ranks number one on my list of the greatest phobias, can I afford to take this chance?*

Kenya swung the Louisville Slugger at the twitching lump. Right on target, the white ash snapped on impact. Split in two, the barrel skittered across the slick playing surface and smacked the basketball hoop support. The metal pole pealed like a call for the faithful to come to church. Watson collapsed on a bench. He sensed dampness beneath his nose. His wrist came away red.

Drops of Kenya's paranasal blood spattered the concrete as he parted the plastic with the bat's splintered edge. He expected to see the shattered Tandoori Box. His mind refused to conjure an image of what more the bag might contain—*something else, something. . . .*

No squashed cuttlefish or decapitated python coiled within the sack—only a dented white takeout carton beside a disposable knife and fork wrapped in brown napkins. As Kenya gaped, the Styrofoam popped up, the molded cups reforming into their original shapes. Fascinated, he pressed upon the clamshell lid to disengage the catch. The top sprang up, exposing. . .*zilch.* The container was empty, excluding a few morsels of basmati rice and a greenish dash of tambuli gravy.

Where is the Tandoori Box? The fucking box is lying where I threw it—on the seafloor with all the other garbage. Then what am I doing out here in the middle of the night freezing my ass off? This is a bad dream. I must wake up now. Yet Kenya felt certain—his palms stung from the big-league swing—that he was wide awake.

His dad's mother had unmasked disturbing traits toward the end of her life. When Kenya was in third grade, Grandma Eleanor went missing several times. Reported on the local news channel, these incidents induced much disruption and embarrassment. One summer evening, the police found Meemaw floating face down in Evans Pond at Wallworth Park. Not drowned, she merely "fancied a midnight skinny-dip." Eleanor could not recall how she had gotten to a public park thirteen miles from her home. And then there was his mom's brother, who was never referred to at family gatherings in anything higher than a whisper. Last month, the night nurse at the upscale Sunny Side assisted living facility discovered Uncle Elliot prowling the women's memory wing. The attendant, realizing the bearded panty raider was not a resident, called the sheriff's department. These days, Uncle Elliot was undergoing psychiatric observation at Princeton House. Mental illness coursed throughout both of his bloodlines. Watson muttered, "I am losing my mind."

A square object shifted at the base of the takeout box. Kenya nudged aside the puffy grains—*are they moving?*—and slid his fingernail under the edge. He flipped the thick paper, even now knowing what it was—a photograph.

Kenya identified himself in this image by the bulbous contours of his head and the rumpled sleeves of his white T-shirt (correct color this time). In the picture, he walked along the footpath leading to the basketball court. His outstretched arm held the leaky bag over the lawn. At the corner of the frame, he spied Mrs. Lampert's pink hair rollers and flowery robe. The aerial perspective paralleled the angle of a swooping barn owl or a hovering drone rigged with a high-definition camera. Watson's eyes shot upward, only glimpsing a slice of the Moon and the trillion stars sparkling in the Milky Way galaxy.

Flurries stuck to his clothes as leaden clouds covered the upper atmosphere. Kenya noticed a stripe of melted snow alongside the walkway. Near the building, a larger patch had yellowed where he was chatting with Mrs. Lampert. Ribbons of earthworms wriggled across the wet cement as if escaping a forest fire—an astonishing sight in the dead of winter.

On Sunday morning, the Tandoori Box reclaimed its rightful place on a bay windowsill inside the Baxter Woods apartments with a blue flash and a muffled bang. Kenya did not see or hear any of this. After he beheld the mass invertebrate exodus, he ran up to his room, packed a duffel bag with necessities, and hustled outside. Scared to tears, Watson had spent the rest of the Sabbath driving aimlessly, worrying about the Tandoori Box, and pondering what he should do next.

The sun revealed its orange crown as Kenya pulled the Honda into a parking space at the rear of a Walmart Supercenter on Monday morning. He notified Marisa by email that he was not feeling well—a true statement—and would not be in to work. The exhausted young man climbed over the center console and tumbled into the backseat. Insulated by Grandma Eleanor's afghan blanket, he fell into a fitful sleep.

Kenya arose shivering and lonesome. The windowpanes were fogged with his respiration. Metal banged the Civic's fender. He used a sleeve to swab the drool from his mouth and the condensation off the glass. A cooing mother extricated her colicky infant from a car seat. Watson, abashed by the tiger mom's icy stare, stretched the green and yellow yarn over his face. When she had departed, he got out of the automobile and trudged through the parking lot.

Within the discount department store, Kenya washed up in the restroom sink. He blew his nose in a tissue, relieved to see only a residual glob of dried blood. Watson bought an Extra Value Meal at the built-in McDonald's. He fretted about his distressing circumstances at a table across from a grizzled man dunking hash-browned potatoes in ketchup and sluggishly licking off the red paste with his flaccid tongue. Kenya was surprised to see that the car's odometer had recorded an additional 300 miles. The only thing he remembered from the previous day was stopping for gas.

Kenya did not have many friends to confide in. He contemplated divulging his atypical dilemma to Russ but dismissed the idea instantly. *Fisher will make fun of me and tell the entire department.* Sally Green? *She already believes I'm an oddball.* The business analyst would certify him as a nutjob.

Fifteen years ago, his biological parents, Dorothy and Earl, had divorced over the sudden loss of their second son, Edward. They were now respectively remarried to submissive Donald and overbearing Melinda. The whole clan lived in central New Jersey. Kenya tried to contact his folks once a month by phone (his mom and dad were old-school baby boomers who refused to learn the intricacies of texting or social media). Still, they were always too engrossed with their adopted families and rarely dropped a dime to call him. When they did connect, he detested the one-sided, drawn-out praises of his half-brother, Jordan, his stepbrother, Kevin, and his three stepsisters, Margaret, Michelle, and Megan.

If Kenya dared to mention the Tandoori Box to his hands-off father, Earl, his stepmother, Melinda—who had her big schnoz in everybody's business—might stop everything to set up an appointment for him with Josef, her latest in a long succession of New-Age shrinks. His mother, Dot, would sigh and read him a Bible passage from the Book of Revelation. And his stepfather? During their infrequent phone calls, Don's heavy mouth breathing always deteriorated into throaty snoring. The overworked man had enough headaches handling his own daughters (Maggie, the eldest, had caught the heroin bug, Shelly had totaled his Eddie Bauer Range Rover while Snapchatting, and little Meg was preggers).

Five days had passed since Kenya had won—by luck or misfortune—the White Elephant at Delphic's holiday party. He now thought of the mysterious cube as the Tandoori Box—this exotic name derived from the restaurant receipt found in the plastic bag it came in.

What is it? Preposterous as it sounded, the Tandoori Box predicted the future. The device—*a camera?*—produced images—*photographs?*—of imminent events. Insomuch as Kenya always appeared in the prints (along with whoever interacted with him at the moment of record), he deduced that as the owner, the divinations were directly linked to him. With no more than four pictures to tally, his reasoning was impossible to validate; yet, so far, this preliminary data inferred a trend.

Where did the Tandoori Box come from? At the holiday party, the White Elephant shared the stage with twenty-two other entries. The present had been encased in a plastic sack turned inside out, stating: HEAVEN IS WHERE ALL CHEFS ARE INDIAN. Come to think of it, the Tandoori Box had been the only article on the table still in a bag. Pamela had probably missed seeing the item on account of its diminutive proportions. Or had subliminal instincts repelled the admin from unveiling the odd gift for all to evaluate? Kenya hadn't paid close attention to the date on the Tandoori House and Meat Shop's sales slip. *Was the takeout meal a recent purchase?* Too late to tell. He had thrown out the slip of paper. *Do any of these factors even matter?*

Who had given away the White Elephant? Someone at DIS. *But who?* Kenya mentally rostered the attendees. No significant person stuck out as the donor. He worked with several Asian Indians, most of whom were based in the Bangalore office. The few locals, as far as he remembered, had skipped the celebration. *Everyone eats Indian food. It could be anybody.*

Is the Tandoori Box bad? Is that black block evil? Fuck yeah, it's evil. It is abso-fucking-lutely evil! That motherfucking Tandoori Box, or whatever the fuck you wish to call it, almost burned down my fucking apartment!

Watson gobbled the remaining crumbs of an Egg McMuffin. He wiped his mouth and reassessed his initial reaction. *To be frank, although the humming woke me up a couple of mornings (I had to pee anyhow), and viewing those weird images can, to put it mildly, be unsettling, the fire didn't start until I dumped the cube on the couch.*

The geezer in the next booth asked Kenya if he wanted his leftover hash browns. He courteously declined, unknowingly avoiding a chronic infection of Hepatitis B.

Watson, his concentration interrupted, and disgusted by the jaundiced man's poor table manners, exited the fast-food restaurant.

As Kenya weaved amongst rows of nested shopping carts, his rationalizing mind concluded that in the long run, receiving daily pictures of his future might not be so disagreeable after all. Thus far, except for minor sofa damage, no harm had come to him or anyone else. *Luckily, I doused the flames before they spread to the curtains.* The scorch marks—*in actuality, just discolorations*—on the loveseat's cushions were his own fault. *I shouldn't have attempted to get rid of the White Elephant.*

Watson extracted the prints from his jeans. The first photograph showed him dozing at his workstation. *I've got to quit staying up late.* He held the second picture nearer. *I like this one of Sally and me in the breakroom. She's so hot!* He didn't review the third and fourth prints. These only exhibited his efforts to discard and demolish the Tandoori Box—definitely a fool's errand.

Could it be that this unusual, anonymous token is not a pestilence hand-delivered to me by Satan but, in truth, a long-awaited—and well-deserved—blessing from God?

Kenya's medulla oblongata throbbed with the infinite possibilities. A grin cracked his face as the insufferable weight lifted from his shoulders. Watson keyed the ignition, turned the radio to a funky tune, and, singing along to "Brick House," cut every corner racing home.

Chapter Four

KENYA SAT ON THE LIVING ROOM COUCH. Upon arriving home, he had overturned the damaged cushion, effectively hiding the singed section of fabric. An open window vented any lingering traces of fried polyurethane foam.

Watson set the photograph of himself curled up in his car's rear seat on the side table and picked up the Tandoori Box. He rolled the six-sided gadget in his palms. It rattled as if there was a loose screw inside. The shape was equivalent to a Rubik's Cube (as Deiter Steuben had so facetiously suggested). Jordan, his teenage half-brother, developed an intense affection for the multicolored puzzle and, after taking second place in Maine's Regional Rubik's Cube Challenge, had qualified for the upcoming US Nationals.

Kenya hefted the abnormal object, for the first time registering that the box's size and weight had changed. *At the holiday party, I swore it was smaller and lighter than a standard Rubik's Cube.*

The color—or absence of color—which Kenya formerly categorized as flat black, was not fundamentally black at all. Iridescent, *or prismatic,* came to mind as the spectrum of the rainbow scintillated on the block's exterior. He peered closer. The lustrous hues dwindled, leaving what his primitive psyche interpreted as a hole or a *deep void.* The hexahedron's corners blended into the overall structure. Watson perceived the element's mass through the nerves in his hands; yet, despite this tactile evidence, the Tandoori Box's visible properties waned. The cube had not dissolved—the article remained solid enough—it was just no longer *there.* And then, before his disbelieving eyes, *it was.* He tapped the square against the coffee table, reassured that the hard edge left a detectable mark in the soft pine. *I am seeing things.*

Kenya ran his forefinger over the device's *skin.* The smooth texture reminded him of a fourth-grade class trip. At the Adventure Aquarium, he had leaned into a shallow saltwater tank to pet the creamy belly of a friendly bat ray. The box's six facets were rounded from continual use—a surviving relic of a bygone age. He used a thumbnail to scratch the outside. Unsuccessful, Watson went to his desk, returning with a miniature sword letter opener and a pair of magnifying goggles. The dagger skated across the Teflonish coating and pricked his palm. Kenya kissed away the red droplet and clamped the magnifier's band securely to his forehead. Under the harsh glare of the attached LED lights, he saw minute depressions pitting the cube's top—*craters.* Scores, *or claw marks,* gouged the sides. Like a baby mouthing a new pacifier, Kenya touched his tongue to the corner of the box, tasting bad medicine and receiving a low-voltage jolt.

A rectangular hatch centered the back. *The battery holder?* The compartment lacked a latch. Watson chuckled, discerning the MADE IN INDIA letters engraved into the tarnished base. He had saved the front—the slot where the pictures came out—for last.

Kenya used the letter opener to pry the two-inch strip embedded in the Tandoori Box's *face.* When freed, the flap snapped shut. *There must be hidden hinges and springs.* He lined up the rectangular photograph with the thin groove. The print did not fit the recess, as it was an inch too wide. Watson rechecked the other sides, finding no distinguishable openings other than the sealed "battery compartment."

He had never witnessed the exceptional contraption dispensing any of the pictures, but he reckoned that these daily miracles always transpired at midnight. Kenya idly wondered if the Tandoori Box would spring forward or fall back for daylight savings time. If he carried the gizmo on a cross-country trip, were its internal electronics clever enough to handle time zone changes? Watson adjusted the alarm on his wristwatch, vowing to stay up and observe the machine in action.

Kenya propped open the box's tab with his thumb. He squinted into the orifice, expecting to detect a transport mechanism. There were no gears or rollers evident; however, he glimpsed minuscule globules of iridescence drifting in space. The wormy specks moved when Watson blinked. He realized that the aggravating floaters were aberrations within his own eyeballs.

An odor evocative of his mom's homemade lasagna wafted from the slit. Sentimental memories brought a smile to Kenya's face—happier days when his parents were in love, and his brother, Edward, still lived. His contentment faded as the appetizing aroma soured into the cloying bouquet of his stepmother's cheap perfume. Melinda had ruined everything. That jezebel had ensnared his father—stolen him right out from underneath his mother's satin sheets. As Melinda's diary (stuffed into the Watsons' mailbox by her first husband, Mario Sanders) explained in graphic detail, Earl Watson had not been at the office every night burning the midnight oil. Dear old Dad had been at the Red Bull Inn working up a sweat with all the other cheaters—*fucking that bucktoothed floozy.* And the sinful fruit of his father's overstimulated spermatozoon and that trollop's superfertile breed berries? Mr. Smarty Pants himself—Jordan, his nitwit half-brother.

Kenya rubbed his eyes, gritted his teeth, and pressed the magnifier's lens to the narrow aperture. Inside the Tandoori Box, under a sweltering sun, a mammoth tree pervaded his vision. The fat, exposed roots—*legs*—impaled the mud-cracked bottom of a dry lake. In the foreground, the tangled ropes of a fishing net spilled from a dugout canoe's charred interior. Beneath a tattered teepee, skeletal chiefs held palaver even in death. The tree's pine needle-spiked branches—*arms*—stretched dramatically into the darkening sky. Watson sucked in sulfur gases as devil winds twisted alkali dust into a funnel. The snug knot of a hangman's rope swung from the thickest bough. Below a new moon, flashes of discharging negative ions illuminated the face of the condemned. He slammed the tiny door and threw up.

"Man, you look like crap," Russ apprised. "Were you out partying?"

Kenya, who seldom drank liquor stronger than beer and shied away from recreational drugs, responded, "Nah, I'm having difficulty sleeping."

Fisher reached into the tight pocket of his skinny jeans and scooped out a fistful of mixed pills. Atop the flat of his palm, his pudgy index finger sorted the pharmaceuticals into piles by size, color, and shape. He selected a pair of blue tablets with S190 imprinted on the powder. As the hardware engineer held out the sedative hypnotics, Watson saw a series of scars—most healed, a few scabbed, and one fresh—underneath his pulled-back sleeve. "Sorry, I'm out of Ambien," Russ apologized. "No worries. These Lunesta will zonk you out. Tonight, you'll sleep deader than Elvis Presley sitting on his porcelain throne, reading about the Shroud of Turin. Just don't fly a jumbo jet or do any neonatal brain surgery."

"What do I owe you?" Kenya asked, opening his wallet. He didn't want the pills but wasn't in the mood to put up a fuss.

Russ laughed at his naiveté. "They're on the house, Doc. Whenever we visit Valeska's aunt and uncle, I clean out their medicine cabinets. Dippy and Zippy are too stoned to catch anything missing. You can't tell me I never gave you nuttin'."

"Thanks." Watson surreptitiously slipped the Z-drugs into his shirt pocket and yawned.

"Man, you gotta snap out of it." His coworker divvied out two more round pills, these branded M.

"What are these?" Kenya inquired, rolling the white tablets between his fingers.

"Kiddy coke, otherwise known by the drug dealers at your local CVS as amphetamines. Valeska's relatives adopted a nine-year-old girl from Romania or some other Baltic state. Spoon-feeding the kid Ritalin is the only thing that keeps Kermit the Frog and Miss Piggy from tearing their own hair out."

"I'm fairly certain I don't have ADHD, and Romania isn't anywhere near the Baltic Sea," Watson said, adding these narcotics to his stash.

"Tell that to Mrs. Reichel, my eighth-grade geography teacher." Fisher shoveled uniquely formed lozenges into his mouth, chomped, and swallowed. He moaned in pleasure.

"What are those? Ecstasy?"

"Flintstones chewable vitamins. They taste like Skittles soaked in cough syrup—very addictive. What're you doin' for lunch?"

Kenya stalled before answering. Last night had been taxing, yet extremely invigorating. When his wristwatch alarm had chimed at 11:45 p.m., he'd gotten up excited to see how the Tandoori Box worked. Hunched in the armchair, he'd trained one eye upon Jimmy Fallon staging a political skit with Seth MacFarlane on *The Tonight Show* and had focused the other eye upon the bag containing the cube.

At twelve o'clock, as anticipated, the black box had hummed. Watson had leaped up and opened the sack—*missed it.* The newborn photograph had lain in a steaming puddle of goo. He'd plucked a slimy corner, shaken off drizzles of milky vernix, and held the print to his nostrils. As a university student, Watson had kept a leopard gecko in a glass terrarium by his bed. Martin's runny stools, avocado-tinted and malodorous, were analogous to the secretion coating—*a fully developed and in-living-color rendering of himself and Sally Green seated in a window booth at what appeared to be his favorite burger joint!*

By the time Watson had returned with a dishrag from the kitchen sink, the sticky residue had evaporated. The enchanting photo now smelled of grilled onions and French fries. He had fallen asleep in the padded chair with the picture clutched to his chest.

When Kenya replied, he suppressed his elation. "Sorry, Russell, but I have plans today."

After the all-hands meeting, Kenya approached Sally in the hallway. Ordinarily, he became nervous dealing with the opposite sex, especially in interactions with the brainy ones. This morning, the man stood strong and cocksure.

Watson was by no means a virgin. He'd had a girlfriend in college. They met in the Algorithms in Programming course at the University of Southern Maine. Due to a not-so-random selection ironically generated from a computer algorithm glitch, Professor Taylor had paired Kenya and Hannah Schrock on the final assignment. The additional member of their group (nowadays, the barefoot, hoodie-wearing CEO of the well-funded startup, Pleezeme) had sporadically shown up for class, leaving the two to collaborate on the project. Watson, during late-night cram sessions in Schrock's dorm room, had learned that she had been homeschooled by authoritarian parents in a Pennsylvania Dutch community. Hannah had told him that the Amish tradition of Rumspringa had coaxed out her "inner wildness," and after "racing around for a year like a nymphomaniac," at sixteen, she had run away to live with a shunned second cousin in Portland. A scholarship based on Hannah's excellent SAT scores and past public service had cinched her a free ride into USM.

At first, Kenya and Hannah had enjoyed an ideal relationship. The happy couple had moved off campus into a cozy studio apartment affording a view of Deering Oaks Park. Throughout that blustery winter semester, his grade point average had descended as fast as his sexual awareness had risen—his youthful prowess a result of her experienced hands-on instructions. Hannah had learned much living amongst the "English." Watson, strategizing for their bright future—which included a crop of incredibly intelligent and talented children—had washed enough dirty dishes in the school's cafeteria to scrape together enough cabbage to buy a modest-sized engagement ring.

Then one cold winter morning, Hannah's Nokia had rung, awakening Kenya from a pleasant slumber. *Who is calling at this hour?* He heard the shower and the echoes of an upbeat song. Watson gave in to the darker voices in his head and read the green text bubble at the top of the liquid-crystal display. The message had not been sent by Hannah's best friend, Denise, or that whack job, Charlease.

Dominick's text slang queried: *S dat fckr stil der? Cn I brng ovr jelly donuts? I can't W8 2 cream n yor hole!*

In haste, Watson had scrolled upward, inspecting weeks of vulgar text message exchanges and titillating selfies. *She doesn't do those kinky things to me.*

Nauseated, Kenya had stomped into the clouded bathroom and, yanking aside the polyester curtain, confronted the love of his life. He had been unable to comprehend the logic for Hannah's infidelity and had implored her to end contact with the other man. "What have I done wrong?" the boy sobbed. "What can I do to change?"

Hannah performed a reverse striptease for Kenya, unhurriedly wrapping her voluptuous curves in a towel. She pushed him across the wet tiles, saying, "Take your piece of crap IKEA dresser, your dopey Beanie Babies collection, and be gone by the time I return from class. I never, ever want to see your ugly face or that stinking lizard again."

The milestone event, which had broken his heart, had taken place nearly a decade ago. Kenya had not gone out on a single date—excluding internet video chat rooms—since college. Here and now, he stood before Sally Green with the Tandoori Box picture in his pocket as proof she would accept his invitation. Watson felt his confidence bloom. *I've been alone for so long. What have I got to lose?*

"Yikes!" Sally exclaimed. "I can't believe he asked you to do that. What was your response?"

In the 1950s-style decor of Hal's Burgers, Kenya and his lunch date sat beside the same window, in the corresponding white-and-red vinyl-upholstered booth shown in today's Tandoori Box photograph. He imitated the picture's depicted effect by donning the same blue shirt and black slacks, whereas Sally came dressed differently than he had expected. Apparently, the hereafter was not written in granite, and if the planets refused to align in a perfect array, slight variances could manifest. The waiter wrote down their food orders and delivered two delicious malted milkshakes.

"I told Glenn to stick it up his ass," he replied.

"You did not," she said in a low intonation.

Every word Sally spoke sounded sexy to Kenya.

The straw sputtered as he sucked the ice cream slush from the soda fountain glass. Watson leaned rearward and admitted, "You're right. I said it to myself. I had completed the source code, and the program was ready for testing. All I had to do was send him a link to the latest file. Walker left me in peace after he checked that box off his project plan."

A server put paper-lined baskets containing Hal's Deluxe Cadillac Burgers and sides of baked sweet potato fries on the Formica tabletop. The accommodating teenager inquired whether he could fetch them anything else.

Kenya looked to Sally, who needed both hands to hold the unwieldy sandwich, and asked for extra napkins.

"I'm so fucking hungry," Sally declared. "I always wanted to come here."

Watson respected girls with potty mouths. He found Sally's potty mouth pretty irresistible.

She questioned, "Where did you work before Delphic?"

"For a year, I was at a company run by an Iranian. We installed point-of-sale software in Taco Bell franchises. I traveled the whole country. You'd be amazed at how many staff members are caught pilfering big bags of meat and cheese."

"Ha! Anyone on minimum wage must use the five-finger employee discount to get by. In high school, I worked at a Burger King for one day. The supervisor—as part of my 'indoctrination'—had me scrub out the restrooms. Caca from floor to ceiling. *So grody.*" A white dab of mayonnaise rode the curve of her lip. Kenya pondered whether it would be more polite to inform her of the intruder, hand her a napkin, or remain quiet. "When I finished my shift, I jammed the mop in the toilet, tipped the pail, and walked out. I kept the ghastly uniform for a Halloween costume. Why did you quit?"

"I was laid off when sales hit the skids. The application had lots of bugs—more than the restaurants."

"Hard to fathom." The tip of Sally's tongue discovered the condiment. "Then you came here? To your dream job?"

"Not yet," Kenya answered. "I obtained advanced programming language certifications and took my first job as a developer at a company specializing in prison library software."

Her plate picked clean, she stared at his uneaten fries. "I thought most jailbirds are too busy pumping iron in the yard or, for fun, shivving each other in the showers with sharpened toothbrushes to have time to read *Don Quixote*."

Kenya laughed. "The convicts leaf through the old masters if all the *National Geographic* magazines are checked out. Some of the smarter ones—the 'jailhouse lawyers'—spend hours studying legal books. To troubleshoot software issues, I spoke to the prison librarians by telephone. Because the inmates' fingers aren't allowed anywhere near a keyboard, the guards had to type in the actual commands. One guy wanted to come visit me after his release—*no way.* There are good reasons why those people are locked up." He pushed the basket of fried sweet potatoes across the table.

Sally popped an orange fry into her mouth. "Let go again?"

"Nope. Fired. Well, kind of. Two brothers, fraternal twins, were running the company into the ground—a couple of real jackasses. One afternoon, I snuck out early to interview with Marisa at Delphic. Somebody snitched on me—told the boss. When I strolled into the office the next morning, she had a security detail waiting for me. They packed my gear and escorted me out of the building. My manager blamed me for each person in her department giving notice. Christ, I was the only employee stupid enough to still be working there."

"My, what a rabble-rouser you are, Mr. Watson. Luckily, you got this job."

"I guess. What are your goals, Miss Green? Can you see yourself retiring at DIS?"

"Portland is a small town. This position is a stepping-stone. To what? Who knows? Maybe Silicon Valley or San Francisco. Since our company's benefits plan covers part of the tuition, I've considered getting a master's degree. I filled out the paperwork, then lost my motivation. After a ten-hour day, all I want to do is go home, kick up my feet, and turn on *Entertainment Tonight*."

Kenya totally understood her feelings of underappreciation. He, too, desired more: a promotion to a senior salary level, a reliable vehicle that did not bleed his paltry savings account, and a beach cottage commanding a view of the Atlantic Ocean—the little odds and ends, when summed up, might give him a shot at happiness. Watson hoped the Tandoori Box was his ticket to financial freedom and, most importantly, the end of his loneliness. *She seems into me. Perhaps I can trust her enough to tell her how—*

Sally combed golden brown hair from her brow and twirled it behind her ear. "You'd like to fuck me, wouldn't you, Kenya?"

Shaken from his woolgathering and by her bluntness, Watson choked. "What? Excuse me?"

"That's not gonna happen," she said, swatting a fly arising out of the cup of ranch dressing. "Sorry, but I never eat where I shit."

Undeterred, the insect buzzed around Kenya's side of the booth. "Don't you mean, 'you don't shit where you eat'?"

Sally nodded. "I always reverse that ancient Chinese proverb. It's the same thing if you think about it. Either way, you won't be dipping your company pen in my company ink." She loaded the trash onto her tray and stood. "Thanks for lunch. Let's do this again sometime."

Chapter Five

THE LUNCHEON WITH SALLY HAD NOT GONE AS WELL as Kenya had hoped. She obviously had no interest in him. Testosterone-fueled gossipers in the cube farm had speculated on Sally's relationship status. Gregory Barnes had heard that her fiancé, a well-connected financier, had abandoned her at the altar. Jack Gantz alleged to have "kept her warm but not dry" in the backseat of his Chevy Suburban during a snowstorm. "Remember the afternoon Dave Hutchings let us go early when the roads were closing? Everybody went across the street and got wasted at McGee's. Because I'm such a gentleman—" Gantz had paused to wink. "I gave Sally a ride home she won't ever forget." While Watson had not believed this sleazy incident to be factual, the offhand boast had turned his stomach. Russell Fisher had wondered whether Sally might be open to a threesome with his wife, Valeska. *Like that would happen!*

Not much out of the ordinary came to pass—if one didn't count owning a mechanical prognosticator—through the hectic days leading up to Christmas. Kenya left his job to rub elbows with the other procrastinators at the shopping malls. In futile efforts to buy his parents' love, he bought his dad a high-tech Callaway putter at the Harris Golf Shop and, at Cross Jewelers, selected a flashy rose-gold Movado timepiece for his mom. And, to make a passive-aggressive point, he picked up inexpensive gifts (hosiery from Ross Dress for Less) for his two stepparents and five stepsiblings.

In the office, work peaked midweek and then tapered off. Nobody wanted to do anything more than spike Pamela's spiced eggnog with rum and discuss their plans for the holidays. Once in a while, Watson bumped into Sally in the hallway. Although she cordially greeted him, when he tried to chat, she seemed withdrawn.

Kenya set his alarm in optimistic attempts to observe his future roll hot off the press. Sucked into orphic, peculiar dreams, he missed the alert on Wednesday and hit snooze on Thursday.

Nonetheless, every morning, Watson, eager to scrutinize the Tandoori Box's latest photograph, sprang out of bed and hastened into the front room. Captured each day at various locations and times, the pictures chronicled his daily routine: Wednesday showed Kenya eating beef nachos in the cafeteria with Russ and Russ' new best pal, Deiter Steuben. Thursday, Christmas Eve, exposed a more woebegone shot—a scrawny, unshaven man sprawled upon the couch watching Angela Lansbury, the amateur sleuth, solve yet another droll ninety-minute murder mystery.

Both forecasted ticks on the clock transpired without Watson having any recollections of the explicit moments they'd occurred. And the most distressing aspect? Sally did not appear in either image.

As his coworkers bid merry farewells for the three-day weekend, Kenya braced the door as Sally rushed into the wind. She wished him happy holidays, adding, "I'm heading over to McGee's to celebrate with a friend."

To Kenya's left, at the head of the food-laden dining room table, his dad, Earl, hair cropped military style, rasped a carving knife across a wet stone. In the chair to his right, his stepmother, Melinda, wearing a hideous red-and-white snowman sweater, expounded on the turkey's enormous size. "This bird is so big," she gloated, "I made Dad buy me a bigger oven." On the opposite side, partially obscured by the garish Christmas ornaments centerpiece, Jordan and Kevin, both built like NFL linebackers, argued amicably over this season's fantasy football picks.

The seven-hour, four-hundred-mile journey from Portland to Cherry Hill had been humdrum, save for the five heartbeats Kenya had lost spinning through the epicenter of a ten-vehicle pileup on an icy overpass. Under the hand of God—the steering wheel had been ripped from his hands during the first revolution—the Honda had skidded to a stop in the correct orientation and without a scratch.

The Tandoori Box's most recent and most often viewed photograph—born (Watson adopted this word to describe how the pictures arrived) early Christmas morning—had ridden beside him on the passenger's seat. In this violent image, Kenya sat astride Jordan's ribcage, holding a silver knife to his half-brother's throat.

Kenya had sped southward, breaking the speed limit. He held no animosity toward Jordan, or anybody else for that matter—merely a general malaise, knowing that in several hours, he'd be forced to interact with his blended family.

Right now, in the thirty-eight-hundred-square-foot house that Melinda had won from Mario Sanders in their messy divorce settlement, slow-burning resentment flared in Kenya's chest. Above the "big bird," his father's deadpan expression held the concentration of an army medic sawing off a gangrened leg. Conversely, his stepmother's rouged cheeks dimpled as she passed bowls of steaming mashed potatoes and sautéed mushrooms to Kevin and Jordan.

Earl asked, "Kenya, how's it going at Delco?"

Kenya took note of his dad sending the platter of white meat away from him. Although he was the hungriest, having skipped breakfast to beat the holiday traffic, he knew he would be the last individual in the room to raise a fork. "Dad, the company I work for is called Delphic Industrial Sciences."

"Deltic. That's what I said. Is your boss keeping you busy?" His father forked a hefty turkey thigh onto his firstborn's empty plate. "I recall how much you love gnawing on the drumstick."

Kenya, sensing his family's eyes upon him, poured himself more Chardonnay. The sweet wine lessened his distaste for dark meat. "The job is fine. When I have my review, I'm hoping to be promoted to senior software engineer."

"Lord, it's about time," his stepmother muttered. "You've been there since the Bush administration."

"Melinda, I've worked there for two years," Kenya corrected. He watched Kevin feed the wiener dog juicy strips of turkey breast.

"Don't spoil him, pumpkin." Melinda giggled, covering her gap-toothed mouth with a palm. "Oscar is getting too chubby to jump up on the bed. I need my little tootsie warmer close by now that Earl's sleeping in the guest room."

As a child, Kenya's parents had not allowed him to have a pet—unless the short-lived goldfish he'd won at the local firehouse fundraiser counted. A pang of jealousy speared his heart.

The remains of the dinner conversation—and dessert, a brown Betty cobbler—centered on the drama of Jordan's Rubik's Cube competitions, Kevin's pre-acceptance letter from Columbia University, and his dad and stepmom's ten-day/five-island luxury cruise to the Caribbean.

The family extinguished the candles, carried the dishware to the kitchen, and adjourned to the living room. Kenya's pulse decreased as the distance from any sharp-edged instruments increased. Earl sank into his Barcalounger, unfastening his belt before swearing the same yearly New Year's resolution.

Christmas presents ringed the twelve-foot artificial blue spruce. Melinda had arranged the tagged gifts by age, and naturally, the youngest had an impressive heap. She asked Jordan if he wanted to go first.

"Yeah!" Jordan cried. He unwrapped a flat, rectangular box and raised the slimmest and most powerful version of Apple's iPad high. The next package contained a framed photograph of Earl and Melinda's son holding his square trophy overhead at the Regional Rubik's Cube Challenge. After a lengthy procession of progressively impressive tributes, including a Sony PlayStation 4 and a hoverboard, the teenager chose Kenya's offering. Watson's jaw clenched as his half-brother disregarded the diamond-patterned stockings and double-checked the paper for more. "Uh, thanks, Kenya. You can never have enough argyle socks."

Jordan clawed at a longish item encased in cardboard and sealed with packing tape. Stymied, he whined, "Mom, I can't cut this!" Melinda returned from the kitchen with the hand-forged steel knife her husband had utilized to slice the turkey. This handy tool had been in the Watson family for generations. Kenya retained acute memories of Grandpa Clarence warding off pushy door-to-door salesmen and pesky debt collectors with the stag-handled "pig sticker." With the help of the honed edge, the adolescent freed the gift. Jordan's face lit up when he saw the blued barrel of a hunting rifle. "Thanks, Mom and Dad!" He laid down the blade and aimed the Remington Model 700 at Kenya.

The remainder of the presents opened without a hitch. Kenya received a half-dozen pairs of boxers and a gift certificate to Maggiano's. He doubted the restaurant chain operated in Maine or if any of their main courses cost less than a sawbuck.

Jordan plugged the supplied cables for his new Sony PS4 console into the television inputs. He invited Kenya to play *Black Ops III*.

Kenya had no aptitude for first-person shooter video games, and it came as no surprise that Jordan gained the upper hand. He was mastering the controller and was engaged in the action when he heard his half-brother remark, "Kenya, you'll never be part of this family."

The overwound spring coiled in Watson's brain snapped. He seized the butcher knife, leaped through the air, and pressed the tip to Jordan's quivering Adam's apple. "What the fuck did you just say?"

Kevin grabbed Kenya by the shirt and tossed him against the couch. "Bro, have you lost your marbles? Jordan only said, 'You'll never be fast enough to get me!'"

Kenya took the week off between Christmas and New Year's. He devoted these days to putting the disastrous episode in Cherry Hill behind him. When he got home, Watson unplugged his landline, and if his cellphone rang, he hit the red ignore button. He deleted his family's voicemails without listening to the recordings. Kenya felt sad about what he had done to Jordan, but he did not suppose the altercation could have been dodged. *The Tandoori Box predicted the outcome. Who am I to challenge fate?*

Watson stayed inactive that whole week—listless and forlorn. The software engineer crawled into bed early (he no longer had the energy or interest to see how the cube worked) and slept late into the morning. He attended a blasé movie sequel at the theater, napped on the loveseat, and clocked too many hours viewing reality TV. Kenya also spent a good amount of the break brooding over the Tandoori Box, which, incidentally, produced no results of great significance during this period.

A noteworthy concern did arise during the holidays. Dozens of migrating birds crashed into Kenya's apartment's bay window. If he was home, occupied in the kitchen preparing supper or folding laundry in the bedroom, the sudden, meaty thuds made him drop what he was doing and dash to the living room. Angelic imprints of dusty feathers or specks of blood marked the glass. Below, he'd spot a dazed black-capped chickadee or ruby-crowned kinglet lying belly-up on the snow. In every instance, except for one, the winged creatures regained consciousness and flitted away to warble at the next sunrise.

Kenya was quite proud of his newest investment. As a preventative measure, the wildlife lover affixed an ultraviolet silhouette of a hawk to the windowpane. The package claimed that birds avoided the area after seeing the glowing predator. At the moment he applied the static decal, a large loon swooped into his face, cracking the center of the glass. Outdoors, underneath the snowcapped shrubs, Watson gently laid the stunned red-throated waterfowl in a carton. Upstairs and indoors, he detected a faint flutter of wings brushing against the cardboard. He peeked into the container. Crimson eyes reflected his own. In terror, the loon darted between his hands and flew three squawking circuits around the room before smashing into the same fractured pane of glass. As Kenya wrung the flailing bird's neck, he blamed the animal's demise (and the costly window repair) on the Tandoori Box.

Late Thursday afternoon, on New Year's Eve, Kenya reclined in his easy chair. Ruminative, he sipped a beer while staring out the window. The final rays of a muddy sunset shone through the Tandoori Box's translucent bag, highlighting the reversed letters printed on the inside. Intrigued, he transposed the words. "Heaven is where all chefs are Indian."

Watson noticed a scrap of white lying under the sofa. He moved the ottoman aside and, on his back, thrust a forearm into the swirling cloud of dust bunnies. His scissoring fingers snagged the curled receipt. *It must be the piece of paper I dumped from the sack on the morning of the fire.* This Tandoori

House and Meat Shop sales slip listed an order of chicken curry, shrimp saag, and a side of garlic naan.

Kenya dialed the telephone number, hearing the jarring "doo. . .dah. . .dee. . ." musical tones and brusque recording indicative of a dead line. He acted on the crotchety android's advice by checking the numerals and re-punching the digits. Frustrated, he hung up, opened his laptop, and entered 2 PARK STREET, PORTLAND, MAINE in Google Maps. Watson switched to Street View, landing at the intersection of Commercial Street near the Maine Port Authority.

The dingy Boat Supply storefront and the tacky Crab Shack restaurant filled his screen. Kenya moused about, rotating his viewpoint one hundred and eighty degrees to find the side of a neglected two-story building. Constructed of brown bricks and browner siding, the clashing color of the purple roof caught his eye. A vinyl banner swung from the eaves advertising LUNCH BUFFET NOW OPEN 7 DAYS A WEEK. Navigating along Park Street to the frontage of the restaurant, he saw a more permanent sign for THE TANDOORI HOUSE AND MEAT SHOP – FINE EXOTIC INDIAN CUISINE. This signboard advertised the identical phone number he had dialed. Watson judged from the sun's high angle that the Google Maps camera car had driven by at noon, and examining the foliated trees shading the parking spaces and the wilting posies in the flowerbeds, he extrapolated the season to be midsummer. The mobile camera's CMOS sensors froze pedestrians in midstride. At the eatery's entrance, beneath a torn awning, a man of average height in a white button-down shirt and black trousers smoked a dark cigarette. As Kenya zoomed closer, the face blurred, an effect of Google's identity protection.

Chapter Six

ON NEW YEAR'S DAY, KENYA STOPPED THE RED CIVIC by the Boat Supply store and Crab Shack restaurant. Both businesses were closed. He traversed the road and stood before the gutted two-level structure at 2 Park Street. In the onshore winds, shreds of a melted lunch buffet banner flapped from the purple roof. Plywood boarded up the windows and entryways. Yellow crime scene tape sagged across the blackened walls. In the refuse-strewn parking area, an incinerated Volkswagen Bus languished on corroded rims. Watson clambered up the rubble to read the orange warning sign stapled to the front door. The Fire Department condemned the building on December eighteenth.

A chain-link fence surrounded the perimeter of the property. Kenya mounted a dumpster and dove over the barbed-wire strands into a snowbank. The wood barrier splintered as he kicked and pried his way inside the Tandoori House and Meat Shop. Even with the temperature in the negative digits, his nostrils tickled with the stench of scorched studs, plastic, and metal. The pungent, oily traces of kerosene persisted underneath the typical odor of combustion.

The only illumination came from the open doorframe. Watson, stepping on his own shadow, maneuvered among overturned tables and chairs. At the meat cases, behind slanted panes of smoggy glass, aluminum trays cradled the cremated bones of chickens and lambs. He distinguished the dull luster of stainless-steel appliances through the circular portholes of commercial swinging doors.

Kenya scolded himself for not bringing a flashlight. He bypassed the dismal kitchen and followed a glimmer to the end of a narrow hallway. Past the restrooms, a stairway led to the upper level. His billowing breath clung to the moldy wallpaper as he negotiated the debris littering the creaking treads.

On the threshold of the four-room apartment, Kenya trampled on a miniature snowdrift. Ragged shafts of sunlight—let in by the firefighters' chopped access holes—floodlit the secondhand furnishings. He perused this morning's Tandoori Box photograph. In this contrasty image, Watson balanced upon the top rung of a stepladder, his right ear pressed against the ceiling, and his left arm stuck into an air-conditioning vent. The ladder was stored in the hall closet beside a brand-new American flag. Kenya borrowed a coin from the cast-iron piggybank on the dresser to unscrew the A/C register from the bedroom wall. He stretched his fingers deep into the sheet-metal duct and touched a cardboard carton.

Seated on the bed, Kenya removed the chalky lid. Two photo bundles fit into the red Nike shoebox. As he tugged the brittle rubber band off the larger set, the elastic snapped, and the pictures spilled onto the quilt. These prints had the same attributes as those produced by his Tandoori Box.

The square images documented a lanky, bearded man in varied phases of daily life: jogging with a raven-haired woman—*his wife?*—on a trail by the bay, counting out change into a female customer's outstretched hand at a cash register, at a dog park with a small girl—*his daughter?*—hugging a sizable Rottweiler, sitting at a sidewalk café with three male companions puffing thin, brown, string-tied cigarettes (Watson found a pack of

Ganesh Beedies on the bathroom sink), in the parking lot signing a deliveryman's receipt for a pallet of rice, driving somewhere with an elderly lady—*his mother?* (a folded wheelchair filled the backseat), asleep on a couch with the same burly canine, posing with a cluster of people—*this must be his whole family*—in front of the Taj Mahal, and hundreds of other candid views. Kenya, bothered by something he had seen, separated the animal's photos. In every shot, the Rottie's amber eyes stared into the lens. *It's as if the dog is looking right at me.*

The second collection of pictures—forty-eight, to be exact—contained subjects of a much more disturbing nature. Shashi Chatterjee (Kenya established the owner's name from a mound of unread mail on the kitchen table and his family's relationships from a group portrait in the front room) was observed: at the beach standing atop a bloated whale with his wife (she appeared squeamish, he didn't), strapping his screaming daughter's bare backside behind an overflowing dumpster, smearing his hairy armpits on a stack of flatbread, singeing an intricate design—*a dog wearing a football helmet?*—into his own forearm with a soldering iron, robbing a terrified liquor store clerk at gunpoint, et cetera, et cetera. And the worst memento of them all? The image that provoked Kenya to pitch the prints back into the box? Chatterjee in a hospital room, forcing a pillow over his mother's gasping mouth.

Did the Tandoori Box influence the restaurant owner to commit these atrocious acts, or was the device passive—a simple machine programmed to record future events? *I could never stoop so low. Shashi Chatterjee must have gone mad.*

Kenya rifled through the entire flat, pulling out drawers, checking under beds, and thumbing through documents in a file cabinet. He discovered a battery-operated lantern in a cupboard stocked with dog food.

Downstairs in the restaurant, Watson unblocked the kitchen doors. In the darkness, the beam flickered and went out. He smacked the plastic housing against his palm to restore the light. The charred, airless chamber stank from crates of vegetables rotting in the walk-in freezer. As Kenya crunched across broken dishes and shattered glasses to the antiquated Chester cooker, a stringy object grazed the tip of his head. In trepidation, he crouched, aiming the torch at the ceiling. What brushed his hair wasn't a gigantic spider's web—only a cord dangling from a fire sprinkler pipe. Watson fingered the manila rope's frayed fibers and chuckled. His eyes focused on a photograph fastened to a silver order wheel. He unclipped the picture and held the dying lantern close enough to see. . . .

In his apartment, at the dining room table, Kenya started his laptop and browsed the internet for information on the Tandoori House and Meat Shop. The initial results listed the address and hours, a few exterior photos, and a two-star average rating on Yelp.

The earlier reviews, going back three years, were generally positive. Ralph Q. said: "My pregnant girlfriend craved spicy Indian cuisine. Man, there's nothing like stuffing your gob with tasty naan, tandoori chicken, and mango ice cream." Patrons declared the food came fast, or they gushed about the friendly atmosphere.

Three to four months ago, the food quality and customer service declined. Ronald T. offered this negative criticism: "Caution! Do not eat here. Really, I AM NOT KIDDING. Dirty and disgusting! I brought my wife to this cesspool for our tenth anniversary dinner. We've been chained to the toilet for twenty-four hours. It had to be the chicken curry." A week after Thanksgiving, Naomi B. bitched: "The place was practically empty, but it still took an hour to get our lunch. Meat raw. Vegetables overcooked. My friend choked on a bone in the mulligatawny soup. I slashed my tongue on a piece of glass hidden in the basmati rice. We asked to speak to the manager. A scruffy guy stumbled over and gave each of us a half-off coupon for one entrée (with the purchase of a regular drink). When my friend raised her voice, the schmuck walked outside and drove away in a VW bus. This joint used to be great. What the hell happened?"

Kenya dug up a brief news article in the *Portland Press Herald*.

> Breaking News – Posted December 16, 2015
> BY BILLY BRUNT – STAFF WRITER
>
> *Indian Restaurant Burns*
>
> Old Port – Portland firefighters are battling a two-alarm blaze at the Tandoori House and Meat Shop. The Congress Street Firehouse responded to a call from 2 Park Street at 2:15 PM. An unnamed diner claims the fire originated in the kitchen and rapidly spread throughout the restaurant.
>
> Thick smoke is impeding the Wednesday afternoon commute on the Casco Bay Bridge. No injuries are reported at this time.

After Kenya skimmed a grim religious commentary condemning a Buddhist bhikkhu's self-immolation, he came upon a follow-up column printed in *The Portland Sun*.

> Published Date Thursday, December 17, 2015
> Written by Staff Reporter
>
> *Maine Fire Marshal Investigating Suspicious Fire*
>
> The State Fire Marshal's Office stated this morning that preliminary investigations suggest arson as a contributing factor in the destruction of an Indian restaurant. The death of the restaurateur, a Portland man, has been ruled a suicide.

> Fire Marshal Jim Thompson said his department's senior inspector has determined there is no evidence indicating a crime in the suffocation death of Shashi Chatterjee, the restaurant's current owner.
>
> The kitchen flareup started yesterday afternoon at the Tandoori House and Meat Shop in the Old Port Exchange district of Portland. First to the scene, a paramedic borrowed a neighbor's extension ladder to save the family's Rottweiler.
>
> Distraught relatives are relieved to learn that Chatterjee's wife and daughter were not residing on the premises at the time of the fire.
>
> Although firefighters were unable to save the structure, the automatic sprinkler system prevented the flames from spreading to the attached apartment and adjacent industrial properties. Extreme temperatures and icy conditions made fighting the blaze a challenge.
>
> Authorities urge anyone with knowledge of the Chatterjee family's whereabouts to contact the Portland Police Bureau.

The Tandoori House and Meat Shop burned down on the day of our holiday party. Watson looked at the photo he had found in the Indian restaurant's kitchen and shivered. The lips of the man hanging from the fire sprinkler pipe appeared to be conveying a message of grave importance.

Kenya got up on Saturday morning, unaware that a marketer in the greeting card industry had named the ninth day of January "National Play God Day." Over his customary bowl of Froot Loops, he studied a photograph of himself accepting a ticket from a short-haired woman standing before a PORTopera poster for *Madama Butterfly*. Watson used the magnifying goggles he kept at hand to pick out details. The digits on the cash register totaled $256.05, which, on the company's website, after adding additional charges, equaled the price of a single orchestra ticket. He never had much fondness for the arts and wondered why the Tandoori Box required him to make this exorbitant investment.

From the bus stop at his apartment, Kenya rode the METRO for twenty minutes to Elm Street, then walked to Merrill Auditorium on Myrtle Street. At the ticket counter, the gal with the pixie haircut was busy helping a difficult customer, so he used his credit card to purchase a fourth-row seat for Thursday (the production's next and last performance) from a different sales assistant. Percy handed him the receipt to sign and said, "Enjoy the show, Mr. Watson. I'm confident you'll find *Madama Butterfly* both utterly beautiful and poetically tragic!"

The following morning, Watson employed the magnifier to evaluate the subsequent picture. Minutes later, he stuffed the *Madama Butterfly* ticket into an envelope addressed to Dr. Carlton Hastings in Cape Elizabeth. Since the image did not show a stamp, he did not mail it.

On Monday evening, Kenya parked in a ritzy development at Smugglers Cove. The Hastings occupied a six-bedroom Georgian colonial on Shore Road. He hunkered down beneath a windbreak of burlap-wrapped evergreens and watched. Many of the lights in the house were switched on. Directed by the third photo in the series, Watson knew his assignment: deliver the opera ticket. He crossed the lane, hurdled a flexible flyer left on the flagstone pathway, unlatched the storm door, and eased the brass cover of the mail slot open. Heated air thawed his frozen cheeks. Kenya peered past white pillars into the grand foyer. Somewhere in a back room, a child wailed for her mother. The envelope slipped from his numb fingers into a wicker basket.

The next several days were serene. Kenya completed his yearly performance review and submitted the online form.

On Friday, Watson sat at attention in front of Marisa's desk. "You're doing extraordinarily well," his boss praised. "In reward of your rapid professional growth, I am giving you the highest rating—a five. You will get a 7% raise, plus a $10,000 bonus. To top it off, I am promoting you to the senior software engineer level. Thank you so much for your dedication!"

Kenya left his supervisor, humming a sweet little ditty. His review could not have gone any better. The newly elevated senior software engineer swung by Russ' cubicle to take him to lunch.

In the cafeteria, Fisher scarfed down a second chili dog and mumbled his congratulations. "Now, you'll need to quit playin' with your pud and actually earn a living."

Kenya laughed; it was the happiest he had felt in ages. "Evidently, the more money you make around here, the less work you have to do."

"Tru dat," Russ agreed. "Wait 'til you're a manager. Then you can lock yourself in your office and drink Maker's Mark until you can't see straight. What do you think about Walter Conrad?"

Watson found Conrad irritating, yet realized that after his recent promotion, he and his fellow senior software engineer would be required to pool resources on conjoined projects. "What of him?"

"Have you been holed up in a cave? It's all over the news. Last night, a plastic surgeon went ballistic at Merrill Auditorium. He shot up the audience."

Suddenly, Kenya's sandwich smelled not of ham and cheese, but of bitter almonds. *Cyanide.* His insides lurched. "What?"

"The doc double-tapped his wife during the intermission." Russ extended his index finger, cocked a thumb, and fired twice. "Blam! Blam!" He blew on the tip of the imaginary barrel and grinned. "The police released a statement that Romeo is still alive and kicking. He's at Mercy Hospital in critical condition."

"What's this got to do with Walt?"

Fisher snickered. "Walter was the one schtuppin' the good doctor's wife!"

"Anybody else hurt?" Kenya whispered.

"Yep. A stray bullet hit a woman in the neck."

Watson's abdominal region groaned. He tottered to his feet. "I have to go."

As Kenya raced toward the men's room, his friend yelled, "Good luck with the new job!"

Watson, tasting the gastric acid from his vomited lunch, returned to his workspace and logged on to the computer. A news item in the *Portland Press Herald* reported that an off-duty police officer "was in the right place at the right time to neutralize Doctor Hastings before he succeeded in reloading his revolver." A funeral service would be held at Sacred Heart Church for Olivia Hastings, his wife of eighteen years. Mayra Jurado, the innocent female bystander, bled out in the aisle at the opera house. A family member from Chicago claimed her body. Physicians predicted that after multiple surgeries and months of extensive physical rehabilitation, Walter Conrad might walk again with the support of leg braces. The Hastings' surviving daughter, five-year-old Sophia, had been placed in a foster home.

The euphoria of his promotion a distant memory, Kenya hid in his cubicle. *Why did I buy that Madama Butterfly ticket? What is happening to me?* He vaguely recalled going through the motions: the bus trip to Merrill Auditorium, speaking with Percy, addressing the envelope, driving to Cape Elizabeth, and finally dropping the ticket into the doctor's mail slot. However, those moments seemed more like a bad dream than reality. Watson had acted blindly in accordance with the Tandoori Box's pictorial instructions, never considering the consequences. Now, he was responsible—albeit indirectly, he justified—for four casualties.

Kenya understood one thing for certain—*the damned box must be destroyed.*

Chapter Seven

BELOW THE NEO-GOTHIC STEEPLES ON CUMBERLAND AVENUE, Kenya's brow furrowed with misgivings. The programmer had prayed long and hard about coming here. Many years had slipped by since he'd last tread upon hallowed ground. In the toasty narthex, Watson peeled off his leather gloves, all the while obsessing over the previous time he had seen the inside of a church—the day of his brother's funeral.

He peeked past the tall rosewood doors into the magnificent Cathedral of the Immaculate Conception. Even on this cloudy morning, the seventy-foot-high arched ceilings were several shades whiter than the snow blanketing the annexed soup kitchen's roof. In the nave, the few parishioners dotting the pews stared pensively ahead, or with hands folded, bent forward on the padded kneeler boards. Kenya walked down the center aisle, passing an inebriated mail carrier and a trio of sobbing schoolgirls.

An obese priest entered through an entryway and limped to the side chapel expressly reserved for weekday services. The ecclesiastic, making signs of the cross, commenced the noonday mass with the Act of Penitence. Watson took a seat between a downcast hotel maid who was thumbing a worn string of orange rosary beads and a stinking oldster who had given up personal hygiene for Lent a year ago and hadn't handled a bar of soap since. He drifted into torpor as the monotonous voice read The Liturgy of the Word.

Kenya had sized up various methods to rid himself of the Tandoori Box. He pictured mounting the black block to a rocket's nosecone and launching the abominable payload into outer space. Or, minus NASA's budget to finance such an expensive mission, he deliberated airmailing the cube to the Nikola Tesla Museum in Serbia with the enclosed note: *"Please add this Future Prediction Device to your private collection of humanly impossible inventions such as the Death Ray and the Wireless Energy Transfer Machine."* More realistically, Watson visualized himself riding the Casco Bay Lines ferry to Cliff Island and leaving the execrable box on the fishing jetty for hungry seagulls to peck to pieces. For a second, he weighed turning the White Elephant gift over to the police—definitely one of his craziest ideas. But as Kenya sat in the sacrosanct chapel reflecting on his prior failures—hurling the thing in the bay and trying to smash it to smithereens with a baseball bat—he acknowledged that depositing the Tandoori Box in God's house was by far his most sensible scheme.

The speakers squealed with feedback when the priest adjusted the microphone stand's height in preparation for The Liturgy of the Eucharist. Jolted from his daydream, he grimaced as the man of the cloth exhorted, "Pray, brethren, that my sacrifice and yours may be acceptable to God, the almighty Father."

Kenya carried the Tandoori Box in its original plastic bag, now double-layered within the same green Woodward Supermarkets reusable tote he had utilized to transport the Swedish meatballs to the holiday party. On his way into the cathedral, Watson had noticed a metal vault for clothing donations. *Maybe I should toss the gadget in the one-way slot and run away.* Once Goodwill collected his "gift," it and thousands of other unwanted items would be trucked to local thrift shops or, safer still, locked in a shipping container and ferried overseas.

Kenya scanned the immense interior for places to discard the cube. A confessional in an alcove caught his attention. Having no desire to confide his lengthy list of sins to a stranger, he could not see himself creeping into the walnut-stained booth's stuffy confines. Kenya stifled inappropriate giggles, envisioning himself, a raving lunatic—or funnier yet, a completely naked raving lunatic—prancing to the altar with his unholy offering.

A railing screwed to the back of the pew held Bibles and hymnals. Slots contained quantities of tithe envelopes. Kenya wrote FORGIVE ME, FATHER with the supplied pencil stub on the blank side of a card. He slipped his atonement into the green sack and tucked the Tandoori Box underneath the bench with his boot. With one voice, the congregation recited the Lord's Prayer as he left the building.

Watson lingered across the street, anxious to witness who might depart with the bag. He jerked up his hoodie and shifted from foot to foot on the chilly pavement. As the hours slowly unwound, his uneasiness mushroomed into remorse. He restrained his popsicle toes from sprinting indoors to retrieve the box. At three o'clock, a hearse rolled up to the church. Six pallbearers labored to haul an ebony coffin up the rock-salted steps. Kenya gave up his shivery vigil and returned to the office.

On Friday evening, after a grueling week of work, Kenya pulled into his carport. He switched off the engine and got out. A well-dressed couple stood upon his front stoop. The pair looked up from their mobile phones, nodding to one another in agreement. They were here for him.

A sharp-angled female in her mid-forties with gunmetal eyes lifted a UPS package from the doormat and handed it to him. "A special delivery for you, Mr. Watson."

The mustached male, several years her junior, with similar hard facial features, presented a badge. "This is Detective Anita Ortega, and I am Detective Carter Savage. Sir, may we come in out of the cold and ask you a few questions?"

The box thumped as Kenya unlocked the door. "What's this all about?" Not receiving a response, he ushered them into the living room and set the parcel on the windowsill. "Can I get you folks a drink?"

Savage lit a Pall Mall and answered with the coffin nail hanging from his mouth. "I'm good."

"Put it out, Carter," Anita reprimanded. "Hot tea will be most appreciated, Mr. Watson." She leaned over the radiator, blowing on her jagged fingernails. "I can't wait for spring."

As the man stubbed out the cigarette in the sink, the woman circled the apartment, inspecting anything not nailed down. She glanced past her shoulder. "Sorry, it's a bad habit I picked up on the job."

They sat in the dining area, a corner which Kenya now associated with the claustrophobic properties of an interrogation room. He dunked a tea bag in the microwaved water and gave the cup to Ortega.

"Why are you here?" Watson asked. He had anticipated this moment—the dreaded arrival of the police—since the night he'd awoken, realizing that he had signed his full name on the merchant's receipt for the individual ticket Doctor Hastings had used to gain entry into the opera house. At the time of procurement, Kenya had had no inkling that he had been instigating a chain reaction.

Ortega slid a photocopy across the tabletop. "Did you buy this ticket?"

Kenya stared at the info on the stub: *Madama Butterfly*, 01/14/2016, Orchestra, Section 2, Row D, Seat 5. She passed a separate reproduction—a PortTIX receipt for $256.05. No handwriting expert would be necessary to analyze his very legible signature. Watson paced the room. He had rehearsed many responses, but with such damning evidence, he could not argue the facts. "Yes, I did. Why?"

Savage's lips tightened. "The ticket you purchased is linked to the shootings in Merrill Auditorium."

At the window, Kenya read the package's mailing label. T. D. Johnson had shipped the box UPS Next Day Air from Flint, Michigan. As he used a knife to slice the clear tape, gelid mist seeped through the seams.

Watson turned to the detectives. "I heard about that incident on the news. Horrible." The lie escaped his mouth so easily. "I sold the ticket to a man for three hundred and fifty dollars."

"Where?" Savage's flint-colored eyes narrowed. "What did he look like?"

Kenya used memories of the doctor's online photograph as a guide. "Stocky. Gray hair, from what I recall. It was nighttime, so—" He pulled the cardboard flaps aside, exposing blocks of dry ice. Then mysteriously, as though rising out of a Scottish bog, the outline of the green Woodward shopping bag emerged from the boiling fog. "The man was outside the theater begging to get into the show. I made a hundred off the sale."

Ortega gnawed on the remains of a pinkie nail. "Why did you buy the ticket if you had no intention of attending the performance?"

Kenya waved his arms. "Look at this shithole. I wanted to earn some extra money. Is reselling tickets a crime?"

Savage coughed, gawping at a red speck on his palm. "Don't do it again," he mumbled.

Watson extracted the supermarket tote and peered inside. No more HEAVEN IS WHERE ALL CHEFS ARE INDIAN polybag—solely the Tandoori Box. The cube vibrated subsonically as he moved to the light—*it belongs to me now.*

"What do you have there?" Savage inquired. His face whitened—the bloodless pallor of someone who just remembered they left their little angel in a hot car with the windows shut.

"Nothing special." Kenya advanced to the investigators. "It's only a puzzle."

Detective Ortega stood first. "Thank you for your time, Mr. Dobson. And for the—" She set down the teacup. In a daze, she about-faced and sleepwalked outside.

Detective Savage robotically pushed his chair under the table. "Sorry for the inconvenience, Mr., ah. . . ." He mimed a butler by bowing stiffly at the waist. "Please contact us if we can be of any more service."

"Will do." When they were gone, Kenya backed against the locked door, waiting for his pulse to normalize.

At the windowsill, Watson removed a packing slip from the carton. Next to the X'ed non-returnable checkbox, a space for gift comments stated: *"Happy birthday and best wishes!"* With everything going on, Kenya had forgotten that today, he turned thirty-two.

On Monday morning in downtown Portland, an obsidian all-wheel drive SUV glided down the ramp into the Delphic Industrial Sciences building. In the subterranean parking garage, Kenya inched the automobile between a support column and the wall. No one was getting close enough to ding his baby.

Yesterday, he traded in his twelve-year-old Honda Civic for a Lexus NX. At the dealership, the appraiser had picked at his car's flaking enamel and had given him a backhanded compliment: "Mr. Watson, you certainly got your money's worth. My highest offer for a vehicle in this condition is six hundred dollars." The auto finance manager, assessing the value of his customer's shabby attire, asked whether he could handle the installment payments for an eight-year loan. Kenya had paid for his new car with cash and pocketed the keys.

Last Wednesday, Watson was astonished when, after weeks of repetitive images of daily chores—scrubbing the toilet, pumping gas, and plucking nose hairs—the Tandoori Box spat out a picture of his fingers holding a Powerball lottery ticket. At the Circle K, he marked in his five preordained numbers and the Powerball number on the two-dollar betting slip. Kenya nearly ruptured his spleen when Seth Arlings, the hyperactive Powerball host, announced that four of the five white numbered balls, plus the red Powerball, matched his choices. The purse did not approach the one hundred and twenty million–dollar jackpot, but he still won seventy-five thousand opportunities to change the course of his life.

When Kenya shut the Lexus' door, he noticed bird shit dappling the polished hood. As a gossamer of slaver drooled from his lips onto the biggest splatter, a metallic noise spooked him. He pivoted abruptly, the saliva string blotching his jacket. Sally stepped out of a green, classic Ford pickup truck. *How long was she parked there?*

Sally tugged a laptop bag from the passenger's seat and walked over. "New car?"

Watson blocked her view of the bubbling stream running along the fender. "You startled me. I wasn't expecting anybody else to come in this early."

Sally, reading the sticker price, raised her eyebrows. "Holy cow! You must have received a substantial raise to afford this." The essence of a new car paled in comparison to her intoxicating scent.

He thought of the Tandoori Box and said, "The payments will most likely kill me."

Sally moved nearer and saw the gritty mess. She rooted around in a milk crate strapped to the truck bed. "Here, try this."

Kenya used her rag to wipe the white poop off.

As they climbed the stairs to street level, the business analyst inquired, "How was your weekend?"

"Boring. I didn't do much."

She chuckled. "It couldn't have been too dull. You bought a really nice car."

He fabricated a high-speed getaway: police sirens, exchanged gunshots, and windows down—his foxy accomplice's undone hair blowing in the wind. "Um, yeah. I suppose you're right."

Sally halted in the building's entrance. "Joyce Benning from HR is throwing a surprise birthday party for her husband. Tim is turning fifty on Sunday. Do you want to go?"

Kenya, not in a position to play hard to get, responded, "Sure. Is this a date?"

"Try not to think of it that way. We'll be two coworkers going to a party at another coworker's house."

"As friends?"

"As coworkers," she stipulated. "Text me your address. I'll pick you up at eight o'clock."

"What shall I bring?"

"Don't worry about it. Just bring yourself." Sally reconsidered. "Put on an ironed shirt and buy a bottle of decent wine."

Kenya could not believe his good fortune.

The workdays dragged, and the nights were restless. Early Thursday, Kenya heard howling outside his bedroom window. Annoyed, he peeped past the slats of the Venetian blinds. A large animal bounded through the courtyard's shadows. "People shouldn't let their pets run loose," he grumbled and went back to bed.

Watson did his wash on Saturdays. Pinned to the laundry room's bulletin board, stuck between a want ad for WHITE-FACED OR RED-FACED HEIFERS OR BULLS – CALL KATHY and a solitary ankle-length dress sock, he saw a poster of a missing dog. King. The Rottweiler looked familiar. He ripped the sheet off the wall, carried his basket of clean clothes home, and dialed the phone number.

"Hello?" a gruff male answered.

"Can I speak to Nick?"

"This is Nick."

"Hi. I may have seen your dog at my apartment complex."

"Today?"

"No. Wednesday night." Kenya corrected the date. "I mean Thursday around three in the morning. His barking woke me."

"Great! Where are you located? I'll be right over to get him."

"At the time, I didn't know he was lost. He ran off."

"Are you calling to tell me he's still missing?" the man asked. "That's my dog, you moron!"

Kenya put down the receiver after listening to the insectile buzzing of the disconnected telephone line.

On Sunday morning, Watson checked the Tandoori Box for any clues about his upcoming "date" with Sally. He extricated a photograph from the primordial goop and set it to dry on the picture easel that once held a family group shot. As the image crystallized, the amber eyes of a broad-shouldered Rottweiler peered between the bars of a kennel.

Kenya entered the animal shelter. In the spacious lobby, bronze puppies and kittens played above the information counter. A woman wearing a CUMBERLAND COUNTY ANIMAL CENTER VOLUNTEER apron inquired, "Are you seeking a lost pet or simply interested in adopting?"

"Just looking," he responded, "but I am hoping to adopt."

She beamed and welcomed him in. "Do you prefer a feline or canine forever friend?"

"A dog. I always wanted a dog when I was growing up."

The volunteer gave him a clipboard and a pen. "The canines are through that doorway. If you see any you fancy, please fill out this form and turn it in to June at the adoption desk."

As Watson wandered down the bright corridor, the plaintive baying of hundreds of abandoned and stray dogs assaulted his eardrums. Animals of all breeds, colors, and sizes packed the rows of metal cages. While a few pooches snoozed, most pranced in excitement when he neared. Even though Kenya longed to bring all the critters home, he had come here for a particular runaway.

By the food preparation area, Watson stopped. As if awaiting him, an imposing Rottweiler dominated a large cage. The attached label stated that KING, a two-year-old male, had been checked in on Friday night and was immediately available for adoption. Kenya answered the personal questions, signed the bottom, and submitted the paperwork.

June led him to the Visitation Room. A minute later, she returned with King. The dog trotted up and slobbered on his face.

"I'll take him," Kenya said, scratching the big head.

June, concerned by the haste of her client's decision, asked, "Would you like to spend more time interacting to be certain you're both compatible?"

"No. I need this one." King wriggled his hindquarters from side to side, wagging his undocked tail. Kenya inquired, "Who brought him here?" A partially healed scar marred the perfection of the hound's muscled flank.

June scowled in antipathy. "Somebody left him in a nighttime drop-off kennel."

"What about the name? Did you name him King?"

"No, he came collared," she replied. "There was an ID tag."

Watson paid the seventy-dollar adoption fee, gratefully accepting the complimentary leash and bag of kibble.

"You're ruining my upholstery," he chided, as King tracked mud and slush into the backseat.

On the way home, Kenya saw Shashi Chatterjee's dog watching him in the rear-view mirror.

"Come here, boy!" he coaxed.

King thrust his bulky frame between the headrests and plopped into the passenger's seat. His uncropped ears grazed the roof liner.

At the apartment, the animal sped indoors and canvassed the rooms, much as Detective Ortega had done two weeks earlier. Instead of using his relatively poor eyesight, his fine-tuned snout examined every nook and cranny. The hound ceased circling and snuffled the green supermarket tote on the windowsill. King stared over his shoulder at his new master and woofed once. The Rottie squatted before the Tandoori Box as though shielding it from harm.

"That's a good boy," Kenya praised.

The knock came none too soon. King growled and jumped off the ottoman. Kenya seized the dog's studded collar and soothed him with a rub. "It's okay, boy." He straightened a pillow, patted his hair, and opened the door. Sally looked fantastic in a black dress. He felt sloppy in his finest shirt and slacks. "Hey there! Come on in."

The Rottweiler nuzzled her hand. "Is this your personal guard dog?" She scrooched down and cooed, "You're a good fella, aren't you?"

"I drove him home from the pound this morning. He does act ultra-protective."

Sally rubbed the animal's thick neck. "What's his name?"

"King."

"Why did you choose that?"

"Someone else named him," Watson responded. "I figured I'd change it to—"

"Don't. See how he stands? He's royalty for sure. I had a cat named Omega. She was the queen of my household."

"As in the Alpha and Omega?" After Hannah dumped him, Kenya started reading the Bible. He'd thrown in the towel seven bloodthirsty chapters into the Book of Leviticus. The tyrannical God of the Old Testament had given him the willies.

"Nothing so symbolic. When I was a kid, my dad built a darkroom in the basement. He used an Omega enlarger to print 8x10s of his photographs." Sally, resting on the kitchen countertop, read the lost dog poster. She exclaimed, "Is this King? *Kenya, are you a dognapper?*"

"No. King was on the lam. A fugitive. I called the number, and the owner sounded mean. Today—by chance—I found King at the shelter. I saved him from a miserable existence."

They took her vehicle to the party. While Sally finessed the finicky 8 ball gearshift, Kenya asked how she had acquired the classic truck.

The radiance of the chromed speedometer bathed her face in a golden glow. "I inherited Turtle when my father died. This 1956 F-100 was his pride and joy. He spotted the pickup rusting away in a barn and bought it from the farmer. For years, Dad worked on the truck each night after supper. As I got older, he'd let me help—hold a light, get a wrench, anything he needed. When the Ford was restored to its original condition, he let me take her on the first test-drive."

"Turtle," Kenya said, sliding his palm across the smooth green dashboard. "It's cool that you got along so well with your father."

Sally twisted the big steering wheel to avoid a pothole. The high beams spotlighted the bare limbs of white birches bordering the lane. Kenya put the skeletal afterimages—reminiscent of the shuddersome tree he'd seen inside the Tandoori Box—out of his mind. He questioned, "What happened to your dad?"

"That's a conversation for another time," she answered as the truck fishtailed around a sharp curve. "Now, I live with my mom."

The GPS application on Sally's smartphone beeped when they reached the coordinates of their final destination—a line of cars parked upon the road's shoulder.

With the temperature well below zero, the snow squeaked underfoot as they trailed a set of recent tracks through a vacant lot. On Sebago Lake, an ice-fishing shantytown gleamed beneath the full moon. Along the shore, the footprints turned northward, passing a shuttered boathouse, and toward a welcoming light.

Kenya aborted his daring grab for Sally's hand when a female voice urged, "Hurry!" A plump woman frantically motioned them closer. "Run! Tim should be home at any minute."

They skipped up the steps to the porch. Joyce Benning, Delphic's human resource director, thanked him for the bottle of Cantemerle. In the dim kitchen, the two shook off their coats and joined the dozen people—some recognizable as DIS employees—cozying up to the wood-burning stove. Joyce placed the gifts on a counter and distributed party poppers. The electrical whir of a garage door opener suspended the low-pitched chatter.

Joyce shushed. "Quiet, everyone."

A beanie-hatted man carrying paper bags jostled into the mudroom and, extending his elbow, flipped on the fluorescent light.

The revelers, showering him with confetti, screamed, "Surprise! Happy birthday!"

Tim dropped the groceries and clutched his chest. "You scared the bejesus out of me!" His wife, towing a bunch of black funeral balloons, rushed forward and kissed him hard on the lips. A friend gave the guest of honor a double shot of bourbon to settle his nerves.

Kenya poured Sally a goblet of wine and uncapped a beer for himself. They mingled with the other invitees, snacking on cheese and crackers. Normally, he was subdued in social situations, but after three potent Allagash Ales, his personal opinions flew freely. Following the delectable catered dinner, the Delphic staff members gravitated to the living room. Gregory Barnes congratulated Watson on his promotion. Susan Thorpe and Frank Walker remarked on his new car. Tipsy, he gagged his tongue from blabbing about his Powerball win. Kenya kept Sally's glass topped off with red. The gap between them shrank, her palm often touching him to emphasize an essential point.

"Sorry we're late, Joyce," a slurred voice apologized. "We came from another party."

Kenya turned as Russell and his wife, Valeska, entered the front doorway.

"Your dipshit friend and his better half are here," Sally murmured out of the side of her mouth.

Watson, observing the Fishers weave through the crowd, wanted to hide under the coffee table.

"Doctor Watson!" Russ shouted, putting forth his right mitt. "I'm shocked your mommy let you play on a school night." He hoisted Sally off her feet and, crushing her in a giant bear hug, created farting rumbles with his fat lips. Valeska blushed in embarrassment.

"Hey," Watson muttered. "Glad you could make it."

"So, are you guys an item?" Russ inquired, tilting his head and widening his eyes. His exaggerated expression pantomimed overwhelming amazement.

As Kenya framed his platonic response, Sally squeezed his fingers and smiled. "Yes, Russ. We've been hot and heavy for months now."

After three minutes of small talk, Russ dragged Valeska to the bar. Sally, still holding Kenya's hand, guided him down a hallway and snuck into a bedroom. She shut and locked the door. In pitch-darkness, she asked, "You know we're not going steady, right? I said we were together to get that buffoon off your back."

Kenya reached into the void, finding emptiness. "I understand."

Sally pushed his shoulders to the bedspread, crawled on top, and straddled his hips. Her sweet breath warmed his cheeks before he welcomed the gentle probing of her tongue. Kenya wrapped his arms around her waist. For an instant, she pulled away, the feverish rustle of clothing falling to the floor. Sally clasped his groping fingers and placed all ten firmly upon her breasts.

The stenciled digits on the outmoded flip alarm clock hesitated at midnight. Kenya pictured King alone at home, his ears perking as the Tandoori Box squirted out today's fresh prophecy. While Sally unbuckled his pants, he pondered the ultimate price for this brief moment of ecstasy.

Chapter Eight

THE GRAPHICS ON THE METEOROLOGIST'S MAP illustrated a polar front dipping from Canada, and to the north, the turbid clouds substantiated her dire forecast. Late to his job and hungover, Kenya's mood did not improve as he slunk into the building through the delivery entryway.

Tim Benning's birthday celebration had been fun, especially the ultra-passionate five minutes he and Sally had shared in the back bedroom. The eighth level of drunkenness—*The Journey Home*—had not been pleasant. As the exhilarating effects of the fifth stage—*The Hookup*—had worn off, and the sixth and seventh phases—*Relentless Party Mode* and *Feed Your Hunger*—had been skipped due to Sunday being a work night, that left the bumpy ride to his apartment. The "date," as Kenya had optimistically labeled it, ended with Sally dodging his goodnight kiss.

The ninth and final stage of dipsomania—*Regret*—hit him harshly when, stomach churning and head throbbing, he peered at the latest Tandoori Box photograph. This grainy image required careful interpretation and reflection, which is why he did not attend Marisa's daily stand-up meeting. The picture showed Kenya in Delphic's main hallway, walking away as someone exited the Technical Services lab. Under the magnifying glass, he determined the sex of the individual, female, and the contents of the carton she carried—*Samsung solid-state hard drives.*

In the past several weeks, rumors of missing computer hardware had circulated in the office. Some had speculated that the cleaning crew loaded their pushcarts with more than trash. Others had accused the underpaid site support agents in Technical Services of developing sticky fingers. Kenya now knew the identity of the thief. It was the woman who had invited him into her house—Joyce Benning, Delphic Industrial Sciences' director of Human Resources.

In a Delphic conference room, Detective Ortega stuffed three chunks of Bazooka chewing gum into her mouth. "Who took this picture? Is it from a security camera?" She handed the print to Detective Savage.

"No clue," Kenya replied as the hangover's swelling pressure centered behind his eyes. "I found it on my workstation this morning." The Tandoori Box had not explicitly expressed its objective. He worried about surrendering the photo, dumbfounded and a little relieved that they could see what he saw.

Marisa informed, "I talked to the head of Security. Video cameras are installed outside, but none inside. Clive Collins is auditing the tapes, or whatever storage technology is used nowadays."

"Mr. Watson, you look familiar," Savage mused. When he tapped the photographic evidence on his clean-shaven jaw, his nostrils flared. "Have we spoken before?"

"Carter, I remember him. Mr. Watson won a Good Citizen award by helping us catch that home invader—the freak who dressed up as Clarabell the Clown. He identified our suspect—his father-in-law—from a wanted poster. This man's Crime Stoppers' tip led to an arrest."

"You got the wrong guy," Kenya contradicted. "I'm no hero."

"He's absolutely right. It wasn't him," Marisa concurred. She fiddled with her hair. "Joyce Benning is stealing our hard drives. Can you get them back?"

Savage released the print and itched his throat. "Possibly, if she didn't already fence them on Craigslist. Do you keep a list of the serial numbers?"

Marisa answered. "Technical Services might. I'll check." The telephone rang as Kenya's supervisor reached for the receiver. She listened and hung up. "That was Clive. Multiple exterior surveillance cameras caught Joyce putting the loot in her trunk."

Ortega spat a pink wad into Marisa's wastebasket. "I'll need to speak to whoever took the picture. It's as if somebody was hiding in the ceiling."

"Why did the photographer give the photo to you, Mr. Watson?" Savage asked.

"Carter, are you having an allergy attack?" Anita inquired. "You're blowing up like a balloon."

A blistering rash spread across the investigator's face.

"May I return to my cubicle?" Kenya requested. "There's nothing else to tell you."

Detective Ortega dismissed him with a flip of her palm. "By all means, Mr., ahhh. . .Thompson. We'll contact you if we have more questions."

As Anita tended to Carter's psoriasis outbreak, Kenya nabbed the photograph and slunk to his cube. An hour later, Kenya stood alongside coworkers pressing against the lunchroom window. The crowd watched Joyce Benning give one last glance up at the building before Detective Savage slammed the patrol cruiser's barred door.

Kenya roused to a foot of fresh snow and an image of himself digging in the white stuff. He spent half an hour shoveling out his car and another ninety minutes skidding to the office. Finally, he sat at his desk.

Midafternoon, Watson recoiled as someone touched the nape of his neck. He swiveled the chair and slid off the noise-canceling headphones.

As Pamela massaged his shoulders, she remarked, "Kenya, you're so tense."

The stroking felt increasingly inappropriate. "Sorry, didn't hear you. I was busy solving a syntax problem."

The admin's hands dove beneath Kenya's collar. For leverage, she clamped onto his clavicles with her fingers and pushed downward with her thumbs. "NOAA issued a blizzard warning. The weather stations are predicting a foot of accumulation on top of what we got last night. David Hutchings is letting everyone leave early today. If you can work remotely, fine. If not, make up your hours during the remainder of the week." Pamela concluded her painful pinching and moved on to notify the next employee.

Kenya powered off his machine and was getting his gear together when Russ barged into the cubicle. "Pack it up, Doc. We're going to tie one on at McGee's."

With all the hullabaloo of Benning's termination, Watson never got a chance to talk to Sally. He could not depart without seeing her. "Don't you want to go home while you still can? I heard there's been a slew of accidents on the highways."

"The radio announced that the school is closed. Danika and Zoria got today off—a snow day. There's no way I'm driving to that hormonal hell until I've reached the proper blood alcohol level. Hurry the fuck up!"

Kenya jammed the laptop into his canvas backpack and snagged his jacket. "I'll be there soon. There's something I need to do first."

"Dude, take a dump at the tavern. Their bathroom stocks the finest quilted toilet paper. Not the cheap sandpaper they have here that's formulated to shred your turd birther." Russ snatched Kenya's bag and tossed it onto the desk. "Step on it, cheesedick. I'll buy you a beer. We've got to get over there before the kitchen runs out of hot wings!"

Watson, giving in to Fisher's incessant needling, tagged after him through the revolving doors and into the horizontal gusts. Sleet peppered their faces at the entrance to Monument Square. Ice frosted *Our Lady of Victories'* leafed crown and coated a human-shaped form huddled on the statue's marble base.

The two followed a jubilant party of men and women into McGee's Grill Pub. Commuters, reluctant to brave the glacial streets, milled around the noisy room.

Russ wheezed. "I think I froze my left nut off!"

Kenya wiped his wet boots on the doormat. "Did you see that homeless guy out there?"

"Where?" Fisher asked.

"Lying by the monument."

The hardware engineer tugged off his fleece-lined mittens. "You saw a bush or a garbage bag covered with a snowdrift. Nobody—not even you—is thick-headed enough to sleep outside tonight. Who cares? Let's grab a drink." Russ signaled the bartender for two tankards of Guinness.

"You're probably right," Watson said with uncertainty.

The pair claimed stools along the wall. "Cheers!" Russ toasted, crashing the foamy steins together. "Fuck!" he swore, as the coffee-colored stout splashed the crotch of his khakis.

Kenya tossed his coworker a wad of napkins and surveyed the space. At the packed bar, Gregory Barnes joked with Milton Mumford. Mumford's mutton-chop sideburns slanted rearward as he roared with laughter. In a private booth, Suzy Thorpe cuddled up with Frank Walker. The intern giggled as the project manager (who was old enough to be her father) spoke softly into her upturned ear. However, the person Kenya needed to talk to—Sally—was not here.

"What were you doing in the boss's office yesterday?" Fisher inquired. He blew on his pants zipper. "Was it about Joyce getting axed? Just the other night, we were singing 'Happy Birthday' to her old man."

"Who would've picked the HR director for a kleptomaniac?" Watson asked, passing over more napkins. "Marisa wanted to know who took the hard drives. I told her that, like everybody else, I heard some hardware walked off, but I had no idea who swiped it."

Russ gave up blotting the indelible beer stain, which now resembled the great state of Florida. "Good, I didn't peg you for a ratfink. Save my seat. I'll be back before you can spell gonorrhea backward." He strode to the bar to discuss political revolution with Deiter Steuben.

Although Kenya stressed over his role—in actuality, the Tandoori Box's role—in Joyce Benning's dismissal and arrest, he morally accepted that she received the punishment she deserved. He winced, envisioning himself at Christmastime pressing the carving knife against Jordan's quaking Adam's apple. Watson contemplated his involvement in the massacre at *Madama Butterfly*. The muscles in his thighs trembled. Perspiration beaded his brow. *I only purchased an opera ticket!* Desperate for air, he hopped off the pedestal and pushed past the throng.

Outdoors, underneath the saloon's awning, Kenya shielded his eyes from the streetlight. In the midst of the storm, he glimpsed a shadow moving near the bronze statue. He skated across Monument Square's frozen bricks and stepped over the chain links. A knoll raised the proud *Lady* to a superior elevation. Watson slipped and plunged headfirst into the snow. He held to the edge of the platform, gaining enough traction to scramble onto the ledge. The whiteout's silvery opacity hindered his ability to distinguish the features of the individual enfolded in the sleeping bag.

Kenya aimed his iPhone's flashlight and shouted, "Hey, mister, are you okay?"

In the LED's bluish lambency, a Caucasian male in a patched army jacket squinted through clouded pupils. Ice crusted a shaggy beard. Wild hair whipped around his head. Tarnished dog tags swung from the open shirt. "Who dat? Zat you, son?"

"Sir, let's get you indoors. You'll freeze to death out here."

The transient's cataracts suddenly clarified, his different colored eyes projecting intelligent luminosity. A voice deeper than the deepest well intoned, *"Kenya, you must find the Forever Tree."*

An arctic blast sucked the oxygen from his lungs. "Do I know you?" Kenya leaned into the tempest, searching for recognition and discovering none. "What tree? Who are you?"

The man squeezed into the mummy sleeping bag. His dirty fingers zipped up the fitted hood. Within seconds, white precipitation buried the thin fabric. Watson tunneled into the snow and yanked the corner of the sack. The puffy bundle rolled off the sill and knocked him off-kilter. Kenya tumbled down the embankment, ringing his bell on an iron pole.

Kenya drove a recreational vehicle, a forty-foot land yacht built before he had been born. The desert highway stretched into the shimmering horizon—long, straight, and narrow. As the moribund sun fell beneath the snowcapped peaks, the radiation of a newborn moon colored the Winnebago's plush interior an unhealthy green. When he fumbled for the headlight switch, the useless knob fell off. Fountains of fluorescent fluid drenched the floor mats—a plague of teething rats had perforated the radiator hoses. He turned on the windshield washers, worsening visibility. The red engine light, centered on the dashboard, buzzed three times, and then the big V8 shit the bed and conked out. Ravenous rodents invaded the RV's cabin as Kenya and King fled to the cooling asphalt. Camped in a dry wash, Hells Angels mounted Harley-Davidson motorcycles and, gunning infernal engines, exploded onto the roadbed. He politely ignored the leathered men's unsolicited mechanical advice. Kenya and his mystical beast traveled westward, seeking an open service station. Elusive night creatures kept pace behind a hedgerow of flowering sage. The Rottweiler, ears back and hackles spiked, chased the varmints into the darkness. Kenya sang out, "Come back, boy!" He cocked his head to listen. Red and blue armies clashed in far-off badlands. Flashes of mortar fire delineated the warriors' frontlines. The ragged outline of an expanding arcus thunderhead—the angry conglomeration of a thousand separate storms—flared with jets of heat lightning. His mother's upraised family Bible acted as a shield. Grandpa Clarence's stag-handled "pig sticker" warded off evil. The identification tags coiling upon his chest rattled like snakes. A gigantic tree grew in the center divider. Even at this considerable distance, Kenya understood that this rare species, so distinct from the native Joshua trees, had lived way before Joseph had laid eyes on Mary. Deliverance in sight, he dashed into the stinging rain, wailing out his own epitaph. Kenya hunched inside a sizzling ring of electricity, his molars aching from instantaneous booms of thunder. He unsealed the holy book. Every page, except for the last (this in a foreign tongue), was blank. Electrostatic discharges set the tree's topmost limbs ablaze. Branches as thick as sewer pipes splintered to the earth. When the massive trunk fractured in two, Kenya retreated to the cover of a boulder. The rending sounded alive.

"Kenya, wake up!"

He heard masculine chanting and peeked past the rock slab. The Monument Square vagrant stood in front of the burning tree. A monk's robe, sodden with melting snow, hung from his extended arms. The prophet's bare feet levitated above the soil. In one hand, she held a black box, the other a—

"Please wake up!"

Kenya blinked as snowflakes tickled his eyelashes. His skull pounded. An ethereal face drew near. *Am I dead?* he wondered. *If so, this isn't so bad.* He tried to focus. "Sally?"

"Jesus, Kenya," Sally cried. Her eyes brimmed with tears. "I was afraid you'd never come to."

"We were about to measure you for a pine box," Jack Gantz professed. "It's lucky we happened by when we did. Why are you out here, anyway?"

The couple lifted Kenya to his feet and brushed off his parka.

"I came outside to help a homeless guy." Watson pointed at the concave depressions in the snow. "Guess I must have fallen off the statue."

"There's no one here," Handsome Jack stated, checking his wristwatch. "Wanna come with us to McGee's? Happy Hour is over in ten minutes."

"No, I just left there." Kenya dabbed the soggy knot on his scalp. "You go ahead."

"Ooh, that's a nasty cut," Sally observed. "Are you all right?"

"Yeah," he responded. "I was born with thick skin."

She frowned. "Are you sure?"

Watson stared at the ground and nodded.

Handsome Jack laughed and pulled her away. Kenya hoped Sally would turn back. As the pub's door clapped shut, he wished his father had never asked his mother to slow dance at the May Day ice cream social.

Watson saw the sheen of metal at the base of *Our Lady of Victories*. He swept off the sparkling powder and slipped a forefinger under the loop of ball chain. In his car, Kenya strung the battered dog tags—*a talisman*—over his head, gunned the engine, and drove recklessly into the blizzard.

On Wednesday morning, snow accumulated at the Baxter Woods apartments. Herculean Public Works trucks plowed and sprinkled salt in ineffectual efforts to clear the streets. Kenya stayed home along with the majority of Delphic's workforce. He connected to the company's virtual private network but lacked the incentive to work on any of his projects.

Watson dwelled obsessively upon Sally Green and her Prince Charming, Jack Gantz. *What is she doing with that smarmy bastard?* He attempted to access her social media posts but lacked the proper permissions to see anything beyond her name. *I've got to flush that slut out of my brain.*

He unwrapped the chain securing the dog tags from his fingers. The embossed letters and numbers stamped into the faces of the twin identical oblong disks read:

JOHNSON
T. D.
2691514 AB
USMC M
NO PREF.

Kenya ran a thumb across the ridges of raised text. Corroded, scratched, and bent, the steel looked to have survived hand-to-hand combat. On military sites, he learned how to read the compressed format: T. D. Johnson inherited an uncommon AB blood type, used a medium-size gas mask, and listed no specific religious preference. The seven-digit number revealed the Marine had enlisted before 1972 and had served in Vietnam. Strangely, the service number was not registered in any public database. *Didn't I receive a package from someone named Johnson?* He sighed and draped the medallions around his neck.

Watson's attention returned to Sally. He had to admit that she'd acted genuinely upset to see him hurt. *That doesn't mean jack shit. In all likelihood, the wind caused those crocodile tears.*

Today's picture rested on top of the growing stack: King resting on the floor in a "lion's pose," and his master asleep on the loveseat with his arms hugging a pillow in quiet desperation. In a blue funk, Kenya spun himself into his purple Snuggie and remained cocooned until the March equinox.

Chapter Nine

KNOWN AS THE SEASON OF REBIRTH, RESTORATION, AND RESTLESSNESS, the defrosting citizens of Portland, Maine, welcomed springtime like a long-lost lover. After endless months binge-watching *Breaking Bad* on Netflix or achieving unheard-of levels of self-gratification playing *Candy Crush Saga* on their phones, the arthritic, overweight masses ventured outdoors to exercise. Before hitting the streets, bicycle riders in flashy jerseys and spandex shorts oiled rusty sprockets and inflated flat tires. Runners in the latest track shoes kneaded atrophied calf muscles and stretched taut hamstrings.

Kenya, out for a stroll with King, passed the BAXTER WOODS APARTMENTS sign. Six weeks had elapsed since the big blizzard of 2016. Today, as the weather turned pleasant, the lingering heaps of gray snow thawed into the gutters. The Rottie, raring to bathe in the odoriferous mud, clawed up a flowerbed of yellow daffodils.

Not much materialized during the final gasps of winter. As the scab on Watson's scalp healed to a scar, he wondered if his vision of the homeless war veteran was a symptom of the concussion—a hallucination. At Delphic Industrial Sciences, management hired a new human resources director and installed security cameras in the corridors. The software engineer kept to himself, doing his job and cashing regular paychecks. Sally approached a couple of times, eager to talk. Kenya controlled his temper, taking the high road and walking away.

On the matter of the Tandoori Box, several events of relevance arose over this duration. One weekend, Kenya drove to the Old Port Exchange neighborhood. He wanted one more look at the Tandoori House and Meat Shop. Now, totally demolished, the restaurant's remains formed a sad pile. On a retaining wall, an aspiring artist with an aptitude for stylized graffiti had spray-painted a stick figure—head, torso, arms, and legs—hanging from a gallows. The red block letters TANDOORI filled the eight dashes—the poignant answer to a hangman's guessing game. Watson imagined the tagger had left the message for him.

Kenya never ceased fulfilling the Tandoori Box's "requests." On Valentine's Day, he deposited a Benjamin in the tip jar at Armando's, a local Mexican restaurant. Twenty-four hours later, on President's Day, he snuck into the alley behind the same taqueria and snipped a green wire connected to the alarm system. At the Maine Shopping Mall, on Good Friday, he duct-taped an antique straight-edge folding razor under a bench by the children's play area.

Watson tried not to think about how his conduct—*the actions he recalled*—might alter the courses of other people's lives.

The man and dog followed the Bri-Mar Trail up Rattlesnake Mountain. Kenya paused to rest and squirt water from a bottle into King's mouth. The morning air stirred the leaves—crisp and clean. Silver dew glistened on sweetly scented honeysuckle petals. Early-bird hikers heading downhill waved hello. Watson prayed to God that he had not missed her, yet he remained convinced that their meeting was inevitable.

Kenya had bonded with the Rottweiler during the previous few months. At first, he'd harbored serious doubts about the animal's loyalty. Was King here to guard the Tandoori Box or to protect him? Would the brute, sensing betrayal, rip out his throat in the dead of night? Watson accepted the fact that the cube had arranged the adoption. Everything the black block did appeared to be part of a bigger picture—a blueprint Kenya unwittingly adhered to without exception and without understanding. He had no premonitions of how this fable might end, but for now, he was content to keep King at the end of a short restraint.

Kenya flipped the image and reread the imprint (a new Tandoori Box feature) for the hundredth time: 9:47:08 a.m. With only eight minutes to go, he broke into a trot. At a split in the trail, King chose the right fork. This path entered a shady grove of tall conifers. A soft matting of dried needles murmured underfoot until the grade toughened. They clambered across roots and boulders. On the far side of a burbling creek, the land dipped and then plateaued. In the thick of a sunlit meadow, three white-tailed deer dined upon new shoots of wild barley. As Watson hurried to focus the camera, King wrested the loop from his hands and took off. All four animals hopped over the limbs of a fallen tree and vanished into the impenetrable woodland.

"King!" Kenya hollered. "Come back, boy!" His feet flattened the grass as he ran to the last place he had seen his dog. By the log, Watson gaped at the woods, the photograph, and his wristwatch. *I'm late.*

A female called in a dominant tone, "King! Get over here. Now!" Nettles parted as the Rottie emerged from a copse of aspen—*with Sally.* She recognized the owner and set him free. The deerstalker dragged the strap through the flowering plants, leaping to muddy his shirt.

"How did you know it was King?" Kenya questioned. He combed clumps of thistles from the canine's fur.

Sally jingled the brass identification tag on the dog's collar. "Plus, your pal remembered me."

"You are rather hard to forget," Kenya said with a smile.

"Aren't you going to ask me why I'm here?" An orange case hung from a strap on her neck, and a tattered copy of *Bird Neighbors* poked out of her nylon backpack.

"It's fairly apparent to me that you're birdwatching," Kenya replied. In the Tandoori Box print, they stood atop a rock ledge, where Sally used field glasses to peer into the distance at a Pac-Man-shaped lake.

"Very perceptive," she said, tucking the book into the flap. "What are *you* doing here?"

"It was King's idea," he answered. "He's a nature buff. Who would have thought?"

Together, the trio hiked beneath the quaking leaves. Sally's ash brown hair flashed under the millions of heart-shaped shadows. Soon, they perched on the granite shelf overlooking Panther Pond. The unobstructed view of the valley was outstanding.

"I didn't picture you as a kooky birder lady," Kenya said. His blood still boiled hot, but here, with her shoulder touching his, he would gladly yank out every one of his fingernails for another moment in her arms.

Sally patted the binocular case's scuffed leather. "This was my dad's. He got it from his grandfather, who was an ornithologist." She handed him a spiral-bound notebook. Beautiful colored sketches of birds with detailed descriptions filled the well-thumbed pages.

"Did you draw these?" Kenya inquired.

"I did the illustrations in the back—the crappy ones. My dad worked as a graphic artist. *He* was talented. On the weekends, he'd teach me how to observe and record. We had fun sneaking around the backcountry. When I'm out here birding, I feel near to him."

Kenya towed King away from poison ivy vines. "You said you'd tell me about your father."

"I'm not sure how he died."

"What do you mean? Was your dad ill?"

"My father was a health nut. Ate gluten-free long before it became a fad diet. He ran frequently and competed in marathons. Dad kept himself in decent shape. Something else happened." Sally used a twig to pry out a pebble lodged in her boot's waffled sole. "During my senior year in high school, we lived in Englewood, New Jersey. Each morning, like clockwork, my father rode the 7:29 Red and Tan Lines bus into New York City. He freelanced at a prestigious advertising agency on Madison Avenue. When Dad didn't come home for supper, my mother phoned his boss. Mr. Eckhoff told us he never came into the office and did not call in sick. The police interviewed the bus driver, who recollected letting him off at the Port Authority Bus Terminal. He worked by the Empire State Building, a five-block walk. Somewhere along the way, my father disappeared from the face of the earth."

A boisterous family tromped through the underbrush. The rambunctious boy chucked sticks at tree squirrels. The giggling girl tossed a candy wrapper upon the ground and begged for more sweets. Sally stared icily as the carefree parents lit cigarillos and opened beers.

"My friend got mugged in the men's room at the Port Authority," Watson said. "Robert was standing at a urinal when a crack addict bashed his head against the wall and stole his wallet. Rob got twenty stitches." He envisioned his younger brother, Edward, and the hillside grave in Locustwood Cemetery. Kenya had not gotten up the nerve to visit the plot since the funeral. He wrangled the escaped tumor of guilt into a solitary cell in his brain's right frontal lobe and slammed the gate shut. "Did you discover what took place? Why do you think your father is dead?"

"The detectives investigated for months. They confiscated video surveillance and checked bank records. We contacted the hospitals and morgues. My schoolmates and I posted signs throughout Midtown. The media broadcast his face on the news.

Nothing ever turned up—not one trace. He must be dead. Dad wouldn't simply wash his hands of us. I realize this sounds naive, but he wasn't that sort of person. I roll out of bed each morning believing today is the day he'll walk in the front door." Sally palmed a fist-sized rock and flung it at the sun. "Then, after I give my father a big hug, I'll make him tell me where the fuck he's been all this time."

"When did you relocate to Portland?"

"A year later. My mom wanted a fresh start. We had relatives up here, so we moved in with my uncle until we rented our own house. I transferred to a new school. It sucked donkey balls."

"You said my Swedish meatballs looked like donkey balls."

"You heard that?" Sally laughed. "Well, they did."

The rowdies wandered off to bully additional wildlife. They had the lookout to themselves. Aside from Kenya's mandatory sessions in seventh grade with the elementary school therapist, he had never spoken openly of Edward. His mother and father had also evaded discussing that heartbreaking topic. He suspected that his parents' deficient communication skills had kindled his dad's infidelity and triggered the ugly divorce. These days, they had too many other kids to give their deceased son a second thought.

"I had a brother, and I killed him," Watson said. He turned to gauge her reaction.

Sally appeared more concerned than appalled. She asked him to repeat the statement.

Kenya stared at the mountains, oblivious to their grandeur. "Edward just turned ten. Eddie was smart, athletic, and always happy, a good kid. It was a Friday. We were riding the bus to school. I still picture the new blue-and-black plaid shirt and Lee jeans my mother gave him for his birthday. My brother wanted to stay with me, but he was two years younger than I was. 'Forget it,' I said. 'Go sit with the fifth graders.' I hung out with my friends in the back seats. . .a bunch of losers. We were horsing around, using straws to shoot spitballs at the girls. I needed to get a laugh, so I yelled, 'Hey, Eddie, look outside. Quick! Kaylee's out there.' He talked about her constantly—his first puppy love. My brother climbed on the cushion and lowered the glass. He leaned from the window, stared backward, and shouted, 'Pickles—that's what Eddie used to call me—I don't see her!' I knew Kaylee wasn't anywhere nearby. She went to the Catholic school across town. The bus cut a corner. The wheels jumped the curb. A telephone pole clipped his head. The driver pulled over, blood everywhere, everybody screaming. I'm—" Kenya clutched his throat and grimaced. "I hauled my brother inside."

Sally's colorlessness indicated horror. "Was he—?"

"Eddie was decapitated by the impact."

"Are you serious?"

"Dead serious," Watson answered. "His death was my fault, and I've been paying for my sins ever since."

Kenya heard the clatter of heavy hooves. Curious, he stuck his head out the stagecoach window. A swirling cyclone of bone ash abraded his face and stung his eyeballs. The coachman, a barrel-chested skeleton cloaked in a flowing cape and top hat trimmed with raven feathers, drove the twelve frothing stallions toward their terminal station—the belching smokestacks of a colossal crematorium—with pistol-shot cracks of a forty-foot whip. Kenya ducked as the spiked arms of a towering saguaro cactus scarred the coach's leather sides. The color of the wagon's lacquered interior, as well as the silk finery attiring the two males and one female seated alongside him, matched the exterior, driver, and horses—a shade blacker than coal soot. Bloated carpetbags and waterlogged stateroom trunks stacked the cabin's floor—conspicuous trappings of the passengers' overindulgent lifetimes. A priest unpinned a rose from his ankle-length cassock. He sniffed the delicate bud and, to his captive audience, decreed, "Some of us may live tonight, but most of us shall surely perish. Those fortunate enough to survive certain death will earn a second opportunity to experience life to the fullest." When the Jesuit plucked the remaining red petal, he smiled sadly and gave the thorny stem to Kenya. "For all we know, the times of our passings are already written in stone." The woman placed a white cornet on her horned head, the crowning vestment of a nun. She shrilled at the coachman, "Faster, Jacob! Give the fiends a taste of the whip!" The accelerating stagecoach careened around eroded headstones and jounced over robbed graves. Ignited by the sparking wheels of iron, embers of coffin wood and embalmed flesh floated through the flapping doors. Cinders scorched holes in the breast of Kenya's waistcoat. He tore off the ruined garments and examined his ribs for burns. "Does anyone wish to disembark?" the sister inquired. "The All-Powerful has notified me that we will be taking a slight detour. Speak now or forever hold your tongue." She gyrated goatish eyes and bleated. "However, I must forewarn you: the brakes on this ancient hearse failed millennia ago." Dread gnawed the shriveled sac insulating Kenya's heart. Consumption gurgled in the depths of his lungs. Again, he hung his head outside the window, seeing the steep escarpments of a canyon. The wagon wheels chattered, ready to break the gravitational pull of this world—silence followed by the whistling lull, the endless fall. At the foot of the cliff, the ultimate reckoning awaited—the wreckage of souls. Would his punishment be an eternity in Hell, or might the Master show mercy and grant him the Big Sleep? The goat-woman blared, "What is taking so damn long? *Jacob, flay them to the bone!*" The vicar bellowed with fervor, "Something awaits on the horizon! Brace yourselves! I beseech thee, bid farewell to everyone and everything you ever loved!" The priest forked a fleeting benediction, and when the carriage tilted forward, he grabbed the nun's cloven hoof, and they leaped to safety. The spokes of the giant wheels reversed direction as the coach launched into space. Luggage hovered weightlessly throughout the cabin. In free fall, Kenya caught a small black box and clasped it to his chest.

When Watson awoke, he remembered the whole nightmare. He repeated the Jesuit's words out loud. *"Some of us may live tonight, but most of us shall surely perish."* At the toilet, by the time he peed his last drop, his mind retained only a sharp image of the rose's thorny stem.

Pink water swirled between Kenya's toes and swished down the shower drain. The blood and grime beneath his fingernails were scrubbed off with a toothbrush. He increased the temperature, put his forehead upon the cool tiles, and let the hot stream soothe his sore shoulders.

Watson had just driven home from Parkside, one of the few "rough" neighborhoods in Portland. The Lexus, fresh from the all-night self-service car wash, dripped soap suds onto his parking spot. To his dismay, cleaning up the mess in the cargo area had been more labor-intensive than he had expected, requiring an industrial vacuum and carpet stain remover. The SUV's windows were left ajar to ventilate the chlorine fumes of liquid bleach.

Kenya dried his shaved scalp with a towel, no longer needing eyeglasses to see himself in the bathroom mirror. What reflected in the fogged glass satisfied him: a handsome man—*a confident man*—with places to go, people to see, and things to do. The unsightly bags under his crystal-clear eyes were gone, and the chiseled cheeks above his strong chin glowed with vigor. Watson flexed and rippled the muscles in his chest and arms. His flat abdomen even exhibited the beginnings of a six-pack. *Apart from these bug bites, I never felt this great! Thank God for the therapeutic properties of that little cube.*

Tonight had not proceeded as foreseen. Kenya merely wanted to scare the car thief. The Tandoori Box photograph showed him chasing a man from his Lexus. He knew the locale—

his carport at the apartment building—and the precise minute when this incident was destined to transpire: 11:48 p.m. Watson armed himself with a Martha Stewart meat tenderizer and hid underneath a hedge of budding rhododendrons.

The waiting gave him the jitters. On edge, he rubbed out a leg cramp. Kenya glanced at his wristwatch. *Any minute now.* He snapped off twigs to enhance his line of vision. Water sprayed the green strip between the sidewalk and the street. Watson zipped his windbreaker against the dampness, closed his eyes, and listened. The irrigation paused as the system switched to a different zone. Motorcycles revving down a distant boulevard were pursued by the wail of police sirens. Hissing exhalations lifted his eyelids. A hooded snake rose from the bark chips—*a cobra?* Venom spit from curved fangs. Kenya scuttled rearward as the fully extended sprinkler head soaked his face with reclaimed wastewater. "Yuck!" he sputtered, releasing Martha's textured mallet.

An engine spun to life, and a door clicked shut. Kenya raced toward his automobile. Someone was inside, their hand on the transmission lever. He heaved open the passenger's door and lunged for the ignition button. The robber, a goateed male dressed in a black tuque and gray Adidas sweatshirt, karate-chopped Watson's wrist with the hard edge of his palm.

"Get out of my car!" Kenya shouted, wrestling for the gearshift.

The booster, his innards reeking of garlic steamed clams, cursed, *"Jebi se!"*

Just as Watson succeeded in killing the motor, a fist punched him in the nose. The man grabbed a compact electronic device, kicked the driver's side door open, and hurtled over the parking lot's speed bumps. Kenya crawled into the driver's seat, restarted the engine, shifted into drive, and laid tracks across the slick lawn. On Hartley Street, an opaque shape absconded into

Baxter Woods. He braked the Lexus in a gravel lot by the trail-head. Only two other routes went in or out of the thirty-acre nature preserve. Watson floored the gas pedal and drove to Evergreen Cemetery, the nearest exit. He parked next to a water delivery van. Upon his center console, a thin metal bar glinted in the glare of the cabin lamp. Kenya gripped the discarded slim jim and crept into the park.

To avoid being spotted, Kenya turned off the iPhone's light. A motif of oak leaves patterned the sky, and deeper into the forest, pine needles whisked away the stars. It was too dark to see anything beyond the tip of his beak. If he strayed off the footpath, sapling branches switched his face, and brambles trapped his feet. Watson, stock-still, tuned into the secretive ambiance of night: below in the detritus, the furtive rustles of mice, by his left ear, the persistent buzzing of a mosquito—*slap*, off to the right, faraway, a car alarm, its repetitive warbling ending abruptly, and high aloft in the leafy canopy, the hair-raising, banshee screech of an owl. Even with his ears cupped, he did not pick up any human footsteps. Maybe the thief took an alternate tack. *Should I go home? I got my car back. Do I really want further confrontation?* Kenya regretted not bringing King. The Rottweiler would have ferreted out the foul-breathed motherfucker—*and torn him a new butthole.*

A quarter of a mile along the track, Kenya barked his shinbone on an iron bench and, falling to his knees, dropped the lockout tool. As he raked a cluster of ferns, a faint scuffling interrupted his foraging. Watson homed in on the source, a flicker of light in the trees. The swinging beam of a penlight illuminated the pathway. He shielded his cellphone by holding the screen close to the soil. Kenya extracted the slim jim from an ant hill and set up an ambush behind a rotten stump.

The attack was swift, one-sided, and, once the torch's bulb shattered, unobservable to anybody not wearing infrared goggles. Watson swung the two-foot length of spring steel in great arcs, knocking the thief flat. He continued striking, initially hitting dirt, and then, as blind fury guided his aim, the tool sliced flesh, carved cartilage, and struck bone. Kenya never sensed the colony of fire ants inching up his sleeve, yet at the apex of his wrath, a vivid image of Sally Green glimmered through the malevolent blackness. Sally looked extremely disappointed. Drained of rage, his arm sank to his side, and the crooked slim jim slipped from his grasp.

The woods were now tomblike quiet. Kenya pressed the man's neck. A weak pulse fluttered beneath the ravaged skin. His fingers probed the notched skull and squeezed the spongy face. "Pretty bad," he muttered, "but not dead." Watson stood, started down the trail, and halted. *Don't croak on me, shithead.* He gazed at the bloody lump of clothes. *That asswipe must weigh a ton.*

Kenya made a hasty trip to the apartment complex's laundry room, doubling back to the park with an appliance dolly. He used the offset tightener to strap the man's waist to the hand truck. A twist of twine prevented his knuckles from scraping the ground. The cart's narrow wheels were not designed for off-roading. After much cussing and cajoling, Watson managed to trundle the robber to the rear of his SUV and dump him into the cargo area.

Roko Petrović regained consciousness at the infamous Parkside intersection of Mellen and Grant Streets. Beatrice McCormick, a shopworn prostitute widely known around the ward as the "Whistler," took pity on the broken man. Bea, motherly and in need of a good pimp, helped Roko to his feet and carried him home.

Chapter Ten

WITH HIS HEELS PROPPED ATOP HIS WORKSTATION, Kenya rapped the Powerball lottery ticket upon his palm. The dancing fir tree stamped on the paper's upper left corner smelled like greenbacks. The tantalizing motto at the slip's bottom promised, PLAY LUCKY FOR LIFE. Once more, the Tandoori Box had divined the winning numbers. That Wednesday, en route to the office, he'd purchased this sure winner at the Rite Aid, contributing an extra bone to get the Power Play option. The Maine Lottery website estimated tonight's jackpot at ninety million dollars. Watson tucked the stub in his wallet and took out his iPhone.

Kenya typed with the tips of his thumbs: *Wot r u doin 2nite?* His forefinger wavered above the send button. He ignored the rabble of butterflies battering his stomach and sent the message.

As Watson stood by for a response, he linked a box of paperclips together, forming a daisy chain. Impatient, he sorted project documentation. Irritable, the software engineer dumped the entire pile in the blue recycle bin. Kenya flipped the keyboard and whacked the edge against the tabletop. Disgusted, he used canned air to blow the flecks of food, skin, and boogers onto the floor.

The cellphone hummed. Sally texted: *Y watsup?*

Stoked, Kenya tapped: *U shd cum over.* He backspaced, giggling childishly as he edited the letters *"cum"* to *"come."* Then he added: *We cn watch a mvie 2geder.*

The company telephone rang. MARISA LANKA registered on the display. Staring at his iPhone, he let the call go directly to voicemail. Watson inventoried his limited collection of DVDs—no appropriate viewing material for an important night with a respectable young lady. If she said yes, he would stop at a Redbox on the way home to pick up a chick flick.

The phone buzzed. *Sry sum bozo wz askn me a dumb :-Q. Il brng ovr a <) n sum (B),* filled the dialog balloon.

Elated, he typed: *Gr8! King wil b :-) 2 c u.*

"Kenya, are you busy?" his manager demanded over his shoulder.

Watson expressed amusement at the yellow winky face emoji he received before shoving the smartphone into his pocket. "No, Marisa. What can I do for you?"

His boss jogged her head toward her office. She sat behind the cluttered desk, ordering him to shut the door and sit down. Marisa looked tuckered out or discouraged. "Not too long ago, you received a decent raise and bonus. Since then, you've slacked off. What happened? I may have misjudged your readiness for a promotion."

Defensively, he questioned, "What are you implying? I complete my assignments. Ask anyone."

"Kenya, there's no need for me to 'ask anyone.' Project managers *came to me* complaining about *your* lousy attitude. You're often tardy, and I've seen you leave early. You used to be so punctual. Frank Walker says you neglect his meetings and no longer finish your tasks on schedule. When I walk by your cubicle, I see you wasting time surfing the internet or playing with your cellphone. How can you expect to reach your performance goals?"

He felt the lottery ticket burning a hole in his wallet. The winnings could allow him to quit. *Then, I will tell this nag to go screw herself.* "Are you firing me?"

Marisa's face softened, breaking into a wry smile. "Not if you get back on track."

"I'll admit, I'm moody. My mother's been bedridden for the last few months." Watson expanded upon the lie. "Her doctor diagnosed her illness as angina with a touch of phlebitis."

"Oh, I am sorry to hear that," his supervisor consoled. "Our company provides excellent mental health assistance. All the benefits are listed on the Human Resources website."

"Thank you, Marisa." Kenya, burrowing into his toy box of terrors, flashed back to a sixth-grade dodgeball game—the one when his gym teacher, a sadist by the name of Ryan Hinkley, nailed him in the family jewels with an over-inflated basketball. He peed blood for days. This painful memory brought tears to his eyes. "Mom being sick is hard on Dad. My parents are very close. Sometimes, I require help coping with my emotions."

"Kenya, helping is what we're here for. My door is always open if you ever want to talk."

Watson assured his boss he would "buckle down" and returned to his cubicle. He browsed rentals on the Redbox site. In the ROMANCE genre, he perused the love triangle plot of the movie *Aloha*. A rubber band snapped his neck.

"What's so enchanting, Doctor Watson?" Russ inquired. "You got yourself a man crush on Bradley Cooper?"

Watson hastily tabbed to another window and swiveled. "I was just—"

Fisher looked his coworker up and down. Confounded, he exclaimed, "Where are your eyeglasses?"

"I got laser eye surgery."

"Are you liftin' weights?"

"Nope," Kenya responded. "I started taking the stairs. Oh, and I gave up drinking regular soda."

"Sucrose is white death," Russ concurred. "Valeska keeps bustin' my balls about my weight. Said I'm turning into a fat slob."

"I heard the 'dad bod' is a growing trend," Watson informed. "Chubby husbands make wives appear skinnier in selfies."

"What a great concept. Valeska should appreciate what she has. Everyone knows American men are the best husbands. Why can't I have a night out with my buds and have a good time? A bucket of extra crispy chicken and a case of beer? I earned it." Russ dug a pinkie into his belly button and showed him the gray lint ball. "Christ! I ain't Superman—I'm fucking married!"

Kenya, tired of this mundane chitchat, turned to his monitor. "See ya. I gotta dial into a meeting."

Sally arrived with a large pizza and double four-packs of Bissell Brothers Bucolia Ale. She tore off two cans before putting the rest into the refrigerator. Kenya filled King's bowl with dog food and got the dishes. They shifted to the table in the dining room.

Sally popped a 16-ouncer and guzzled the sticky hops. "I hope you like your pizza with everything on it." She opened the cardboard box and served him a thick slice. "Go on, ask me."

"Ask you what?" Kenya bit into the wedge. He washed down the stringy cheese with a gulp of beer.

"You're dying to know what I was doing with Jack Gantz."

"On the night of the snowstorm? It's none of my business."

Sally buzzed her lips. "Then why were you avoiding me? Whenever I tried to speak, you stormed off."

"Me? You made it clear you're not interested in a meaningful relationship—not with me, at any rate."

She tipped the can, clenched her eyelids, and drank. Sally set the container on the tablecloth and said, "I have my reasons."

"Such as?"

Sally reluctantly replied. "I met someone online. His profile listed all the qualities of being a nice guy. I fell in love, we moved in together, yadda, yadda, yadda. . . . A few months later, he—*that asshat*—hooked up with some tramp on Tinder. One afternoon, I came home early and caught them in *my* bed. They stole *my* cat and ran off to New York City. From what I've learned, he's now a successful trader on Wall Street." She scowled to herself. "Thank God, I didn't marry that douchebag!"

"Your boyfriend kidnapped Omega?"

Sally nodded. "You remember her name?"

"You said she was the queen of your household and named after your dad's photographic enlarger." He dished out two more slices. "Are you saying you're currently single?"

"After getting burned, I've been skittish." She tapped her head twice. "Trust issues. It'll be a while till I'm ready to mount that horse again."

Kenya locked eyes with her. "I've heard rumors regarding you and Gantz."

"Do tell!" Sally slanted her chair rearward. "What's the scuttlebutt?"

"Gantz said you had sex with him in his Suburban."

She snorted. "You fell for that bullshit?"

He shrugged. "Why not? You left me out in the cold."

Sally finished the pint. At the refrigerator, she opened two cans, gave him one, and sat. "What about you? Are you a monk, or—?"

"No." Kenya related his version of his relationship with Hannah Schrock. He omitted that he was still stuck on her.

"That Amish gal sounds like a real piece of work. You haven't gone out with anybody else?"

"No one special," he answered. "For a long time, I thought Hannah would want me back."

"Ha! I am well acquainted with that insane level of insecurity. Why did you ask me over here?"

"To watch a movie."

She leaned forward. "No, really. Come clean."

The next words spilled from Watson's lips without his consent. "Bumping into you on Rattlesnake Mountain wasn't altogether an accident."

A tail thumped Kenya's leg as Sally fed King crust beneath the table. "It seemed odd. How did you find out I'd be up there? Were you stalking me?"

Kenya had consumed a quart of the full-bodied brew. He wanted to disclose the truth, but did not think divulging his secret would be wise for either of them. Watson attempted a sheepish expression. "I followed you there."

"From where?" Sally's eyebrows arched in mistrust. "You don't know where I live. Do you?"

"I, uh—"

"You tailed me to my house?"

Kenya took another sip. "It was easy. Your vintage pickup truck sticks out on the road." He glanced at the clock. "Let's start the movie."

Sally shut the pizza box. "We need to discuss your inappropriate behavior."

"We'll talk afterward." He stowed the leftovers in the fridge and recycled the empties.

Watson inserted the *Aloha* Blu-ray disk into the player and joined her on the couch. King sprawled half-asleep between them.

Five minutes into Bradley Cooper's petulant monologue—something about satellites, billionaires, and broken legs—Sally seized the remote and jabbed the pause button. "Oh my god—*so lame.* Did you imagine I'd enjoy this dreck?"

Kenya lifted his arms, naively presuming every red-blooded female adored every romantic comedy ever made.

King wriggled closer to Sally. She punched the play button.

Midway in, Sally again stopped the disk and said, "Any dolt can tell the girl is Bradley Cooper's daughter. Those two women will fight over him tooth and claw." She laughed. "I am kinda curious to see who wins the war—Rachel McAdams, no doubt."

"I have my money on the," Kenya made air quotes, "Asian lady."

Sally raised her shoulders. "Why in the world did the director cast Emma Stone for this role? Aren't there any legitimate Asian actresses in Hollywood?" As the romcom approached its wacky conclusion, she froze the screen for the final time. "Nothing went on between me and Jack Gantz that night or any other time."

Kenya remained reserved.

She inquired, "Remember the blizzard we had a couple of years back?"

"Uh-huh. I just started working at Delphic."

"Like the one this February, everyone walked to McGee's to wait for the trucks to plow the streets. When we left, my engine wouldn't crank over—a dead battery. Jack offered to drive me home. It was late, and he kept pestering me to—"

He raised a hand, interrupting her. "Sally, you don't have to tell me this. It's all water under the bridge."

"I caved in—it was freezing—and we got in his car. Jack fumbled in his jacket, pretending he had lost the keys. Right away, I figured out his angle. When I reached for the door handle, the drunken twerp grabbed my arm. I told him to knock it off. He skipped first and tried to steal second base. I applied a finger lock, and he let go. Jack apologized. I called Triple-A."

"What's a finger lock?" Kenya questioned, picturing a woven Chinese finger trap.

Sally stretched across the snoring Rottie and took his hand. "This is gonna hurt you way more than it's gonna hurt me."

"I am not going to—yow!" He yelped as she bent his index and middle fingers toward the back of his wrist. King's head raised at the sudden outburst.

With an impish grin, Sally released him. "You're lucky. I could have broken your fingers with a slight twist."

Watson sucked his bruised knuckles. The joints ached, but he loved serving as the object of her attention. "It still doesn't explain what you were doing with Gantz the night you stumbled upon me at Monument Square. Didn't you already learn your lesson?"

She frowned. "A woman puts up with a lot of crap in the workplace. You've had a demonstration of how I can defend myself. When Pamela gave us permission to leave work early, Jack came by and asked if I was going over to McGee's. He appeared remorseful for his earlier actions. I've gotta work with the guy, so I went to the bar with him. Kenya, I felt crummy leaving you out in the snow. You gibbered about a homeless man. There wasn't anybody there."

Watson sensed the gravity of the pendulous metal dog tags underneath his shirt. "I saw somebody that night." He reviewed the time: 10:55. "Do you mind if we catch the lottery? I bought a Powerball ticket."

"Sure," Sally replied, transferring the remote. "Nothing like voluntary tax—"

"—ation on the poor and stupid," Kenya said, finishing the old adage. He flipped the channel to WABI. In the final minutes of the medical drama *Code Black*, a stoic female doctor stood behind a screen, observing a tearful mother comforting her sick son. The frail boy died (after telling his mom to donate his organs to science), and the camera cut to the last scene. Set in a dim hospital corridor, the same physician bantered with a male nurse, each topping one another's hilarious anecdotes of sheer exhaustion. Closing credits scrolling across a neutral background were replaced by a bedpan-full of gloomy pharmaceutical commercials.

At 10:59, the television gleamed optimistic blue. An athletic man bounced between double bingo cages, one brimming with white balls, the other filled with red. The dapper host acted markedly amped tonight. "Get ready, everybody. *This* is Powerball. Good evening, America! I'm Seth Arlings. We have a guaranteed jackpot of *$100 million.* Take those Powerball tickets out. Good luck to you. The first number is—"

Sally called from the kitchen, "Don't you need the ticket?" She opened the refrigerator, deaf to the music reaching a crescendo.

"I memorized the numbers," Kenya called back. He tracked the winning digits as they lined up along the bottom of the screen. Four of the five white balls matched his picks. *Not anything to get excited about—a measly C-note.* The sixth ball, the red Powerball, shot down the metal ramp. *Seventy-five thousand dollars—equal to my previous win.* But what made this game different? Today, he'd paid the sullen counterperson an extra one-spot for the Power Play multiplier. For four winks of an eye, *4X* blinked above the string of final numerals. Seth told everyone to have a great night, and the local news began.

The whole drawing flew by in under a minute. Kenya half-listened to the anchorwoman's dreary summary of the day's tragedies, weather, and sports. *I'll keep my distance from woodchippers and wear a short-sleeved shirt tomorrow.* Watson, preferring to build castles in the air, shut his eyes and, slack-jawed, sank into the sofa cushions.

Sally carried over the remaining ales. "Wake up, buddy. Better luck next time." She cracked open a frosty can and gave it to him. "When Dad disappeared, Mom played the lottery. She hoped God might have pity on us. Shoulda saved that money for my college education. I've got tuition bills up the ying-yang. Let's wrap up the movie."

I just won two hundred thousand dollars, Kenya thought. *Subtracting taxes that leaves. . . .* He did not care how much the IRS scalped off the top—the balance would still equate to a coffin-load of chop suey. Kenya reined in his compulsion to cheer and hit play. By the time the motion picture concluded, Bradley

Cooper had more or less established which costar he loved the most.

Sally and Kenya's mocking critique of the film progressed into a lusty make-out session on the loveseat. The couple, rushing to the bedroom, shed a trail of clothes. Beneath soft candlelight, the man worked slowly, applying the tantric techniques he had gained under Hannah Schrock's careful tutelage. The woman, pleased with her new lover's solid physique and willing desire to indulge her intimate needs, taught him several tricks of her own.

At midnight, as Sally slept upon his side of the bed, Kenya closed the bedroom door, thereby muting the uncanny harmonies emanating from the black box on the living room windowsill.

"It will look peculiar if we both call in sick today," Sally remarked. She passed the jug. "Although I must admit, those craft beers left me feeling a mite swampy."

"Me too. It's the damn histamines." Kenya flooded his cereal bowl with milk. "I heard there's a virulent strain of the swine flu hitting the city of Portland. Intelligent people, like you and me, should stay home." The Tandoori Box photograph prompted him to email Marisa and turn on his out-of-office reply. He got a kick picturing his boss reading the verbose apology, her thin lips puckering into a sour pout.

"Okay, but only this once." Sally phoned her supervisor, reciting a rehearsed message while holding her nose and clearing her throat. "There. Happy? Except for heading back to bed—I'm all for that—what shall we do on our sick day?"

"We'll feel refreshed if we get a little air. How about hiking? There will be lots of birds for you to draw."

King, anticipating he was going for a ride, edged up to the table.

Sally blew on the steaming coffee. "Where?"

"Ever been up Mount Agamenticus?"

"In York? No. My uncle said he skied at Big A in the '70s."

"That's the place," Kenya responded. This information gave the image significance: the green Mount Agamenticus Learning Lodge sign hung from the peaked roof of a structure resembling a traditional ski lodge. "I've never been there either. We can have a picnic on the summit."

They picked up sandwiches at a deli and drove southwest along the coast, past the sheer York Cliffs and the black-and-white Nubble Lighthouse. Both landmarks reminded Watson of an outlandish dream.

Kenya parked at the trailhead and put a leash on the Rottweiler. Halfway up the Ring Trail, Sally halted, motioning for him to hold up. She pulled out the worn binoculars and, after a moment of concentrated viewing, made a notation in her birding journal.

He held King by the collar. "What do you see?"

Sally relinquished the field glasses and pointed. "A pair of woodpeckers. Black-backed woodpeckers, specifically. It's uncommon for this species to come this far south in the spring."

"Is global warming the cause?"

"The temperature is in the upper seventies. Somewhat abnormal for April. Don't you agree?"

Kenya acknowledged the world was on its last legs, and they continued up the path.

At the fork, the hikers took the right-hand way and climbed between hemlocks and beeches. Scrub oak and blueberry patches lined the walkway to the peak of Mount Agamenticus. At the top, they meandered around a paved loop. On an observation platform, underneath the blue dome, Pawtuckaway Mountain in New Hampshire appeared within reach.

"Is that Boston?" Sally asked, focusing her binoculars on tall buildings to the southwest.

"Must be," Watson replied, peering through the lenses. "That's eighty miles away!"

The Mount Agamenticus Learning Lodge was closed on weekdays. Kenya and Sally sat upon the stairs and ate lunch. King porked out on dog treats.

She inhaled the rarefied air. "This is delightful. I could live up here. Perhaps the rangers will hire me as a lookout on that fire tower."

He squinted at the array of antennas installed on the lofty shelter's roof. "You wish to be a hermit? What a lonely job."

"Nah, I was kidding. In reality, at times, my mother gets on my nerves—too possessive. She means well, but I need to find my own place. After Ted cheated on me, I moved back home. Never believed I'd still be there."

"I'm thinking of buying a house. Would you like to live with King and me?"

Sally laughed at his proposal. "We'll sail to a tropical island. You'll carve tiki gods from driftwood, and I'll string necklaces out of puka shells. A fortune will be made selling our trinkets to the gullible tourists."

"Sally, I'm not joking."

She laid the sandwich on the wooden step and turned to him, confused. "Today has been fun, and last night was incredible, but—"

He objected, "But what?"

"Kenya, I hardly know you."

"You moved in with Ted!"

"That was a mistake!"

Watson sulked for a minute before standing up and wading into the wildflowers. King remained with Sally. *Another betrayal.* He stopped at a mound of rocks framed by boulders. A white sign stated that Native Americans had created this spiritual site to memorialize a Micmac chief who'd converted to

Christianity in the 1600s. Kenya, aware of the Rottie's tongue licking his fingers, squatted to pat the wide brow.

Sally held out a chunk of granite. "Let's pay tribute to Saint Aspinquid's memory."

He uttered a silent prayer for his own welfare and tossed the stone upon the cairn.

On the winding Witch Hazel Trail, King led the way down the mountainside. The animal marked his territory as Sally shot photos of the abandoned ski slope's rusted T-bar towers and junked snowcat. Soon, they were back in the vehicle. The Lexus zoomed northward on the highway, an alternative to the leisurely coastal route.

"How can you afford a mortgage?" Sally questioned. "You just bought this new car. Where is all this money coming from?"

Kenya showed her the previous night's jackpot lottery slip. "This ticket is worth two hundred thousand dollars."

"Yeah, right." Sally scowled. "You're asking me to live with you, but you won't even be straight with me."

"I also won seventy-five thousand playing Powerball. Those winnings helped pay for this SUV."

"Kenya, I watched the drawing. You were Mr. Mopey when you lost."

"Was I?"

"You—" She saw his contorted smirk.

He made a snap decision. "I'll prove it to you."

Instead of staying on Interstate 95 into Portland and home, he veered into the 295's fast lane.

Halfway across the Tukey Bridge, Sally inquired, "Can you please tell me where we're going? You're freaking me out."

"Don't worry. We're redeeming my prize."

An hour later—fifty-nine minutes of mutual uncommunicativeness—the NX splashed into a parking lot in a dumpy section of Hallowell. Inside the nondescript Maine Alcoholic Beverage and Lottery Commission building, Kenya signed the back of the

Powerball ticket and completed the required forms. He removed his driver's license from his wallet and slid the documents over the countertop.

"Congratulations, Mr. Watson!" the administrator proclaimed. The other staff members stood and clapped. She returned his ID. "Our records indicate you claimed a prize ninety days ago."

"That's correct," he responded.

The state employee shook her head in astonishment. "Sir, you beat the odds—twice." She presented him with the lump-sum check and requested, "May we take your photograph for promotional purposes?"

"By all means." Kenya tugged Sally in front of a Maine State Lottery banner. In unison, they held the oversized, fake $200,000 banknote and smiled at the camera.

Outside, as the sun set, he ripped the real check for one hundred and forty thousand dollars in two. Watson gave her the bigger piece.

Flabbergasted, she cried, "What is this?"

"I'm giving you half of what the IRS didn't keep."

"Why?"

Kenya grumbled, "How am I supposed to spend all of this by myself?"

"You know I can't accept this!"

He took her torn slip of paper and walked toward the recycle bin.

"Wait! You're acting crazy!"

"Crazy is as crazy does," Watson said. He held the fragments above the blue can. "This only cost me three bucks. No great loss."

Sally latched onto his outstretched forearm. "Stop! Stop! Cut it out, Kenya. I'll move in with you."

He handed her the two parts of the check. "Did the money change your mind?"

She hesitated before replying. "No."

"Now is *your* chance to be honest."

"It's fantastic you won the lottery. Still, I—" Sally perceived King peering at them through the automobile's rear window. "Something is going on here that I cannot make sense of. Something you're hiding from me."

Kenya pulled her close as darkness descended upon the land. "Sally, do you trust me?"

"I'll try to." She pressed against him. "But I'm nobody's fool."

He kissed her forehead and whispered, "Good, because I don't cotton to fools."

Sally nodded in assent. "Me neither. Oh, and another thing. Now that we'll be living under the same roof, you're obligated to meet my mother."

Chapter Eleven

SALLY ANSWERED THE FRONT DOOR of the red-shingled and white-trimmed Queen Anne-style house. Her mother wasn't intimidating in the least—quite the opposite, in fact. In the airy foyer, the refined, energetic woman greeted Kenya with a warm hug, an affectionate act his own mom shied away from doing unless coerced by social constraints. "Please call me Nora," she requested, leading him into the homey study.

In a room filled with books, framed photographs of Sally, taken at various stages of her life, covered the walls and crowded the fireplace mantel. Many prints comprised the standard school or party photos. In the more entertaining action shots, the lithe, ponytailed athlete attacked balls on hockey fields or scored layups on basketball courts. Watson tarried before a large family portrait above the hearth. Upon green grass beside a blue lake, Sally and her mother embraced a strapping man whose clipped van dyke barely contained a huge smile.

"That was my husband, Peter," Nora said softly. She curled a strand of her short, auburn tresses around a pinkie. "Sally's father. He's—"

"Gone," Sally concluded. She elaborated sarcastically, "Dad hit the bricks, flew the coop, or, using the housewives' favorite cliché, he went out for cigarettes and never came back."

Her mom's face tinged an unbecoming shade of shame. "We do not know what happened." She composed herself and turned to Kenya. "Sally told you the long and short of it?" He nodded awkwardly. "We've been living in limbo. It isn't easy for either of us."

Watson, anxious to discuss anything else, crossed the Persian rug to a teak cabinet. Arrowheads, stone axes, pottery shards, and woven baskets lined the shelves. He peered through the glass at a fractured jawbone. "What is this stuff?"

"This is the Green's world-famous cabinet of curiosities," Sally responded. "Mom's an archeology professor in the Anthropology Department at USM. She has a Ph.D."

"That's my alma mater." He pointed at the yellowed bone and teeth. "Where did you get this?"

Nora unlocked the door and reverently removed the weatherworn article. "I discovered this specimen on one of our school's exploratory trips to New Mexico." She overturned the remains and ran an index finger over the jagged notches in the underside. "Can you guess what caused these rough cuts?"

"You got me, Mrs. Green. A mountain lion? A spear?"

She pressed a wobbly canine tooth with her thumb. "We suspect these serrations are evidence of survival cannibalism during the 'starving time' which occurred in Southwestern Indian American settlements six hundred years ago. These are stone knife marks." She whistled a melodic tune while sawing her palm across the mandible.

"Mom, you're creeping him out," Sally protested.

Kenya laughed. "No, I'm good. The past is fascinating." He focused on a round remnant. A dark square ringed by intricate patterns centered the parchment.

"You have an eye for the unusual," Nora noted. She raised the curio. "This membrane is a drumhead. See the piercings used to lace the leather to the hand drum?"

"Very meticulous. How old is it?" He touched the surface, assuming the aged rawhide would be stiff. The smooth material felt as supple as a Gucci handbag stitched from brain-tanned pigskin.

"By analyzing the ingredients of the pigments applied in the design—the double-bonded carbon atoms identified in soot—our assessment is that this percussion instrument was fashioned in the pre-Columbian era, sometime in the late eighth century."

Kenya said in amazement, "Unbelievable. The hide feels like new."

"Marvelous, isn't it? This human skin is perfectly preserved. To this day, we haven't reverse-engineered the recipe for their embalming fluid."

"Did you say human?" Watson scrubbed his palms on his trousers.

Nora moved to a picture frame illuminated by the window. Featured on the cover of July's *American Archaeology* magazine, Sally's mother stood hip-deep in a hole, its four straight walls carved into the rich loam. Excavation tools—a spade, a gardening trowel, a broom, and a dustpan—surrounded the staked-off pit. "Last summer, my class unearthed this rarity in California." Her fingertip traced a circle upon his shoulder blades. "The warriors tattooed and then stripped the flesh from an adolescent male's back while the victim—most likely a captive of a warring tribe—still lived."

Watson shivered, arching his neck in repulsion.

"My mother's pulling your leg, Kenya." Sally sighed. "Moo. It's cowhide."

Nora coaxed her daughter to come nearer. "This tissue is human epidermis. Do you see the moles and tiny hair follicles?"

Aghast, Sally replied, "You told me the drumhead was made of leather."

"It is!" Nora chuckled. "Nowadays, anyone can purchase wallets, belts, even briefcases manufactured from human leather online with one click of a PayPal account. I must profess, they're certainly not reasonably priced."

"You've looked?" Sally questioned in abhorrence. "Mom, that's so fucking wrong on so many levels."

"Watch your language, dear. A British company specializes in the tanning process. Skilled skinners harvest the flesh of willing donors whose relatives are reimbursed postmortem. The business is totally legit."

Kenya envisioned primitive hands aglow in raging firelight, pounding hypnotic rhythms on the dead man's back. His attention reverted to the fuliginous cube dominating the mummified drumhead. "What do these characters represent?"

Nora laid the age-old object on a table and then went to a bookcase. The woman skimmed her forefinger along several gilded spines before tipping a thick tome from the shelf. A tasseled bookmark marked a page of lithographs. She tapped upon an image displaying four columns of equilateral stone slabs—twelve rows in all. "These are classic Mayan stucco glyphs." In each block, an artist had squished an alien-shaped face into a host of grotesque entities. "The Mayas created these pictographic logograms to communicate concepts instead of employing phonetic tones. This one is the script for the word 'jaguar.'" To Watson, the distorted anatomy did not correlate with any cat he had ever seen. "These logograms are similar in form and style to the motifs on the drumhead, yet they don't match any documented translations. I showed them to a friend at Yale, a historical linguist who is deciphering the *Voynich* manuscript. Doctor Evans is convinced these Mayan glyphs were inscribed as a warning."

Kenya recalled a high school World History class. The Maya civilization had mysteriously collapsed. "Warning for what?" he asked.

"He's not positive," Nora replied. "Doctor Evans based his speculations on the inked figures' fearful facial expressions, as well as their raised weapons and shields. Unfortunately, we do not possess a Rosetta Stone to help us transliterate Mayan logograms."

"But isn't the drawing on the drumhead rather distinct?" Watson inquired with a hint of desperation. "The black symbol is a square box, right?"

"Yes, the emblem is definitely some sort of cube," Nora responded, "though its connotation is unknown."

Kenya leaned across the table. "You said you found this in California?"

"Central California," she answered. "The university held the dig at Inyo National Park. Up in the White Mountains."

He plucked at the whiskers his razor had missed. "I understood the Mayan civilization inhabited Central America."

Nora smiled. "As I told you, this material culture is extraordinary."

Sally moaned in boredom. "Enough of the archeology lesson. Let's eat!"

Over a scrumptious meal of Hungarian goulash served with a bottle of Brazilian wine, Nora's thorough interrogation of Kenya's upbringing and occupations evolved into a topic of a more pressing nature. As he reached for a second helping of glazed carrots, she caught his wrist. Her bright green eyes bore into him. "Sally mentioned you two are shacking up?"

With his free hand, Watson wiped his lips with the napkin. "Only with your approval, Mrs. Green."

Nora clamped harder on his forearm and whispered, "Don't you dare hurt my girl. You'll be sorry if you do."

Kenya grinned at Sally and gently pried her fingers away. "Mrs. Green, I pledge to take good care of your daughter."

After pie and ice cream, Watson excused himself and located the master bathroom while the ladies loaded the dishwasher.

With the door locked, he opened the medicine cabinet. Over-the-counter flu remedies, antacids, and anti-inflammatory drugs stocked the glass shelves. He paid special attention to the prescriptions. Kenya, using the newest Tandoori Box picture as a reference, pushed and rotated the childproof lid of a blue-labeled container resting upon the center ledge.

Before coming to visit, Kenya had researched Lipitor on RxList. Categorized as a statin, the drug lowered blood cholesterol to prevent cardiovascular disease. He inserted Russell Fisher's two Ritalin tablets into the bottle and shook the contents. Mixed collectively, the white pills looked alike. Watson screwed on the top, returned the Lipitor to the correct rack, and, cocking his eye, gave the position a final tweak. Satisfied that nothing in the cabinet appeared altered, he shut the door. Kenya did not recognize the creature reflected in the streaked mirror.

Sally moved closer to the monitor and frowned. "Are you sure this is a smart thing to do?"

Kenya paged through homes marked for sale on Zillow. King lay underneath the dining room table, his tail thwacking the chair leg whenever they spoke. "Jointly, we can put down almost thirty percent." He plugged numbers into the mortgage calculator. "Check this out. On a four-hundred-thousand-dollar house, our loan payments will be peanuts."

"Twelve hundred a month isn't chicken feed. What if I prefer to spend my seventy grand on a Tesla?" She took over the mouse, narrowing her search to a photograph of a gray cottage trimmed in purple. "Wow! This one is cute. Maybe my mother can live in the little guesthouse."

"Cool with me, baby," Kenya stated, already planning to convert the outbuilding into a man cave. "How is your mom doing?"

"Oh, jeez, I didn't tell you. I talked to my mother this morning. She had a bit of a scare—thought she was having a panic attack. A neighbor drove her to the emergency room."

Watson's face emoted authentic concern. He remembered peeking in Nora's medicine cabinet but not adding the kiddy coke to the bottle of Lipitor. "Oh no! Is she okay?"

"Seems to be. The doctor adjusted her medications. I wasn't even aware she had a heart condition."

"Parents rarely share problems with their kids. We should drop by and see her."

"It makes me question what more I'm not on top of." Sally tied her hair into a knot. "You realize I was joking about the electric car."

"Yeah, I knew that. I really dig this cottage. The description claims the bay is visible from the upper story. Check out the fancy stonework on the wraparound porch and the built-in fire pit."

"I like the Adirondack chairs they have on the front lawn. This place has been listed on the market for three months. I don't understand why it's not selling."

"Because this house is meant for us," Kenya replied with confidence. He mentally compared his recollection of the Tandoori Box's latest output to the image on the screen. The photos were nearly identical, except the cube's higher angle of view recorded a statuesque woman escorting Sally, King, and him up the front steps. Dressed in a business suit, she had to be a real estate agent. "The owners are probably asking too much. They'll be eager to negotiate the price."

"I hope you're right." Sally selected the remaining thumbnail listings. "None of these other homes appeals to me."

Kenya, knowing they wouldn't, urged her to complete the contact form.

"Now?"

"We must go today."

"It's approaching lunchtime." She yawned and stretched her arms. "And naptime. What about tomorrow?"

He rose and paced. "Sunday is too late. Somebody else will get it."

Sally filled in her name, phone number, and email address. The page showcased the shark-toothed smiles of four agents: three males and one female. Her cursor lingered above the checkbox for Jeff McCoy and hesitated on Steven Roy.

"Pick the lady. Shawna Lunt is the one we need."

An hour later, a man, a woman, and a dog stood on the pointed bow of the *Bay Mist*. The ferry navigated Casco Bay, halfway to Peaks Island.

Kenya gazed between the drapes hanging in the master bedroom window. In the distance, a weather-beaten lobster boat plowing through the Diamond Island Pass left a V-shaped trail of foam. Downstairs, in the dining room, Sally belted out Top 40 hits while unpacking boxes.

The couple had moved into the one-hundred-year-old cottage on Pleasant Avenue ten days ago. Their few possessions scarcely filled the small U-Haul truck, much less the rooms of their new home on Peaks Island.

Watson lifted the green Woodward Supermarkets tote from the windowsill and sat upon the bed. The perplexity of where to store the Tandoori Box racked his mind.

At the apartment on Hartley Street, Kenya had learned to leave the bag on the sunny, southern-facing windowsill in the living room. Terrible things presented themselves if the cube was stashed elsewhere. When he sat on the couch watching television, the eccentric box's proximity to his head had been unnerving. Watson had transferred the sack to a northern window alongside his laptop. Not only did the devious mechanism fry the computer's motherboard, but it also emitted an annoying caterwauling equivalent to rutting tomcats until he returned it to the original location. Once, Sally had phoned to inform him that she was on her way over. Kenya hid the inexplicable item in a dresser drawer. Luckily for him and the other tenants residing at Baxter Woods, she had smelled fumes. He hotfooted to the bedroom, flung his smoldering corduroys into the bathtub, and turned on the shower. As Watson placed the jute bag back on the living room windowsill, he explained to Sally that he had neglected to switch off the electric steam iron. Conceivably, after a long, cold night in the dark, the gizmo required daylight to recharge.

The Tandoori Box heated his palms, a subtle indication of impending doom. Kenya studied the six sides of the apple-sized cube—smooth as polished coal. Yellowish gum crusted the dispensing slot. He scraped the lochia discharge with a fingernail and brushed the flakes off the bedspread.

This morning's distressing photograph foretold an argument with Sally. Their furrowed foreheads, screaming mouths, and reddened cheeks suggested a knock-down, drag-out fight. Watson could not fathom the impetus for the quarrel. The day began fabulously: an hour of sensual lovemaking, buttermilk pancakes at Peaks Café, and a relaxing stroll with King in the woods behind the house. Now upstairs and by himself, he needed a secure spot to conceal the bothersome black block. So far, for reasons unknown, Sally had slept peacefully through the machine's midnight buzzing. *She's a heavy sleeper; however, it's just a matter of time before she questions why I never got rid of this strange White Elephant gift.*

Kenya's thumb detected roughness on the base of the box. Something was gouged into the hard shell. He fetched the magnifying glass. A flashlight held crosswise to the markings accentuated the etching. *This drawing was not here the last time I looked. Or did I somehow miss seeing it? And where is the MADE IN INDIA stamp?* Watson no longer heard cheerful singing rising from the lower level. Only silence.

"Kenya!" Sally yelled up the staircase.

Here we go. Our first real spat. Whatever this is about, I will not lose my self-control. "What's the matter, Sal?"

"Get down here right now!" His girlfriend sounded angry—*livid.*

What did I do? Watson dropped the cube into the bag and set it on the windowsill. *I'll deal with you another time.* He stomped downstairs, shouting, "Coming!"

Sally, dressed in blue shorts and a white tank top, kneeled over an open carton. She fanned out a stack of photographs on the pickled hardwood floor. "What is this shit?"

Kenya stopped upon the bottom step. *She discovered the Tandoori Box images.* He exhaled, remembering he had cached the shoebox in a cavity behind the furnace. Then Watson saw what they were. "Why are *you* snooping in *my* junk?"

Sally bombarded him with the snapshots. "Who is this skank?"

Kenya stooped and gathered a handful of explicit photos. The glossies portrayed a big-breasted, blond girl in a plethora of sundry risqué poses, or worse, performing X-rated acts—*on him.* "That's Hannah." He should have destroyed the prints, but found the feat easier said than done since he cherished the amateur pornography for sentimental and wholly selfish purposes.

"The Amish slut? Why do you still have her pictures? Is there more on your computer? What have you been doing? Are you jacking off to that bimbo?"

"N-no," he stuttered. "I just—"

"What a perv," Sally muttered. She marched through the kitchen, knocking over a chair. The screen door whammed shut.

Kenya sprinted onto the rear deck. "Sal, I'm sorry. I forgot all about them. They mean nothing."

"Is Hannah calling you? Are you texting her?"

"I am not calling or texting anybody. You know how much I hate my goddamned phone!" And then, as another thread of his sanity unraveled, Kenya unlocked his arsenal of hurtful words, chose the sharpest four letters, and hurled the unforgivable insult, "Quit being such a cunt!"

Sally's face flushed, twitching to the side as if physically slapped. "If you're that unhappy, what are you even doing with me? Us moving in together was *your* bright idea!" Watson scorned her anger by not going to her. Instead, in defiance, he went to the garden and sat on a concrete bench. In loathing, she snarled, "Fuck you. We're finished."

Kenya watched Sally walk to the garage and thrust open the weighty door. The front wheel of a red bicycle emerged from the shadows into the sunlight. To his dismay, she glided along the ribbon driveway and, without glancing backward, pedaled down the lane. Akin to a forsaken wish, Sally was gone from his life.

Chapter Twelve

"EVERY MAN NEEDS HIS OWN PRIVATE SPANK BANK," Russ teased. Fisher, measuring Kenya's flourishing level of melancholy by the extent of stubble shadowing his coworker's face, had gleaned the gist of Kenya's breakup with Sally by ratcheting up his obnoxious wheedling. "We both knew that broad was too good for you."

Not hungry—in reality nauseous—Watson twirled the splattered entrails of cooling spaghetti with a fork.

Russ chuckled. "A few weeks after our honeymoon, I got in a little hot water myself. Valeska found a Russian mail-order bride catalog hidden under the bathroom sink. My wife hit the roof! She threatened to go back to Belarus."

Kenya stared up from his ignored lunch. "Did she ever forgive you?" Sally had not returned to work, and at the end of last week, he'd learned that the business analyst had given notice.

"Sure did, pal." Fisher grinned at the memory. "I told her the brochures weren't mine. The dingdong fell for it hook, line, and sinker! That night, we had hot makeup sex—knocked Valeska up."

Watson pushed his tray out of the way. "I thought you only had your two stepchildren. What happened to the baby?"

The hardware engineer stabbed a barbecued shrimp. "Stillborn. Valeska said the fetus had webbed hands and feet." He delivered the crustacean into his mouth. "Our fertility specialist showed us a micrograph of my sperm. The little bastards have two heads." Russ spit out a pink tail. "Get over her, Doc. There's lots of chicken in the sea."

At Sally's house, Watson relied on the handrail to haul his carcass onto the stoop. His brain throbbed, his gut bubbled, and his unwashed clothes stank of last night's smoke. Kenya, drunk on cheap beer and cheaper rum, had burned Hannah's photographs in the fire pit behind the cottage. The blazing bonfire, lacking constant nurturing, guttered out, leaving the man cold and lonesome. He really missed Sally. Kenya had phoned, texted, and emailed all her accounts. No response—*nada.* Her red bicycle—a tangible reminder of her existence—rested upon the porch railing. His shaking fingers pressed the doorbell.

A hand drew apart the white, laced curtains in the door's square window. Through the pane, he heard the unmistakable words "Go away!"

Kenya squashed his nose to the glass and pleaded, "Mrs. Green, can I please speak to Sally?"

The woman cracked the front door as far as the safety chain allowed. "Why? What for?"

"Because I love your daughter, and without her, I am nothing. And that, Mrs. Green, is the sad but gospel truth."

Nora let him into the hallway. "You stink like a distillery. Are you drunk?"

"Uh-uh. Just a bad hangover. Did Sally tell you about our silly disagreement?"

"Of course she did. I advised you not to cause trouble. You couldn't last a week before screwing up."

"Believe me, that wasn't my intent." Watson kneaded his brow and the bridge of his nose. "Do you have any painkillers?"

Nora set a half-empty bottle of Bufferin and a full glass of tap water on the kitchen counter.

Kenya doubled the dosage. The fourth tablet lodged in his throat.

She pounded him on the back.

He choked out the words, "Thanks. Is Sally upstairs?"

"No, Kenya. She's gone."

"To the store?"

"To New York City." Nora poured a tepid cup of decaf into the drain. "She left three days ago."

"Sally is with that prick, the stockbroker?"

"Yes. Ted works on Wall Street."

"She called him a douchebag—*a jerk.* Why did she run back to him? It makes no sense."

Nora raised both of her palms in mutual accord. "Even you're preferable to that lying sack of shit. I attempted to talk her out of it. She wouldn't listen. My daughter was hell-bent on leaving town."

Watson spied Sally's name printed above Ted Jennings' address on a note stuck to the refrigerator with a gold King Tut magnet. He memorized the number on Rector Place while putting the glass in the sink. "I appreciate the aspirin, Mrs. Green. The pills will soothe my aching head, but they won't heal my wounded heart."

As Kenya trudged down the sidewalk, Nora hollered, "Sally said to keep the money if you sell the house!"

He whirled to respond. The door had closed.

In seat 35B of a United Airlines jet, Kenya sat stiffly, crushed between a sniffling teenage girl and a snoring businessman whose pomaded duck's ass oozed dark splotches onto the headrest. The Tandoori Box photo showed him stretched out and asleep on a vacant airline bench, a fanciful expectation considering his present relationship with the ever-fickle karma. When Watson depressed the silver button to recline the seatback, the rear passenger, a three-hundred-pound, dead-eyed thug, kicked him in the spine.

The cube, swaddled in a towel and stuffed in his backpack, was crammed in the overhead compartment. A drooling toddler goggled over the front seat. He shut his eyes and pondered why the otherworldly contraption couldn't have endowed him with a first-class ticket. In the blackness of his own psyche, Kenya beheld a negative image of the emblem scratched into the block's skin: a puggish visage encapsulated in what looked like an astronaut's helmet. *Perhaps the UFO wing nuts weren't moonstruck—the primitive Mayas made contact with technologically advanced extraterrestrials.*

Kenya sat up when the aircraft's wheels slammed against the tarmac at Newark-Liberty International Airport. Inside the bustling terminal, he boarded the AirTrain and then transferred to New Jersey Transit. At Newark Penn Station, Watson rode the PATH train to downtown Manhattan. The railway car's doors parted at the final stop. Kenya jumped onto the platform and melded with the morning commuters spilling out of the Chambers Street Station. With no plan, no place to stay, and no umbrella, he stepped into the pouring rain.

Kenya sloshed toward Sally's current address on Rector Place so miserably soaked that he hardly registered the somber crowds encircling the 9/11 Memorial's North and South Pools. To avoid drowning, he procured a disposable poncho from a feeble woman pushing a shopping cart.

A wiry gypsy, topped in a felt fedora, hawked souvenirs in a European accent: "Come see genuine relics recovered from the terrorist attacks!" He waved a rectangular plastic card. "The Lion Sheik! Osama bin Laden—the greatest jihadi since Genghis Khan!" The slick huckster snagged Kenya's forearm and shook the melted ID badge in his face. "Sir, this item is the real McCoy. See the scorch marks. Smell the jet fuel. Feel the heat."

The printed address, DEAN WITTER REYNOLDS – ALL DEAN WITTER FLOORS 1-2-4-5 W.T.C. – IF FOUND, DROP IN NEAREST MAILBOX – POSTAGE GUARANTEED – 2 WORLD TRADE CENTER, NEW YORK, N. Y. 10048, filled the left side. A photo of an unsmiling Asian woman was laminated to the right side. The employee's name had been—Watson felt certain this person was a victim—Meredith Wong. The abraded back included a barcode and the six-digit ID number 071504.

"Being that you're such a good guy, I'll only charge you five-fifty. I take cash, Visa, MasterCard, American Express, whatever you got, except bitcoins—they're as worthless as tits on a porcupine." The Romani reacted to a policewoman on the beat. "If you act immediately, I'll include a walnut frame for your historical keepsake."

Unsure why he desired this ghoulish memento of a horrible day in American history, Kenya withdrew a ten-spot and held out the soggy bill. "Here. Keep the change and the frame."

"Change? Man, are you high? This piece of Americana is worth five hundred and fifty dollars at Sotheby's!"

The city cop dashed to the plaza, shouting into her radio.

Caught in the act, the wanted con artist took the money, tossed the keycard, and escaped into the oak trees. Watson picked up the rectangular ID card and slid it into his wallet.

At a brick-and-glass high-rise in Battery Park City, Kenya ambled into the swank lobby. The slate walls reminded him of the Tandoori Box's smooth exterior.

"May I help you, sir?" a guard at the security desk inquired. Watson turned his cheek and went outside.

Rector Place encompassed a narrow park. Upon a bench, he scoped the condominium's entryway, not having to sit for long. The downpour ended, and the sun emerged from black clouds as the doorman swung open the side door for a smartly dressed, youthful female toting a briefcase. *Sally!* Kenya fastened the waterproof hood around his face and tailed her from a distance.

She headed north, cutting across Zuccotti Park to Broadway. Sally fussed with her hair and raincoat as if preparing for a crucial appointment. Near the Woolworth Building, she entered the corporate suites of a large telecommunications firm.

The wait for her reappearance was considerable—enough time for his clothes to dry. Hungry and thirsty—breakfast had consisted of a Cinnabon and orange juice at the airport—he bought a hot dog and soda from a food cart. Two hours and three tube steaks later, Sally exited the commercial offices and walked southward to Wall Street. On the patio of a ritzy outdoor café, she embraced a tall, stylish man—obviously, Ted Jennings. The chivalrous son of a bitch pulled out a chair and pushed Sally under the table. He unbuttoned his tailored jacket and sat. Sally vivaciously described her day as the stockbroker leaned in, listening silently. The pair gestured at the menus and ordered lunch. When the waiter delivered glasses of red wine, Kenya recommenced the stakeout at a magazine rack in a bodega.

Jennings paid for lunch, they hugged, and each departed on diverging courses: Sally in the general direction of Rector Place, Ted heading to the Financial District. Watson, wanting to learn more about his adversary, pursued the rich boyfriend. The speculator, instead of ascending the golden towers dominating the East River, descended into the sticky obscurity of the MTA subway system. Kenya, rushing to keep up, purchased a fare and darted onto the Seventh Avenue Express as the sliding doors closed.

When the train screeched into Columbus Circle, Jennings rode the escalator and strutted to Central Park. Via the Merchant's Gate entrance, the man sauntered up to an attractive, blond woman sitting by the USS Maine National Monument fountain. She heard his greeting and looked up from her tablet. Her face brightened in happy recognition. Watson used the guise of a gawking tourist to photograph them with his cellphone. With their arms linked in spirited conversation, the twosome wandered through a secluded section of the park. There, on the highest point of the schist arch spanning The Pond, Ted leaned in once again—this time to kiss and caress a woman who did not remotely resemble Sally Green. Kenya thought the backlit greenery, the Gapstow Bridge's sparkling reflection, and the paddling mallards contributed aesthetic charm to his candid video. *Hold steady now, this shit is priceless.* After that key scene, the rest of this romance feature film was all gravy. He recorded every flirt and blush. Jennings took his main squeeze to a five-star hotel on Fifth Avenue. Watson loitered for a while but cleared out when they never came out for air.

Kenya resisted his first impulse to send Sally the incriminating images. Since twilight approached and he was worn out from all the detective work, he decided to contact her in person the next day. Watson walked past a row of flophouses to the Bowery and, tapped out from buying the house on Peaks Island, checked into the Old World Hotel. At $59 a night, he bargained for few amenities. Kenya climbed up seven flights of stairs, shoved open the door to room 723, and jostled into a cell the size of a closet. He laid the knapsack on the nightstand, unpacked the Woodward bag, and placed it upon the only other available area—the heat radiator. The brown shag carpet reeked sweetly sour—the result of a former guest's losing bout with cyclic vomiting syndrome. Watson divided the paisley-print curtains, pried on the sash, and gave up after seeing the painted shut window frame. He aimed the ceiling-mounted fan at his face, flicked on the thirteen-inch television, and curled up on the lumpy mattress. Kenya fell asleep watching Chinese melodramas.

Kenya—or a version of his cosmic doppelgänger—hovered on the Hudson River in a dugout canoe. Leaks spouting from gaps in the worm-eaten keel pooled around his bare toes. He sealed the worst hole with the sole of his foot. In the brume of the gloaming, the megalopolitan towers glittered like jewels until lightning bolts decimated the power grid. New York City, the "City that Never Sleeps," suddenly became the "City of Eternal Sleep." Manhattan Island, its anchor of bedrock severed by violent tremors, floated toward the Statue of Liberty. Chunks of ice calved off the toppling New Jersey Palisades. Tidal waves extinguished the green lady's torch forevermore. A paddlewheel steamer emerged from the noxious miasma. Merry passengers toasted each other's health on the overloaded hurricane deck. *Is that Sally and Ted dancing the mambo?* Kenya held tight to the rotting thwart as the canting ship's wake nearly capsized his dinky craft. Bioluminescence from millions of mating jellyfish illuminated the contaminated riverbed. Twenty fathoms down, a nineteenth-century sloop—crewed by skeletal cadets outfitted in navy blue tunics—set sail into a vortex of antediluvian sediment. Jettisoned items littered the bottom: Liberace's rhinestone piano, crates of headless Barbie dolls, a still-running Kawasaki jet ski, and, to his great surprise, a dead giraffe. There were too many handguns sprinkled along the channel to count. As the canoe crested a swell, the tip of a black fin carved the churning water. *Something's coming.* An orca, the breadth of a Russian submarine, leaped above Kenya's upturned face. Her silken belly, as white as Siberian snow, passed close enough for him to touch. The graceful beast gyrated in the air, splashing into the river on her back. She broke the surface once more to swim nearer. A gigantic pink tongue curled over the gunwale. The killer whale's mouth opened wide, regurgitating undigested food onto his lap. Kenya reached into the mass of flopping fish and scooped up his guerdon—a black box.

Kenya awoke in abject darkness. His heart hammered as though something frightful had just scurried across his chest. The possibility of a mischief of rats invading this sad, little room was not out of the question. Four feet away, the Tandoori Box buzzed, the birth of a new image ending with an extended slurp. Watson, so used to this nightly routine, no longer confirmed the time. He itched all over. His fingers eventually found the light switch. Underneath the industrial glare, an intrusion of cockroaches scattered beneath the baseboards. Patterns of red bedbug bites dotted Kenya's arms and thighs. In this rundown fleabag, he figured the pests came at no extra charge.

Kenya sidestepped between the bed and wall, blaspheming his pathetic state of affairs. By the steam radiator, he wiped the photograph's odious coating on the stained sheets. He squinted in disbelief, swabbed the rheum from his bleary eyes, and looked again. In hysteria, Watson tipped the night table. The two individuals in this *three-dimensional moving picture* were trapped in an endless loop: a male with a shaved head hitting an older male on the scalp with a brick, the brick dropping as the victim fell, and in the end, the offender rolling the limp body into a waterway. Until now, the Tandoori Box had produced two-dimensional stills. As impetuous curiosity overtook better judgment, he held the animated image to his ear. Kenya heard a repetitive grunt and splash. His earlobe was wet. *Impossible.*

Watson filled his backpack and checked out of the Old World Hotel. In the wee hours, the only people on Chinatown's streets were squatters scouting for sheltered doorways or college students craving munchies after a drunken evening out on the town.

He sat at a communal table in a hole-in-the-wall restaurant aptly named Noodletown. Kenya requested the roast duck noodles and a bottle of Tsingtao from an aloof matriarch draped in a RICE RICE BABY!!! apron. As he waited for the food, he reviewed the photograph from the Tandoori Box. *This can't be me pounding the man's gray matter into pulp. Is that Ted Jennings? It has to be.* Due to the cameraman's high vantage point and poor lighting, it was difficult to identify the victim. *I am not a murderer.* Kenya recalled the night he beat the tar out of the thief in the depths of Baxter Woods. *Is that guy still alive? That episode, although brutal, wasn't premeditated. The dirtbag tried to steal my car.* No matter how badly he needed Sally, he wasn't going to kill to get her back. *Am I?* The duck came just as he liked—hot, spicy, and flavorful—but as Kenya guzzled the chilled beer, he felt like the real cooked goose.

In mental turmoil, Watson rambled the city boulevards, idly passing the time before heading to Rector Place for a sit-down with Sally. A never-ending cavalcade of freshly washed garbage trucks rolled up Canal Street and dispersed to the four corners of Manhattan. He traveled eastward, hankering to witness the crack of dawn and hoping a new day would bring emotional solace.

On the Lower East Side, at a public housing development, whooping hooligans hustled from a flaming dumpster. Sirens blared as Kenya passed under the FDR Drive and walked behind the Pier 36 event facility. He propped himself on a railing overlooking the East River. A man and a woman in a neon green kayak paddled against the tide. Beneath a storm drain, clusters of plastic bottles and tampon applicators spun in an eddy's web. The sky over the Williamsburg Bridge brightened as a colony of seagulls soared overhead. For a moment, his disposition lifted. *When Sally sees the photos of Ted with another woman, she'll surely come crawling back to me. My god, I only saved a few racy pictures of an ex-girlfriend. What's the big deal? She ran off to screw her ex-boyfriend.*

As Kenya's blood pressure skyrocketed in anger, a sharp noise interrupted his inner rant. He swiveled, seeing a refrigerator box bang the warehouse's aluminum siding.

"Go fuck yourself, Ruthie!" a voice rasped. A naked foot—the worming toes reminding Watson of bloated slugs—stuck out from the shipping container. "Not today. . .not today, Ruthie.

Maybe tomorrow *if* you're a good girl *and give me a friggin' break!*" A northbound barge, its exotic cargo of life-size dinosaur replicas shackled to the deck, tooted an air horn. Kenya snatched a length of discarded chain and crept to the open end of the elongated carton.

Inside the cardboard cave, a middle-aged man wrestled with the leather straps of a prosthetic leg. "You worthless whore!" he seethed, sending the wooden appendage crashing onto a pile of empty whiskey bottles. "Ruthie, you continue to betray me with your evil scheming."

"Sir," Watson asked, "do you require some assistance?"

The vagrant turned, his chapped lips baring even teeth. Across the river, a sliver of sunshine squeezed between a grove of tall chimneys. Bright light struck the man's face. His brown left eye's milky pupil shrank to a pinprick. The right pupil, its iris strangely black, remained the same diameter. "Is that you, boy? Have you come a long way to find me, Kenya?"

Did he say my name? No, he couldn't have. Watson hunched to get an unobstructed view of the wizened profile. His features did not match those of the transient he'd seen at Monument Square on the night of the blizzard. This man was black, bald, and beardless. "What's wrong with your leg?"

"What leg?" The fellow massaged the scarred knot of flesh. "I lost my leg in the Second Battle of Fallujah. Went into a schoolyard to pass out candy to the children and stepped on an IED's tripwire. Wasn't nothin' left to bury 'cept my boot. Believe it or not, once upon a time, I had a beautiful wife, a nice split-level in suburbia, and a stable income. My kids—" He clasped the artificial limb and tinkered with the snapped buckle. "My kids reckon I'm dead. Since the Marines discharged me twelve years ago, the only benefit I received from Uncle Sam is this feisty ol' gal to keep me company on wintry nights." The veteran's self-deprecating laugh morphed into a spittle-flying coughing fit. "At least this wench doesn't talk too much." His facial muscles deflated as tears trickled down his cheeks. "Who am I trying to fool? Ruthie never speaks to me at all."

Watson inquired, "Shall I try to fix the strap?"

The ex-soldier mopped the wetness from his face. "Son, hold your horses. I'll get her on." He forced the leather socket onto his thigh and used a cane to struggle upright. "What's the chain for? This old coot is as blind as a bat, but my ears are fine and dandy. They pick up the jingle jangle of a beatdown as clear as a bell. Are you here to rob me, or is homicide this morning's breakfast special? I ain't got much to take. And death? Oblivion will come as a blessing for this crippled jarhead."

The coil of metal links rattled to the earth. "Sir, I've got no quarrel with you. I came to see the sunrise." On impulse, Kenya held out the identification tags and asked, "By any chance, are you T. D. Johnson?"

The vet rejected his offering of mangled tin and hobbled to the meshed fencing. He raised his chin to the sun and sang a short rhyme. "Oh me, oh my, what a splendid day to die." The Marine set the crutch on the walkway and turned around. "Kenya, who do you think I am?"

Watson, again hearing his forename, questioned, "Did you just say my name?"

"You can refer to me as Thaddeus Damian Johnson. I will call you Kenya Alan Watson. In the grand scheme of things, our names are merely arbitrary labels. In any case, today, your destiny is to take a life." The ex-soldier scaled the guardrail and straddled the top bar. "This man's life, if you had any doubts."

Watson flew forward. "No. Stop!"

Johnson unstrapped the leg. "Goodbye, sweetheart." He kissed Ruthie on the ankle and flung her into the waterway. "Kenya, if you wish to find tranquility, you must make a pilgrimage to the Forever Tree." The veteran tilted his head at a slight angle, used a forefinger to tug down his lower eyelid, and popped out his blue eye. "Here, catch," he said, lobbing the synthetic oculus underhand.

Kenya stumbled, grabbing the spinning eyeball. His forward momentum and pinwheeling arms toppled the oracle into the river. A geyser of brown water doused Watson's clothes and shrieking face. Johnson—his cranium striking a submerged rock—surged to the surface in an explosion of red bubbles. The unconscious man bobbed into a forest of sunken pier posts. Steered by the ebb tide, the body drifted through the maze of barnacle-encrusted pilings.

Kenya, yelling for help, vaulted onto the edge of the wharf. He tucked the fake eye into his jeans and kicked off his sneakers. When Watson attempted to remove the knapsack, a sizzling jolt of electricity zapped his spinal column. Paralyzed, he fell to the dock. As Kenya lay on his back watching the Goodyear Blimp's tortoise-like flight across the East River, roiling currents swept Thaddeus Damian Johnson, or whoever he may have actually been, far out to sea.

In Central Park, feral pigeons defecated upon *Peace's* chiseled coiffure. The statue's alabaster arms reached in humility to masculine *Courage* and feminine *Fortitude*. A quartet of Jamaican street musicians drummed syncopated rhythms on upside-down plastic paint tubs. Double-jointed teenagers took turns breakdancing to the frenetic beat on the gum-spackled plaza.

At the USS Maine National Monument, Kenya alighted on the fountain's rim. He relived Thaddeus Johnson's untimely demise while dipping a salted pretzel in mustard. The Tandoori Box's prediction had proven to be, for the most part, correct, but Watson's addled mind refused to accept any culpability. *His death was completely accidental. I didn't kill the old man. He wanted to die.*

At noon, the flaxen-haired female he had followed yesterday sat nearby. Watson threw his crumbs to the birds and stood. His hulking shadow fell on her glowing iPad. The hopeful smile creasing her lips transformed into an irked scowl when she saw his face. “Sorry, I’m not interested,” she rebuffed and resumed browsing the Facebook news feed.

“Leave,” Kenya said.

The young woman strained to peer around him. “Excuse me? Are you speaking to me?”

“Ted’s a scumbag. Go home. You’ll be much happier without him.”

A policeman emerged from the restrooms. He paused to harass a drifter setting up a pup tent.

“Move aside!” she warned, slithering past him to the footpath. The young woman, not glancing rearward, hurried uptown, shouting into her cellphone. Kenya took her seat and waited.

Jennings crossed Central Park West into Merchant’s Gate. The broker isolated his girlfriend’s tormenter and lowered the phone. Red-faced, he strode across the pavement and demanded, “Who the fuck are you?”

“Nobody you want to know,” Kenya replied. Garrulous mallard ducks quacked on the audio track as he played the salacious video of the couple on Gapstow Bridge. For the double feature, Watson queued up the clip of the paramours checking into the luxurious Pierre Hotel.

“What are you, a peeping Tom?” Jennings asked. When Kenya only glared, he grappled for the incriminating electronics.

Watson captured the womanizer’s hand and bent two baby-smooth fingers toward the diamond-encrusted timepiece adorning his wrist. The phone clattered to the cobblestones. “There are additional copies, Ted. Haven’t you heard of cloud computing?” He applied extra torque. “Hurts, doesn’t it? Sally taught me this nifty technique.”

The financier winced and sputtered. "Oh, you're the nerd she's been mooning over." A watchful Japanese tour guide shepherded his rubbernecking flock to the sightseeing coach. "Why do you care? That chick's bat-shit crazy."

Kenya, staying alert for the cop, yanked on Ted's digits until the distended ligaments popped. "Say again, dickswab?"

Beads of perspiration darkened the banker's white collar. "Never mind. Please let go. I'll give you whatever you want. Take my watch."

Watson unclasped the band and tossed the custom Rolex into the fountain.

Jennings fell to his knees in agony. "I swear on my mother's grave—*we didn't do anything.* She slept on the couch!"

"Listen up, dingleberry," Kenya ordered. "When you return to your overpriced bachelor pad, I need you to pressure Sally to pack her suitcase and go back to Portland. Do not tell her you've seen me. Say you found somebody new or that your boss is transferring you to a satellite office in Kazakhstan. I don't give a rat's ass what you come up with. Just be sure she's strapped into an airplane seat tomorrow morning." The man's eyes shut, making it a challenge for Watson to determine his level of attention. "Ted, are you still with me?"

"Yeah, yeah," Jennings moaned. "I'll talk to her tonight and buy a—"

"First-class ticket," Kenya growled. "If not, you'll have more than a few broken fingers to cry about."

The pigeons, spooked by the snaps of brittle bones, ceased pecking *Peace's* stony head and spiraled into the smog-smudged sky.

Chapter Thirteen

TWENTY-NINE DAYS AFTER KENYA LEFT NEW YORK CITY, the doorbell chimed on a Saturday afternoon. He did not need to squint through the peephole to know who was outside. The last Tandoori Box photo gave him a useful heads-up. He grinned, reaching for the doorknob.

For Watson, the previous month had been purgatory. The hours during this period of despair had passed by at a snail's pace. He could not comprehend why Sally hadn't contacted him since he'd sent her the videos of Ted Jennings necking his other squeeze.

After Kenya's return flight to Portland International Jetport, he'd picked up King at the boarding kennel. Upon entering the cottage, the hound had scoured every room with his keen nostrils. The Rottweiler, detecting that his female master's scent had long gone cold, had snarled at his worthless male master, lifted his hind leg, and pissed on the rug. As Watson had blotted the acidic stains with clumps of paper towels, he'd agreed with the canine's foul assessment—*I am such a loser.*

Devoid of Sally's effervescent presence in Delphic's halls and offices, any satisfaction Kenya had compiled from coding applications soon evaporated. The software engineer had kept up with Marisa's assignments to hold on to his job and, in effect, prevent his house from being foreclosed. And as usual, Russell

Fisher had persisted in aggravating Watson with his plebeian jokes and perpetual pessimism.

The pint-size Tandoori Box and Kenya, its full-size elf, had stayed busy. Daily images had directed him on numerous offbeat errands.

A few tasks—petty things, pranks in all honesty—had taken place on the island. One evening, as a light posse of fireflies had swirled around his head, he'd spritzed the tomato plants in the community garden with a gallon of herbicide. Another time, Watson had siphoned seawater into a Boston Whaler's gas tank. Later, he'd read a news article recounting the same boat's dramatic Coast Guard rescue. One of the survivors had been identified as the chairman of the Peaks Island Council.

The preponderance of the photographs depicted Kenya engaged in miscellaneous activities on the mainland. In an entertaining exercise, he'd bid for—and won at $29.95—one of *Playboy* magazine's final nude issues on eBay. After Pamela Anderson's glossy, shrink-wrapped boobies had shown up in the mailbox, Watson, acting as an admirer of neoclassical architecture, had entered the Shaarey Tphiloh Synagogue. He'd counted up three benches on the left side, located a brass plate engraved with the name ETHAN RIVES, and slid Kristy Garett's creased centerfold into the provided prayer book.

Again, in the Portland area, one enterprise had proved to be more ticklish. When Bill's Old Port Barbershop had closed for the day, Kenya had heaved a plastic sack of rubbish from their dumpster. In his garage, he'd deposited the sweepings on the floor. While a political reporter had discussed "America's rampant ethnic and religious bigotry" on National Public Radio, he'd sorted out any nonorganic items, then repacked the choicest protein filaments in a quart-size Ziploc bag. Now came the tricky part. Early the next morning, Watson, disguised in bargain-bin sunglasses and a Portland Sea Dogs baseball cap, had tailgated a sleepy janitor into the rear door of the Brookings

Semiconductor International factory. Upstairs, in a mahogany-paneled corner office, he'd held back sneezes as he'd spread the assortment of human DNA—scalp hair, chin whiskers, long sideburns, bushy eyebrows, and neck fuzz—across the acre of olive-brown Berber carpet.

One weekend, Kenya had rented an automobile and crossed the Canadian border. He'd steered into an industrial park on the outskirts of Montreal, shut off the engine, and waited impatiently for nightfall. Underneath the glare of sodium-vapor bulbs, Watson had spray-painted the symbol he had seen etched into the Tandoori Box onto the side of an aerospace parts manufacturer's warehouse: a squished face encased in a spheroidal astronaut's helmet. In a motor court, he'd tossed and turned for two hours before driving fifty minutes to a rural neighborhood in the Chateauguay Valley. On this moonless night, Kenya had used the starlight from one hundred billion distant galaxies to help him trample lines and curves into a farmer's wheat field. From a superior view, the crop circle's complex design had duplicated the image of the bug-eyed space traveler.

In retrospect, none of these strange, shameful, risky, or criminal deeds seemed real to Kenya. Not even after he'd disabled a fire alarm at the local elementary school had he contemplated the repercussions. His memories of these reprehensible acts had faded as quickly as the aftertaste of a bland meal. Bereft of his soulmate, Kenya had felt empty—a wooden-headed puppet manipulated by an omnipresent being of much higher intelligence.

King, leaping in excitement, clawed at the doorjamb. Flecks of paint speckled the planked floor, blowing elsewhere as Kenya yanked on the knob. Sally arrived dressed in the same white tank top and blue shorts she'd worn the last time he'd seen her—the day she rode off into the sunset on her bicycle. In this heightened emotional juncture, time and space were compressed. To the man and woman entwined in a strong embrace, they had never parted.

As the dog gummed Sally's fingers, Kenya took her backpack. "You have a key, and this is still your house."

"I didn't want to barge in on you in case you were. . .you know." She made jerky wrist movements and smirked. "How was your trip to New York? Did you take in the sights?"

"The Nation's Greatest City sucked. My advice? Don't stay at the Cockroach Inn." He exhibited the bedbug bites on his arm. "How was it for you?"

"The same, except my scars are internal. Look, I brought a surprise." Sally reached around the doorway and dragged a pet kennel into his field of vision. A gray-and-white feline's green eyes stared from behind the bars. "I got Omega back."

In the living room, Kenya let the short-haired cat out of the cage. Omega introduced herself to King by hissing and swatting him on the snout. Her dominance asserted, the queen jumped up on the couch and curled into a ball. The dog, mesmerized by the feisty guest, lay panting on the rug.

"They like each other," Sally observed.

"Do they?" He faced her. "What about us? Do we like each other?"

She set the deadbolt and led him to the bedroom.

The weekend came and went for the reunited lovers. To their merit, the points of contention, Hannah and Ted, were at no time broached—not entirely forgotten but sagely forgiven.

The dog days of August were hot, humid, and lazy. Kenya and Sally unpacked and, when not exploring the island, lounged in refinished Adirondack chairs on the front lawn under an elm tree. During this transitional period, King huddled alongside the couple, apparently concerned that the smallest squabble might instigate another split. Omega, reveling in the amenities of a housecat, watched from the kitchen window.

They were sitting in these aforementioned dark brown seats when Kenya said, "Let's take a vacation." A hazy notion had congealed in his brain two days earlier. "It will be good for us to get away for a while."

"Where to?" Sally asked.

He stared up at a black dot on the sun. "The West Coast."

"Are we going to Disneyland?" The Rottie got up, stretched his long legs, and tried to climb onto her lap. Sally, giggling, pushed his big paws off. "King, you're not a Chihuahua!" She hurled a wiffle ball down the hill. The animal gave chase and retrieved his favorite toy. "I always thought it'd be great to attend the parade on Main Street and ride that thing where you're on a roller coaster inside a mountain."

"The attraction you're referring to is either called the Matterhorn or Space Mountain. We'll visit Mickey and Minnie Mouse if there's time. At the moment, I have different plans."

"I guess Universal Studios isn't high on your list?"

"There is a forest I'd like to hike in."

Sally scratched the top of her head. "California is a desert. From what I've seen on *Keeping Up with the Kardashians*, the landscape is all palm trees, asphalt, and assholes."

"That's the southern part where the stuck-up movie stars live. I understand the north is much greener and much friendlier."

"What of my job hunt?" Sally flattened her beer can and tossed it into the cooler. "I submitted a shitload of resumes." Both concurred that once she gained employment, he would seek new opportunities as well. "How can I interview if we're out of town?"

"You can always speak to the hiring manager on the phone. Your voice is very compelling. . .very sexy."

She batted aside his overeager hand. "I need to be there in person."

"When they see the gorgeous and intelligent Miss Green, you'll be hired on the spot."

"Oh yeah? Mr. Watson has his beer goggles on." Sally threw the slobbery ball farther along the slope. King's feet blurred as he scampered after the perforated ball. "This is important to you, isn't it? I hate to pry, but does it have anything to do with the lottery tickets?"

Kenya wanted to confess his relationship with the demonic Tandoori Box and the mythical Forever Tree, yet he feared what might happen to him—or worse, *to her*—if he blabbed. These were his own enigmas, the heinous secrets he must carry to his grave. Tension tightened a band around his forehead. Watson shrugged and evaluated the length of his fingernails.

Sally asked, "For how long?"

"Not sure. Until—"

"What about your boss? She'll let you take so much time off?"

"If Marisa says no, I'll just resign." He strayed from underneath the elm's leafy umbrella to pace under the sun's baking brightness. "I was about to anyhow."

"Kenya, with neither of us working, how will we pay the mortgage? Or the utility bills?" She went to him. "This is nuts. Is traveling across the country really necessary?"

"Sally, I'm losing my wits." The twinge behind his temples intensified as blackness vignetted the edges of his vision. "We've got to search for—"

"You're sweating." She pulled him to a halt. "Are you feeling all right?"

"I'm a bit dizzy." He leaned over and touched his knees. "The beers, combined with this muggy weather, gave me a wicked headache."

"Well, don't get heatstroke. Please come and sit in the shade." Sally put a cool palm on his brow. "You're burning up! What specifically do you hope to find? The Fountain of Youth? That's in Florida."

The man stood his ground and uttered the burdensome words, "We're looking for a tree. A big, old, ugly tree." Beneath the cloudless sky, he anticipated a bolt of lightning striking his head or a loosened blood clot exploding his traitorous heart. Despite his wariness, neither of these catastrophic events occurred. Kenya whispered in relief, "The Forever Tree."

Sally misheard him. "The forever free?"

Watson felt foolish restating the three spellbinding words. The thaumaturgical phrase had lost its luster.

"A tree?" She responded to the angst screwing up his face. "Okay, okay. We'll do whatever you want. I'll go inside and book airfare."

"No, we aren't flying." Kenya was glad he'd won the lottery money that had bought the Lexus. The wheels would have fallen off his rickety Honda Civic halfway to Ohio. *What if, all the while, the SUV was part of the master plan?* "We'll be driving my car."

Sally's jaw dropped lower. "Driving? Why? It must be two thousand miles one way."

"Closer to three. The journey will be easy if we take turns behind the wheel—a few relaxing days on cruise control." The excruciating migraine had dissipated, leaving him bulging with exultation. "And it'll be fun to bring King along for the ride." The dog stopped circling his two masters. He rested on his hind legs and barked. "That's right, buddy," Kenya said, stroking the animal's muscular shoulders. "Mommy and Daddy are taking you on a road trip."

Sally's lips curved upward until Kenya added, "And by the way, King's grandmama, your mother, shall be accompanying us on this little adventure."

Professor Green waited for Kenya to conclude his dubious reasons for driving out west before questioning, "Why do you surmise this 'Forever Tree' is growing in the Inyo National Forest?"

Sally and Kenya sat upon the camelback couch in her mother's study. The antique sofa was uncomfortable, but the ball-and-claw feet matched the home's classic décor. Across from them, Nora settled in a padded wing chair beside the fireplace. King, on his best behavior, lay near her stockinged toes.

The Rottweiler, pretending to snooze, cracked his eyelids when Watson answered, "I believe it's close to where you excavated the drumhead. And like the drumhead, the tree is extremely old."

Nora asked, "When you were doing your research, did you read about the Ancient Bristlecone Pine Forest? Dendrochronologists ascertained that many of those Pinus longaeva have lived for thousands of years."

"Yes, I did," he replied. "The Wikipedia article stated that that particular species is one of the longest surviving individual organisms."

She nodded. "Wikipedia is accurate on that fact. However, clonal organisms may exist for much longer."

Sally inquired, "Clonal? You mean carbon copy duplicates?"

Her mom smiled. "Precisely. Genetically identical, the individuals originate from a single ancestor. For example, there is a colony of quaking aspen in Utah connected by a distinct root system—the eighty-thousand-year-old Pando, also renowned as the 'Trembling Giant.' Certain bacterial colonies are virtually immortal, as are a limited number of fungi and plants."

"The Prometheus Tree was five thousand years old," Kenya said. "Some stooge chopped it down for firewood."

"This planet is populated with cretins," Nora acknowledged. "What is the link between this special tree and the drumhead I dug up? Is it that tattoo you found so provocative? The black square inked in the center of the parchment?"

"Kenya won't tell you, Mom," Sally muttered. "I'm still in the dark."

"Mrs. Green, I shouldn't have mentioned the tree. I was unwell that day and misspoke—a mistake I regret."

"Cut the crap, Kenya. What you are proposing is mad. . .the harebrained delusions of someone undergoing a psychotic break. You can't possibly expect me to allow my daughter to motor off to never-never land with a maniac." She sat up and crossed her legs. "And quit calling me Mrs. Green. It makes me feel fucking obsolete."

Watson glanced at his girlfriend, who appeared both stunned and amused by her mother's profanity. "You didn't inform her?"

"Hell no!" Sally exclaimed. "I've got enough problems wrapping my head around my role in this insanity."

Kenya wrung his hands and smiled. "Mrs. Green, er, Nora, can you go with us? On an expedition such as this, your talents will come in useful." He tempted her with a question, "Wouldn't you like to add new archeological artifacts to your cabinet of curiosities?"

Fervor flooded the woman's cheeks, yet she remained unconvinced. "Sally told me you saw this tree in a dream?"

"The mental images are nearer to revelations than dreams." He sucked his teeth before adding, "As inconceivable as this sounds, the two guys who told me to go on this pilgrimage might be the same person occupying separate bodies."

Sally elevated her arms in exasperation. "Pretty fucked up, huh, Mom?"

"Yes dear, you definitely know how to pick 'em. Kenya, will you be able to identify this tree? It's not the famous Methuselah, is it?"

"No, I doubt it. I pored over all the photographs I could find of the Ancient Bristlecone Pine Forest. The Forever Tree is similar to the Methuselah Tree in color and shape, but taller and more. . . ." Kenya paused, unable to convey the unease he experienced summoning the monstrous tree to mind: inner ear vertigo combined with stomach queasiness. Sometimes it got so bad, he sensed the cerebrospinal fluid sloshing about inside his skull. Watson ended the sentence using a standard unit of the English language, which did not quite fit: "Imposing."

To everybody's astonishment, especially her own, Nora inquired, "When do we leave? I suppose the department head shall let me take a non-paid sabbatical. Luckily for me, I've saved up my time off."

Kenya raised clenched fists. "Thanks, Mrs. Green!" King sprang to his feet and howled.

"Don't thank me, Mr. Watson," Nora said sternly. "I am only riding shotgun to keep tabs on my baby girl. The moment you start coming apart at the seams, I'll let you off on the side of the highway. You'll have a long walk home."

Sally held her juice box high in a mock toast. "To our first family vacation since Dad left!"

Chapter Fourteen

FOUR DAYS LATER, AT FIVE O'CLOCK ON A MONDAY MORNING, Kenya backed the obsidian Lexus into Nora's driveway. Soon, with the rising sun behind them, they crossed the Massachusetts state line at eighty miles per hour. The NX had appeared roomy inside the showroom when he'd first bought it, but now, crammed with three adults and a large dog—even with the Thule cargo box strapped to the top—the automobile's interior felt cramped.

Before setting forth on their quest, Watson had called both of his parents to inform them that he would be away. When he'd attempted to contact his mother, his middle stepsister had answered the home telephone. "Hey, Kenya. Dorothy's not here. She's at one of her revival meetings." Michelle, chock-full of juicy family gossip, had given him the lowdown, starting with her older sister, Margaret. "Maggie checked herself into a drug rehab center. Yeah, that or get booted out of the house by my dad. Mags can't stand the Twelve Steps. Says she'd rather OD in a back alley than listen to any more religious bullcrap." And the status of little Megan's pregnancy? "Meg cut loose with a guy she met at Goodwill during a shopping spree for infant supplies. We don't know where Meg went or if she's alive. Your mom believes she joined the traveling circus." Kenya had asked his stepsister how she was doing. "Me? I'm fine. Since Dad won't let me touch his Range Rover, I'm saving up to buy a Prius." Shelly had promised to have Dorothy phone him when she walked through the door.

His father had answered his cellphone, speaking in broken Spanish. "Sorry, Son. I thought you were Edgar, the gardener." Upon learning of Kenya's sudden vacation, Earl asked him if he had been fired from his job. "No? Boy, it's too late in life to try to find yourself. Don't you think it's time to pull yourself together?" This heartwarming father-and-son conversation had fizzled out when his dad had claimed that he'd run out of minutes. "I'll call you back as soon as Melinda picks up a TracFone refill card at Wallymart."

Kenya still waited to hear from either of his parents.

Sally's head nodded on the passenger's headrest. Her mom napped in the backseat. King kept watch for other animals through the rear window. Omega, not a huge fan of motion sickness, stayed at home under the care of a pet sitter. Watson pondered whether he'd made a miscalculation bringing them along. He was weary of responding to every one of their well-intentioned questions.

The Tandoori Box, cushioned in the Woodward Supermarkets tote, was packed beneath the driver's seat. Whenever the SUV hit a bump, Kenya realized a scant six inches separated his derriere from a potential ticking time bomb. He remained in a quandary about whether to transport the black cube into the hotel room or let it sleep out in the car.

The predictive machine had revealed nothing of relevance before their departure. Watson could not characterize the device's prevailing temperament. This morning's photograph showed him squeegeeing bugs splattered on his windshield at a Shell gas station. Was the instrument pleased or cross that he had planned this trip? *Probably, like the Creator, the fucking brick is incapable of emotions and, frankly, doesn't give a damn.*

Vexed by his own failings, he floored the Lexus and passed a camel train of eighteen-wheelers.

Kenya pumped high-octane while Sally and her mom shopped for breakfast at the yellow-and-red Food Mart. As he scraped solidified moth guts off the windshield, Watson surveyed the atmosphere—as he always did—in an effort to glimpse the omnipotent photographer. Near the sun, a dot of light sparked and died out. He shaded his eyes, but the sparkle had disappeared.

Sally squinted up and joked, "Do you see a UFO?" She carried a bag of snacks. Nora held three bottles of soda.

"Just stretching my spine." Kenya put on a show of grunting and arching his vertebrae. He wrapped an elbow around her. "Want to take the pilot's seat?"

She gave him a Big Texas Cinnamon Bun and a sweet kiss. "Happy to, as long as I get to DJ the tunes."

An hour after sundown, the Lexus rolled into a pet-friendly Best Western in Gary, Indiana. The road warriors had driven an ambitious one thousand miles on the first day. In an uninspiringly decorated room across from the clanking icemaker, Nora and King opted for the queen-size mattress beside the air-conditioner. Sally and Kenya slid underneath the starched linens in the bed by the bathroom.

As Tuesday ousted Monday, a car alarm shrilled an endless cycle of annoyance. Watson, awoken from an unmemorable yet wearisome nightmare, shuffled to the window and poked his head between the opaque blackout curtains. Rainwater ran in rivulets down the windowpane. In Best Western's parking lot, the headlights of a vehicle in the last row flashed an urgent warning. Kenya, dismayed to discover the automobile making the racket was his own, remembered that he hadn't brought the box indoors.

Sally's mother mumbled, "What is it?" into her pillow.

As Kenya replied, "Somebody's alarm is going off," the honking silenced. "Everything is okay. Go back to sleep." He waited for the woman's respiration to settle into the delta rhythms of slumber before twisting the lock. King, his eyes as black as onyx, headed to the doorway. Watson palmed the dog's boxy head. "Stay here, boy. I'll come right back." The Rottie nosed into the hallway as he eased the door open. "Fine, but be quiet." They descended the rear stairs and splashed into the puddles.

The NX's interior reeked of sardines, and the tempered glass wept with greenish condensation. Kenya disentangled the Woodward Supermarkets bag from the springs beneath the driver's seat and activated the cabin light. Each time he steeled himself to view a Tandoori Box image, his scalp prickled with perspiration, and his bronchioles constricted. Watson often held the photos at arm's length in vain attempts to obscure any distressing details. This morning, he slanted the print toward the dull bulb: another moving picture. . .this one dark and hard to see.

As the storm let up, Kenya locked King in the SUV and skidded down the rough embankment behind the hotel. A pathway roamed into a dense thicket of sassafras trees. The wet leaves smacking his face and the stiff branches snagging his feet smelled of root beer. Further on, the morass ascended onto a gravel trail that terminated at a fence. He ducked between the split rails and stood in a field of seedlings. Atop a hill, an outdoor lamp illuminated two rocking chairs on a farmhouse's front porch. Watson snuck through an herb garden and followed a paved driveway to a group of agricultural buildings.

Within a timber-framed barn, Kenya maneuvered around a new John Deere tractor and a restored Chevrolet Corvair. A pair of horses stared from under the hayloft. He found what he had come for in a Sears tool chest on a workbench in the tack room.

A rutted track ended at a pointed tower silhouetted by overcast moonlight. Halfway to the tall structure, Watson vacillated.

His eyebrows lowering in concern, Kenya returned to the barn. The gray-dappled Arabians, snorting in the night air and yearning for a gallop, whinnied their thanks when he freed them into a pasture.

The road flare felt as heavy and as dangerous as a loaded gun in Kenya's hand. On the front of the massive grain silo, a padlock secured the curved entry door. An external galvanized ladder led up to the roof hatch. Neither of these access points was viable. He knew where to go. The angled aluminum duct of an unloading apparatus was bolted to the concrete storage bin's base. Watson reached underneath the electric motor housing into a discharge chute. He detected the corkscrewed blades of an auger. *Let's get this done. I must get back to the hotel.*

Kenya unscrewed the flare's plastic cap and briskly rubbed the striking surface against the ignition button on the waxed paper pipe. The tip of the pyrotechnics-filled fusee glared blistering red. Molten magnesium spewed onto his sneakers as he shoved the torch into the metal chute.

Watson spun away from the silo and hoofed it past the cultivated rows of sprouting vegetables. He could not explain how the flare would ignite the stored grain, but since he fastidiously followed the actions defined in the Tandoori Box's current motion picture, he never doubted the bin was about to blow.

White-hot sparks carried by an updraft sailed within the spiral blades of the auger and landed on organic waste accumulating in the granary's funnel-shaped sump. The small-scale primary explosion was powerful enough to send a pressure wave at 1000 feet per second through the mountain of corn. A slower fire front vaporized the high concentrations of finely divided grain dust suspended in the air and clinging to the canister's walls. This flammable catalyst triggered the ultimate reaction: a much grander secondary detonation.

The immediate release of kinetic energy took Kenya out at the knees. Compression waves flipped him facedown into the mire. A basketball-size chunk of cinderblock—a man-made meteorite—plummeted into the turf beside his skull. The incandescence baked the side of his face and melted the wax in his ear. As Watson jumped to his feet, corn kernels fell on his shoulders. The remains of the tower burned out of control—a monumental Roman candle shooting scorched popcorn into space. *What did I do?* At the farmhouse, shadows moved across the curtains. *I'd better get out of here.*

Kenya sprinted into a cornfield, crouched among the tasseled stalks, and gasped as the barn's roof burst into flames. *I'm glad the horses are safe.* On the house's veranda, a potbellied man cocked and aimed a shotgun. The farmer, determining he was out of range, swore and dashed into the yard. Pellets fired from the first barrel tore the husks above Watson's brow, showering him with corn juice and strands of silk.

A woman dressed in a long nightgown shouted over the railing, "Harry, come back! I'm calling the police!"

Kenya, hoping he chose the right course, zigzagged through the corn. The next, louder bang leveled the plants near his hip. A single pellet penetrating the denim of his pants came to rest in the subcutaneous layer of cellulite in his left buttocks. The stinging sensation reminded Watson of the night his college roommate shot him in the keister with a BB gun on a drunken dare. He lowered his head and plowed into the columns of vegetation.

On the field's perimeter, Kenya lay on his belly and listened. Apart from the snaps, crackles, and pops of the burning grain silo, he only heard a ringing roaring in his ears. He lunged into the wide-open expanse and dove into the aromatic sanctuary of sassafras.

Fire trucks clanged past the Best Western as Watson crept into the car lot and unlocked the Lexus. King, vigilant and awaiting, yipped when he slid behind the steering wheel and shut the door. Situated upon a beach towel, he shifted to one side and eased down his dungarees. He flinched, probing the tender puncture. The seat cushion vibrated persuasively. Violet luminosity at the shortwave end of the visible spectrum spilled across the floor mat. Kenya, governed by a nameless intelligence, extracted the Tandoori Box and, on base instinct, held the warmest side to the entrance wound. The droning sharpened. His pierced flesh tingled. The buckshot oscillated, dislodged, and, reversing direction, bore a new tunnel in the fatty tissue. This expeditious but painful surgical operation was completed with the hard pellet cleaving to the black cube with an emphatic click. Kenya considered the implications of the lead sphere beneath the dome light, thankful that a tighter cluster of projectiles had not embedded in his tush. He used an index finger to flick the bitsy ball of trouble out the window. The boxers and towel, now rigid with congealed blood, were stuffed in the trash.

Back in the hotel room, Watson inspected his scrubbed backside in the bathroom's steamy mirror. Miraculously, the wound had healed to a tiny, circular scar. His muddy jeans might be salvageable after a thorough washing in OxiClean.

"Where were you?" Sally questioned, rubbing sleep from her eyes. "A noise woke me. I became worried when I saw you weren't there."

"King seemed restless, so I took him for a walk," Kenya answered. He rammed the soiled pants into a dry-cleaning bag. "It was pouring buckets. I slipped and fell in a gully."

"Is that blood on your clothes? Are you hurt?" Sally patted down his dripping body, looking for injuries.

"No—just a boo-boo." Under her inquisitive fingers, he felt his love muscle stiffen.

"What do we have here?" Sally whispered playfully. "Is this where it aches?" She pressed the lock and wedged her terrycloth robe in the gap underneath the door.

Kenya let her lead him to the sink. "Are you out of your mind? Your mother is right outside."

Sally sealed his lips with a firm touch. "Relax, sweetie. Mom sleeps like a rock." She thrust aside the complimentary toiletry articles and hopped onto the countertop. "Come on now, Mr. Watson. Time to feed the kitty."

And for a short while, the fledgling arsonist forgot the blazing farm, the screaming police sirens, and his true master—the Tandoori Box.

"I didn't sleep well," Sally's mother grouched from the backseat. King's big head lolled on her purse. The Coach bag contained a shampoo bottle with a bunch of air holes punched in it. That morning, as she'd enjoyed a nice, hot shower, Nora had sensed something on her ankle. In panic, she'd shaken her foot and swiped at the soap bubble mask. A leech-like bug had crawled up her calf. Before the inquisitive worm's sucker had latched onto her skin, Nora swatted the critter with a washcloth. She'd turned off the faucet and stooped to examine the organism's morphology. The two-inch-long green creature had had the makings of a dozen vestigial legs, four sets of pulsing magenta-fringed gills, a doublet of iridescent wings, and most threatening—a segmented tail tipped with a red stinger. This annelid was not related to any of the varieties she had ever seen. Nora had gently placed the unusual specimen—the insect's eight eyes watched her every move—in the small plastic container for continued study. "Boy, I had some horrendous dreams—real bedwetters. Even in the bright of day, they haunt me."

On this second day of travel, they sped along I-80 somewhere in central Iowa. The monotonous scenery—the low, rolling hills of fertile farmland, sparsely dotted with farmhouses and barns—bored Kenya. Sporadically, he spotted jumbo-size combines harvesting endless acres of unrecognizable crops. Sore from head to foot, a result of his vigorous nocturnal duties, Watson lowered the passenger's seat and his eyelids. *I never want to see another farm.*

"Mom, me too. What were your dreams about?" Sally flashed the high beams at an elderly motorist hogging the fast lane. "Drive it, or park it, Grandpa!" The geriatric cranked down the Oldsmobile's window and extended a bony middle finger.

Nora leaned upon the console and advised, "For Christ's sake, child, go around that slowpoke!" The Lexus swerved about the powder-blue Super 88 and rebounded into the passing lane. "I dreamed of your dad. He was young and still had a thick head of hair. There were others, too—slim beings garbed in metallic costumes. We climbed a volcano. The air boiled, and the earth shimmied. Trees toppled over. A monster was on a rampage. Animals—big and small—stampeded down the mountainside. Pete told me— Ahhh. . . . Every time I'm close to remembering, the words crumble to dust. The dream was so surreal."

Later, as her mother snored loudly, Sally reduced the radio's volume. "What the hell was that? My mom and I had identical nightmares. You know more about what's happening, don't you?" When Kenya sat up, not saying anything, she continued. "In *my* dream, my dad took me birding. Black smoke snaked from a crevice in the mountaintop. I focused the binoculars' lenses. Shiny figures with glass domes on their heads danced around the hole. The smoke was actually colonies of flying bats. My father told me something was in the ground. Something bad. When I turned to ask him what he meant, he was gone. No surprise there! I followed a path downhill. A terrible rockslide forced me into a cave. Strange hieroglyphics covered the walls. While I tried to read the symbols, an evil presence tiptoed up behind me. I ran screaming, finally forcing myself awake. Then, I found you in the bathroom where we, uh. . . ."

Kenya grinned. "That was good, clean, American fun." It *was* curious how the women had experienced similar dreams—explicitly ones featuring spacemen. He'd heard of synchronized menstrual cycles, but excluding Freddy Krueger stalking sleeping adolescents in slasher films, he had not apprehended that real people could share a nightmare. Watson blamed the Tandoori Box for generating these metaphysical symptoms. *The detestable thing is right underneath Sally's seat, radiating God knows what sort of dark matter throughout the car!*

Sally turned to him. "You agree it's weird we had the same dream?"

He thought back on his perplexing visions, all of which ended with him acquiring the black box: deep-diving to the murky bottom of the sea, the rat-infested recreational vehicle stranded in the desert, the hell-bound stagecoach, and the killer whale leaping over his canoe on the Hudson River. These fantasies held no significance for him. Weird was the new normal. "Do you frequently dream of your dad?"

She exhaled. "Not really. Maybe a couple of times a year, usually on holidays. I rarely recall my dreams, but this one felt ominous."

"Hungry? We should stop for lunch." Kenya used the GPS unit to locate a restaurant a quarter mile ahead.

"Sounds great. I could eat Trigger, and that other one. . .the one who—"

"The talking horse? Mr. Ed?"

"Yeah, Mr. fucking Ed. All I had for breakfast was a stale bagel at the hotel and that wretched cup of brown sludge labeled 'Premium Roast' at the gas station. Am I under the impression you don't want to discuss our nightmares?"

"Sal, the resemblances may be coincidental. Yesterday, your mother saw the '69 Camaro on the road and told us how your father owned a similar model in college. That reminded you that it is time to change Turtle's oil, your dad's truck. Perhaps your somnolent brains were just processing the same data?"

Sky-high, fast-food restaurant signs crowded the berms of the next overpass. Sally paddled the right turn indicator and cut across three lanes. "Kenya, our 'somnolent brains' didn't dream of cars or pickups. My mother and I both dreamed of Martians."

She exited onto the ramp. "You won two big lotteries—while theoretically possible, it is statistically highly unlikely—and now we are on a cross-country race to find a magical tree. Who can tell what we'll run into along the way? In this instance, I do not believe in coincidences."

"Simultaneous dreams are fairly remarkable," he said as she parked at Jersey Mike's.

Sally would not let it go. "Are you trying to protect me from someone?"

Nora, roused by the vehicle's deceleration, yawned and unsnapped her seat belt. "Oh, good. I wasn't in the mood for a burger."

As Brenda, the sandwich artist, assembled their giant Super Subs, Sally texted Kenya: *Ur guna hav2 tel me sumtym.*

Early Wednesday morning at the Days Inn's business center in North Platte, Nebraska, Kenya picked a sheet of paper out of the communal printer's tray. Only the Tandoori Box knew who had left it there. He memorized the message. *The address is nearby.* He noted the date and time. *Ninety minutes from now.* A quick Google search confirmed that the telephone number's 963 prefix was a Syrian country code.

A few blocks away, Watson nodded to the night clerk manning the Golden Spike Resort's front desk and rode the elevator to the second floor. He skulked down the long corridor, wary of security cameras; there were none in sight. Kenya, suspecting his delivery of contact information might aid Taliban or Islamic State terrorist cells, debated tearing up the communication or even notifying the FBI. As always, he did what his internal programming obliged him to do: implicitly obey the Tandoori Box's strict code. Kenya tucked the page beneath the door of room 264.

When Watson rose, anxious to retreat to Sally's arms, the DO NOT DISTURB sign hanging from the doorknob fluttered to the carpet. A topless, hairy male clad in a sweat-stained back brace and *Toy Story* pajama bottoms peeked through the doorway.

The fidgety hotel guest inquired, "Are you Rodeomonkey?" The man, not waiting for a response, scooped up the printout from the floor and towed Kenya into the dank chamber by his sleeve. "Come in, come in! No need to be shy. You're a celebrity on the darknet." He scanned the hallway before locking the door and switching on the ceiling light. "Welcome to my playhouse. I go by Freejared. Oh, duh. You already know that." Freejared wiped his moist palms upon the flannel jammies drooping from his waist and reached out to shake.

Kenya, absorbing the racks of computer equipment spread across the dresser and stacked on two folding tables, ignored the offered hand. Overlapping windows of file lists, network traffic graphs, and blinking command prompts filled an array of monitors. Box fans prevented the machinery from overheating. He asked, "What is all this?"

"My server farm," Freejared replied, proudly fondling a computer cabinet. "Terabytes galore. Gotta keep my clients streaming twenty-four seven."

"For an installation of this size, you're not using the hotel's free wireless. How do you get a broadband connection to the internet?"

Freejared raised his pasty arms, smiled roguishly, and, without answering, got down to business. "Rodeomonkey, I've got something right up your alley. Your hot cup of tea, if you will." He hunched over a keyboard, typing a sequence of characters. A window on the biggest screen popped open. Moving images depicted an adult man clad in S&M leather performing unspeakable perversions on a prepubescent boy chained to a cot. Freejared enlarged the video clip to full screen and held out a pair of 3D glasses. "Try these on, champ. High-res MPEG-4. God, it feels like you're right there in that dungeon with them. And for a fellow Husker, I'll throw in this hard drive of hacked nanny cam footage as a bonus."

Incensed, Kenya went to the bureau and hoisted the monitor overhead. Cables swung from the display as he used the giant flyswatter to squash the two-legged cockroach. The pedophile crashed to his knees and, whimpering, backpedaled to the bathroom. Watson dragged a table lamp off the dresser, drew the electrical cord between his fists, and charged after him.

"Take it all!" Freejared cried. "Just don't hurt me. Please, I have a wife and kids to support." Blood dribbled from a gash in his cleft chin. "The primo slurpy is stored on the cloud. I'll give you my administrative password."

On the floor, Kenya straddled the squirming smut peddler. The coil—constricted to asphyxiate—cut a purple groove into the man's fleshy throat. While Freejared's bug eyes squeezed out of their sockets, his arms and legs beat a desperate cadence on the checkered ceramic tiles. Kenya thought of Sally asleep in his bed. *I can't do this to her.* He loosened the garrote and slumped against the toilet. *The fat turd isn't breathing.* Watson pinched the man's proboscis, inhaled, and blew life into the stalled lungs.

With the sharp edge of his right thumb's fingernail, he scribed the letters PEDO into Freejared's forehead.

Kenya found his printed contact info on the nightstand, weighted down by a well-worn Walther PPK. Thirty minutes ahead of the Tandoori Box's specified time, Watson consulted the instruction sticker on the hotel's telephone, got a dial tone, and entered the international number. He listened to mechanical clicking reminiscent of an oldfangled rotary phone, repeated rings, and, finally, dead air punctuated by heated bursts of white noise. Kenya pressed the receiver to his earlobe and greeted in his strongest Arabic accent, *"As-salám aláykum?"* The unresponsive party—if a living human was indeed on the other end—severed the connection.

In the bathroom, he used Freejared's own shoelaces to tie the man's wrists to a sturdy water pipe. Watson dialed 911 and provided the dispatcher with concise directions for SVU officers to make an arrest.

Kenya, his hand upon the knob, hesitated in the hallway. He pushed the door open, crossed to the bedstand, and jammed the semi-automatic pistol, plus a box of hollow-point bullets, in his pocket.

Chapter Fifteen

A WHITE CLOUD OF WIND TURBINES CHURNED THE SKY over Arlington, Wyoming. Nora, her turn behind the wheel, suggested a pit stop. As she ventured into the ladies' restroom at the Wagonhound Rest Area, Kenya and Sally took King for a walk on the sorry patch of weeds designated as the DOGGY POTTY ZONE.

Sally bent to tighten her shoelace. "Did you see those cops at the Golden Spike Resort this morning? It looked serious."

On the way to the highway, Kenya had attempted to distract the women from noticing the fleet of Homeland Security vans and the RV-sized Denver Bomb Squad response vehicle outside Freejared's hotel by insisting that the Lexus' engine had started to make a funny noise. "Maybe someone slipped in the shower, or their room got robbed," he responded, scooping hot dog poop into a bag.

Perturbed, Watson pondered whether his long-distance call to Syria had postponed *or advanced* a terrorist attack on the United States. He awoke on Wednesday, having difficulty reading the bearing of the Tandoori Box's moral compass. The magnetic fields of decency appeared to be reversing poles. Ordinarily, he felt bad—*defiled*—after consummating one of the machine's insidious tasks. Today, he felt good—*clean.* Kenya held his head high. *I assisted in the apprehension of a child pornographer. Honorable, right? I'm a nice guy! A bona fide hero! All the same, fundamentally, did my interference provoke greater harm?* His chin lowered in defeat. *Who am I kidding? The Tandoori Box is using me for a solitary purpose and a solitary purpose only: to propagate its septic seeds of destruction.*

"Kenya, did you hear me? The bomb squad was there. I saw an FBI agent in a blast suit."

"You did?" he asked, remembering the remote-controlled robot crawling into the resort's front entrance. *It might be that the police uncovered enough evidence in Freejared's room to infiltrate a radical organization. In that case, I averted a catastrophe. You're welcome, everybody.* Watson, feeling vindicated, smiled. "I figured those crowds milling around outside were extras in an action movie."

"There weren't any lights *or* cameras." Sally waved to her mother. "Those people in bathrobes were guests!"

"Are you folks hungry?" a feminine voice inquired. "May I interest you in some delicious carne asada tacos?"

They turned to regard a Hispanic teenager dressed in a yellow Wyoming Cowboys sweatshirt and matching sweatpants stationed before a charcoal grill. Savory smoke wafted from the marinated skirt steak. A military-style rucksack brightened with dozens of state flag pins leaned on the wrought-iron bench.

Bothered by the stranger's intrusion, Kenya replied, "No, thank you." A two-pronged metal tool protruded from the end of the girl's right forearm. Watson shifted his gaze upward, differentiating that the eyes peering from the captivating face were of unmatched colors—the left one brown, the right one black. Upon closer scrutiny, he realized a permanently dilated pupil evoked this disconcerting effect. *This cannot be real.* An image of the cypress cross on Calvary and the words *IESUS NAZARENUS REX IUDAEORUM* emblazoned in his mind. *In this age of stellar black holes and "spooky" quantum entanglement, anything—including resurrection—is possible.* "Johnson, is that you?"

"Theresa Desiree Johnson at your service," she affirmed, shaking a bottle of orange-colored seasoning onto the seared meat. "Kenya, you're looking well for everything you've been through. Will you be kind enough to introduce me to your traveling companions?" When he just stared openmouthed, she said, "That's all right. I'm familiar with who you all are."

Sally, her green eyes greener than usual, glanced at her mother as if to corroborate that this chummy exchange had in fact transpired. She thumped Kenya's chest, thereby cracking open the lid of Pandora's Box. "Does she know you? How do you know her? Did you know she'd be here?"

Dazed, Kenya responded, "You can see her?"

Nora, her hands on her hips, swiveled to him. "Of course, we can see her. Why? Is she an apparition? If so, that beef sure smells heavenly."

Sally, also tempted by the mouthwatering aroma, interrupted, "Who is she? Is this bitch Hannah?"

The dark-haired girl smirked. "Does *this* bitch look Amish?"

"She's not Hannah!" Watson yelled. "She's way too young. Hannah is my age."

"Not anymore," the griller said. "Hannah Schrock is dead."

Kenya refuted, "She is not!" Yet his heart held the truth. "What happened to her?"

The wanderer lay four flour tortillas on the grill to toast. She fed King, who had sidled up to the barbecue, raw meat treats. Any passerby—each perceiving contrasting earthly manifestations of T. D. Johnson—would uniformly assume the cook was the animal's master.

Watson pleaded, "I need an answer."

Sally screeched, "Why are you still speaking to her?"

"Your previous girlfriend—not half as pretty as this gal, I might add—died the instant you set a match to her pictures," Theresa said. "Nothing fancy. . .merely a fatal brain aneurysm while watching a *Friends* rerun. She relinquished life as her latest and last beau dialed 911. Trust me, as far as exterminations go, this one was quick and relatively painless."

Sally winced in bewilderment. Bitter bile leaped up Kenya's throat. Nora said to nobody in particular, "Stupid television program for stupid people. That Joey character is Webster's definition of dum-dum."

At the grill, Johnson used the fork attachment on her prosthetic arm to transfer the carne asada onto an aluminum tray. Then, she laid out four sets of plastic utensils, paper plates, and napkins on the vinyl tablecloth. From her camouflaged rucksack, whose interior volume appeared immeasurable, Theresa removed Tupperware containers of pico de gallo salsa, lettuce, shredded cheese, guacamole, and a round of Corona Extras. Lastly, she used a polyethylene flask, imprinted with a gold crucifix and the words HOLY WATER, to fill a bowl. The girl placed the font upon the ground for King. She coaxed them to the table. "Everyone, please be seated. Hope you're all famished. I always make too much food."

Nora added the fresh toppings to the overstuffed taco and bit into the soft, juicy end. She grinned. "This meat is yummy. Tell me, Theresa, if I may be so bold to ask, are you God or simply a darn good cook?"

Johnson choked on a swig of beer. "Thanks for the compliment, Professor Green, but Lord no, neither of those equally fine occupations! On second thought, after the fall of the Nixon presidency, I punched a clock as a short-order cook at a greasy spoon in Washington, D. C. Nowadays, I don't have time to put together a grilled cheese sandwich. And God? Mr. Big Bang passed away—*bless him*—of natural causes during that bleak period in human history known as the Stone Age. Since I'm a team player,

I volunteered to help out when required, keeping the lights on and such, until the board hires a suitable replacement. I bid our recruiters the best of luck in enticing prospects to come in for an interview. With Zion's internal bickering and staffing budget cuts—augmented by the calamitous ramifications of global warming—we haven't found anybody with an ego humongous enough to take on that thankless job. Back in the Middle Ages, we had a candidate with suitable qualities, but—" Theresa spit into her palm and frowned at the gnarly piece of grizzle. "Let's just say, she didn't work out as expected."

Appalled, Nora said, "The Stone Age ended six thousand years ago. It's hard to believe no one has stepped up to the plate."

"Do *you* want to be in charge of *everything* in existence?"

"Are you joking?"

Johnson spread her arms in the symmetry of the cross and smiled. "What do you think?"

Nora scrunched up her face. "No way in hell."

"Exactly my point. So far, it hasn't turned into much of a problem. You guys invented enough false idols to pack all your houses of worship to the rafters."

"What about the Messiah?" Nora questioned. "Why did Jesus Christ have to die?"

Theresa waggled her forefinger and took another bite. Crucifixion was not a topic she cared to discuss while eating.

Nora accepted a second ice-cold cerveza. "If you're not the King of Kings, are you Satan? To me, an insignificant mortal, hearing that you snuffed out a woman's life because of a few racy pictures seems a trifle extreme—more in line with one of Beelzebub's despicable stunts. Sorry, but I must ask. Were you involved with Hannah's demise?" She knocked off the bottle cap on the table's edge and, closing her eyes, drank half of the limy brew.

"The two events occurred concurrently; however, they were unconnected." Johnson conceded, "I mean, sure, I subliminally injected the sentiment of shame into Kenya's consciousness. Yet his guilt compelled him to burn the incriminating photographs. At that same moment, I increased pressure upon a weak spot in Hannah's femoral artery. The vessel ruptured—*kaput.*"

Baffled, Sally inquired, "How can you claim those acts were unrelated? You must be the Devil."

Theresa's face hardened as she suppressed irritation. "Lucifer is upper management. We only see that dude at holiday parties. His minions do the lion's share of the work. Sally, hundreds of thousands of people perish every day *on this planet alone.* On the books, Hannah Schrock still had roughly fourteen healthy years outstanding. As I mentioned, we are grossly understaffed. Even a superhero can only multitask for so long before a preventable accident kills millions. Regrettably, due to time constraints, we are often forced to combine assignments." She said to Kenya, "I was appointed to oversee both you and your ex. Reviewing your records, I saw the romantic link to Hannah. By moving up her expiration date, I saved myself 8 milliseconds and crossed her off my list ahead of schedule. It gave me time to be here with you today."

Nora swatted a bumblebee determined to land in her hair. "Fourteen years isn't a drop in the bucket."

"Yeah! What she said!" Sally exclaimed. "Who are you to make those kinds of decisions?"

"Somebody has to do it," Johnson responded. "Imagine the highway congestion or the lines at Disneyland if everybody were immortal."

Kenya, thrilled by the concept of a personal assistant, queried, "Are you *my* angel?"

The girl flapped her shortened arm and shot back, "Do I look like a flippin' angel?"

In unison, the three humans shook their heads and mumbled, "No, ma'am."

"Are you the Grim Reaper?" Nora asked. "The hooded skeleton wielding the scythe?" To Sally, her mom acted and sounded a little buzzed. "Death, can you tell me how many more years I have remaining?"

Johnson put away the picnic items. She troweled the scraps onto a plate for King. "We're not playing twenty questions, Professor Green. In any event, you'd really prefer not to know."

"Then why are you here?" Kenya inquired. "When you—the other you, the one-legged man—fell into the river, you tossed me your eyeball." He felt inside his pants pocket and, separating out a fistful of loose change, held the blue glass orb up to the sun. "During the blizzard, you left me these." The dog tags jangled as he pulled them out from under his shirt. "What are these disks used for? For some reason, I thought the IDs were a talisman."

"Under befitting circumstances, the tags may be used as an amulet or a charm. Carry them where they are, over your heart. The eyeball is what it is—an eyeball." Theresa pressed a quick-disconnect button on the artificial limb and, twisting slightly, released the fork from the bayonet socket with a click. "Bring this on your journey."

"Is it a weapon?" Kenya questioned, touching the sharp tips. "This fork is too puny to be of any use fighting off the Four Horsemen of the Apocalypse."

"Just keep the tool handy," Johnson recommended. "And be careful. Wrap it in a sock so you don't poke your eye out."

Sally, silent while this bizarre dialogue unraveled, apologized. "Sorry, I jumped all over you, Theresa. Sometimes, I get unduly jealous. What I'm about to ask is rude, but how did you lose your arm?"

"The Marines," Johnson replied, tugging a mechanism from the bag. She snapped a split-hook terminal device into her appendage and used the curved tip to scratch her nose. "Shrapnel."

"You were in the military?" Sally questioned. "You're so young."

"My mother signed the enlistment papers when I turned seventeen. In 2006, on my first deployment, I was part of a convoy transporting medical supplies to a Doctors Without Borders hospital in the Saladin Province. A rocket-propelled grenade hit our Humvee. I got out. My comrades did not."

"This took place a decade ago?" Sally inquired. "You haven't aged a bit."

"The medics amputated my arm. When the military shipped me home to Fargo to recuperate, an anti-war demonstrator shot me the moment I stepped off the bus. Theresa Desiree Johnson never had a chance."

Nora groaned. "I'm confused. Am I to postulate you're using this woman's body as a host? Like Whoopi Goldberg in *Ghost*?"

"*The Exorcist* with Linda Blair won as many Oscars and was much more realistic," Theresa answered, slinging the sack on her back. "I've got to go." She squatted and whispered in King's ear.

"Whoa!" Watson called. "Where do you think *you're* going? Don't abandon us!"

"Kenya, you're a big boy. Too old for me to need to wipe your nose and change your nappy. I keep telling you—*find the Forever Tree.*"

"We're trying," he responded. "What about the Tandoori Box? How does it fit into all of this?"

Johnson hailed a burly trucker exiting the restrooms. "You wish to free yourself of that thorn in your side, right?"

"Please!" Watson replied. "It's driving me insane."

Her eyes on her ride, she said hastily, "Well, you can't. Not now anyway."

"That thing made me break every commandment," Kenya cried. "I'm going to Hell, aren't I?"

Theresa raised her palm to signal the driver to wait. She draped her good wing around Kenya's shoulders and tapped his chest with her metal hand. "Your spiritual aureola shines as unsullied as a newborn's halo. Rest assured, you're not booked on the next night train to Abaddon." Johnson kissed him upon the cheek. "Not on this angel's watch." The girl pushed away and jogged to the idling big rig. She halted halfway, whirled, and shouted, "Beware the evil entities who will stand in your way!" The Marine dashed off and climbed into the truck's elevated cab. Plumes of diesel fumes belched from twin stacks as the chromed car carrier merged onto the highway.

Chapter Sixteen

SALLY SLAMMED THE CAR DOOR and clicked on the seat belt. Then, shutting her eyes, she rocked backward and forward, holding her head in her hands.

Kenya started the engine and sped up the on-ramp. He could not risk losing Theresa. She was his only connection to the Tandoori Box and whatever daunting confrontations lay ahead.

"Where did she go?" Nora asked, craning her neck east and west. The roadway was deserted. The tractor-trailer was nowhere to be seen. A tanker truck barreled toward them on the opposite side of the highway. "That's not it!"

"Slow down!" Sally ordered. The Lexus' speedometer needle hovered several notches over one hundred and ten miles per hour.

Watson took his foot off the gas, letting the SUV coast to ninety. "You saw Johnson?" he questioned. "She was visible to you?"

Sally yanked open and banged closed the glove compartment for no reason. Likewise, her mouth opened and shut without intent.

Nora picked at a daub of green guacamole on her shirt sleeve. "How many 'Ronas did I drink? It's time for my siesta. Wake me up if we bump into Muhammad or Buddha." She lay her head upon King's tummy and passed out.

Sally found her voice. “What is the ‘tandoori beef’ you were speaking of? Tandoori is Indian food. Your strange friend grilled carne asada.”

Kenya replied, “I didn’t say ‘beef.’ I said ‘box.’ The Tandoori Box came in a bag from an Indian restaurant. Voilà, my ad-lib name for the unnamable.”

She solemnly inquired, “What’s in the box? Spicy chicken?”

Despite the tension, Watson chuckled at the farcical image. His constrained tee-hees broke into braying hee-haws. Kenya’s hitching gasps for air burst into a fit of tears. He caught his breath and wiped his face. “Now do you understand what I am dealing with?”

Sally, worried that she and her boyfriend were experiencing conjoined mental breakdowns, squeezed his shoulder. “Are you telling me it’s not stuffed with roasted chicken?”

“No. Nothing remotely edible. When I initially got it, I peeked in the flap. That’s when I saw the tree.”

“That bristlecone pine we’re trying to find? The Forever Tree?”

“I think so. Something in there scared me shitless. I never looked inside again.”

Sally silently snapped down the sun visor, eased the seat to the lowest level, and appeared to doze off. For twenty minutes, she rested in this same position until her eyes shot open. “Where is it now?” she babbled, jerking on his elbow. “Is that thing here in the car with us?”

He unclamped her fingers. “I’m driving! Let go!”

Nora perked up. “Why are you two yelling?”

Kenya realigned the NX between the painted lines. “The box is under my seat.” He blocked Sally’s straining arm. “Not while I’m behind the wheel. I’ll show it to both of you later.”

“Was it here all along?” Sally hollered. “What else does that box do? What’s it doing right now?”

Watson shook his index finger and voiced through compressed lips, "Calm down! You'll see the Tandoori Box when I'm good and ready."

Late Wednesday, the exhausted travelers lugged their suitcases into the La Quinta Inn in Salt Lake City. Sally and Nora had provided Kenya with breathing space that afternoon by doing most of the heavy driving and keeping the conversation light. That night, the Tandoori Box produced a creepy image of Sally and Kenya fooling around while her mom slept in the next bed.

Their cross-country trip concluded Thursday evening after a long, uneventful day on the road. The Owens River Inn in Big Pine, California, offered a magnificent panorama of the White Mountains. Temperatures that had topped one hundred degrees when they'd checked in lowered to the mid-eighties as the sun set behind the Sierra Nevada Mountains. Nora, rejuvenated by her nap, chatted to an Australian couple in the hot tub. Sally and Kenya, the only guests in the hotel's swimming pool, clung to the curved edge. The cement tank's milk-warm water remained inappreciably cooler than the night air, but it was preferable to sitting in the air-conditioned room—*waiting.*

"Please tell me what will happen," Sally implored. "I need to prepare myself for the worst."

Kenya pushed off the blue wall and backstroked to the deep end. She dove beneath the ripples and emerged in a swirl of bubbles in front of him. Her cheeks sparkled with water droplets.

"Sal, you'll have to experience it for yourself. The Tandoori Box is an unnatural phenomenon well beyond explanation. For me at least."

"I heard you tell Theresa Johnson the box was driving you bonkers. If it's such a pain in the ass, why did you bring it with us?"

"I had no choice," he answered. "I have attempted to walk away from the Tandoori Box more than once. The first time, I threw it in Casco Bay. Then, I hit it with a baseball bat. I even left it in a church for a parishioner to trip over. The device continues to reappear. Eventually, I gave in, gave up. Now, I just strive to keep the damn thing happy."

"Is it dangerous?"

Kenya grimaced. "You have no idea. Not in the slightest."

"That freaky shit at the rest area affected me. Although Hannah was your ex-girlfriend, I'm still upset about the nature of her premature death." Sally looked him in the eye. "There is something I must get off my chest. While you were in the shower, I had a meltdown. I told my mother we should vamoose."

"Why didn't you? I wouldn't blame you at all."

The underwater lights illuminated Sally's kicking feet. "Mom said to stop running." Water spilled into her mouth as she sank below the surface. She spat out the chlorine and opened her heart. "Besides, I love you way too much to ever let you out of my sight again."

Kenya often expressed his affection for Sally. Until tonight, she had never responded to his ardent declarations by uttering the three vital words he most needed to hear. He paddled nearer and asked, "Since when?"

Sally breathed her reply in his ear. "Since the day you squirted hot chocolate on my favorite shoes. They really were ruined. I purchased a new pair so you wouldn't feel bad."

Inside the two-bedroom hotel suite, seated in the bare-bones kitchenette, Kenya, Sally, and Nora fixated on the Woodward Supermarkets tote centered upon the dining table. Both antsy and bored, Kenya doodled alien stick figures on a notepad. Stressed out, Sally had developed a nervous tic, an uncontrollable quivering of her lower eyelid. Wired and impatient, Nora monitored her wristwatch every few seconds, each time ticking off the minutes remaining until midnight.

Over the last hour, Watson had informed the women of his prior encounters with T. D. Johnson. Sally now understood what he was doing outside McGee's Grill Pub during the blizzard. Nora's eyes watered at his morose tale of the disabled Marine taking a header into the East River. He stated when and where he'd first acquired the Tandoori Box. Sally recalled his White Elephant gift as being a package of emergency underwear. Kenya explained how he'd used the takeout receipt found in the HEAVEN IS WHERE ALL CHEFS ARE INDIAN bag to locate the cube's former possessor, the owner of the torched Tandoori House and Meat Shop. In conclusion, Watson reiterated the miscellaneous methods he'd used to dispose of the square boomerang—all failures. But he never revealed the profundity of his nefarious acts or reported how Shashi Chatterjee's suicide culminated in King's adoption. *They are not ready to learn that I assaulted a car thief in Baxter Woods or the tragic rationale for tiny Sophia Hastings unexpectedly becoming an orphan.* Kenya remembered seeing his reflection in Nora's bathroom mirror, not recollecting why he stood there for so long.

Sally announced, "The witching hour approaches." She poked at her ocular muscle spasm in frustration. "This eye is annoying me. When will you take the thingamajig out of the bag?"

"I'm going to leave it right where it is," Kenya answered. "The delivery is messy—gooey. I haven't seen the box give birth. Several times, I stayed up—always missing the precise moment."

"'Birth!'" Sally jabbered, almost tipping her chair. "Is it alive? You compared the Tandoori Box to a Rubik's Cube!"

"It is." His thoughts returned to the terrifying night he smashed the eely creature on his apartment's basketball court. "Kind of."

"As a practicing scientist, I must witness this parturition for myself," Nora said, reaching into the supermarket bag. Watson stretched an arm, unable to control her. She held the black block beneath the brushed-nickel pendant light.

"Mrs. Green," Kenya protested, "getting too close may not be such a smart move. As I said before, the Tandoori Box likes to do its business in private."

"This is absolutely—" A belt of purplish fluorescence girdled Nora's hands. "Ouch!" she yelped, dropping the object onto the tabletop. Self-powered, the buzzing cube rolled off the edge, hitting the floor with a thud that rattled the cups and saucers stacked in the kitchenette's cabinets.

"It's moving around under there!" Sally shrieked, lifting her bare feet onto her seat.

The humming spiked, resonating in every corner of the room at once.

Nora, undeterred by the angry blisters rising on the tips of her thumb and forefinger, probed the shadows beneath the table. King leaped from the couch. "Get out of my way!" She shoved the Rottweiler's unyielding shoulder.

The thrumming suddenly ended in a wet gush.

"Stop, you'll hurt yourself!" Kenya warned. He hauled her upright. "It's done."

"What is that awful stench?" Sally pressed knuckles to her nostrils. The dining area held the brackish fetor of stagnant rock pools at low tide. "This reminds me of seaweed rotting in the sun or the dead sea lions at Boothbay Harbor."

Nora murmured, "The Parisian sewers in the summer of 1986. Ammonia and methane. Peter bugged out when I tried to take him on an underground tour. He's claustrophobic."

Kenya opened the sliding glass door. The fragrant air parting the curtains held the essence of desert sage. He wadded a ball of paper towels, pinched his sniffer, and crawled under the counter. Watson emerged into the shaft of light with the Tandoori Box *and* the dripping photograph.

Nora grabbed for the print, blurting, “Give it here!” King leaned protectively against her knees.

Kenya put the cube into the green Woodward bag and planted it on the windowsill. He whispered to King, “Good boy,” and kissed him on the head. Watson pointed at the kitchen chairs and told them to sit down. When they were settled, he slid over the picture.

“Who are they?” Sally asked. Her nose squinched. “Is this us?”

The image was an overhead view of one man and two women seated at a table. A black dog with brown markings on its chest lay on the floor. They all gazed skyward. From Kenya’s perspective, the four represented subjects were clearly in the room. Despite his inner knowledge, he kept his mouth shut, allowing Sally and Nora to discover this disquieting truism at their own pace.

In obvious discomfort, Nora went to the freezer and got an ice cube tray.

“Hang on,” Kenya said. “I’ve got what will do the trick.” He took the Tandoori Box and had the woman hold out her palms. The blood blisters shrank to red blotches as he gently touched her fingers to the top of the pulsing block.

Nora giggled in girlish wonder. She rubbed her fingertips together. “Oh my, it tickles.”

Sally, religious enough to recognize a miracle when it smacked her in the face, or on the contrary, the vile work of the Archfiend, crossed her chest with her right hand while chanting the Trinitarian formula. Her jittery eyeball worsened.

Kenya said, “Sal, come here. I’ll fix your eye twitch.”

“Nuh-uh.” She massaged her eyelid. “You’re not getting anywhere near me with that thing.”

“Okay,” he said, placing the box back on the windowsill. “Let me know if you change your mind.”

Nora analyzed the photograph's composition front and rear. "The shape and resolution resemble a color Polaroid, but this print is not what it appears to be. Am I right?"

"It's a clever imitation," Watson replied. "Real instant film has chemical layers encased in a plastic envelope. This material is too technologically advanced to have been manufactured in one of our factories. Sometimes the images are animated, and I can hear or smell what they depict. Now and then, a time is stamped on the back."

"Nothing here," Nora muttered, checking the other side. "There's no odor present besides the feculence we're still gagging on." She abruptly peered at the ceiling. They all did, including King. Sally's mom stood and thoroughly inspected the top and bottom of the light fixture. "Where is it?"

"Where is what?" he responded, anticipating her next words.

"The miniature camera. It must be up here someplace." Nora spied the smoke detector and moved a chair across the floor.

"There is no camera," Kenya said. "And even if there was, how did I create this print?"

Sally answered, "You used a pocket-sized wireless photo printer."

He pointed his finger down. "Are there any printers underneath this table?"

She hung her head. King, aware of her disorientation, nudged her leg. Sally bent over and stroked his ears.

"Don't you see?" Kenya asked.

"See what?" Nora replied.

Watson's finger tapped thrice on the image. "That's you. There's Sally. And that's me."

"The photograph is backward," Nora noticed. Agitated, she worked out the brainteaser. "No, not reversed—distinctly different. I am sitting across from you, but in this characterization, I am against the wall, and Sally is directly opposite you. How can this be? I've been right here the entire time."

"The seating arrangement is a minor detail. What else?" Kenya questioned. "Come on, Doctor Green. What's actually going on here?"

"I wouldn't call the fact that the image does not reproduce our reality a trivial matter," she answered. "In the photo, we're looking up. We tried to spot the photographer *after* the picture was 'born,' not *before,* which is—"

"Utterly impossible," he ended, tucking the print in his pocket.

Nora's mouth fell open. "Kenya, are you claiming this gadget predicts the future?"

"From the time I won this White Elephant, the daily images always depict me at an event destined to transpire within the next twenty-four hours. The jury is still out, deliberating whether the box passively foresees or dynamically influences what is to come. As a scientist, you should be better at solving that riddle."

Tempestuous, Sally scolded, "You've kept this goddamned thing to yourself until now?"

"I didn't want to involve you," he replied. "The Tandoori Box has proven to be very powerful and somewhat unpredictable. Now that you've heard the whole story, you'll take back what you told me in the pool."

"Wait a minute," Nora said. "It's now August. In the last nine months, you'd have collected over two hundred and fifty pictures."

"Much too long and far too many," Watson verified. "Why? What are you getting at?"

Preoccupied, Nora did not respond.

"May I examine the other photos?" Sally asked. "Do you save them?"

"Yes, I do," he replied. "The oldies are at home. I have the ones the box made since we left."

She put out her hand. "And you'll let me see those?"

Kenya answered firmly, "No."

"Why not?" Sally inquired. "Are you doing something wrong? Something illegal?"

"You heard me admit to Theresa Johnson that I've sinned on behalf of the Tandoori Box. She said returning to normal life is not currently an option. Sal, I can't go on living like this."

"My mom asked why the photograph doesn't accurately portray our seating positions."

"The Tandoori Box must use limited data to make an educated guess of what will take place," Kenya replied. "Outside influences might impact the final result. Normally, its renderings are right on the money."

"Fascinating theory," Nora mused. "How did you learn the cube had the mojo to cure my blisters?"

"Just a hunch. I wasn't certain it would work. To be upfront, I believe the cube's abilities are boundless."

"Tuesday morning, there were bloodstains on your jeans," Sally said defiantly. "You told me you slipped and fell while out walking King. Yet I didn't see any wounds on your body. Not a scratch." She thrust out her jaw. "What really happened? Whose blood was that?"

"Mine. I had a shotgun pellet in my butt. The box hummed, so I placed it on the wound."

Sally shouted, "Somebody shot you?"

"Kenya," Nora questioned, "I get that you don't want us to think less of you, but can you please walk us through this specific incident? The particulars may help me come up with a solution to your uncommon dilemma."

"I'd prefer to give an account of what occurred last night. For once, I achieved a positive payback and felt good about myself." Watson spoke rapidly, touching upon his stealthy outing to the Golden Spike Resort, finding Freejared's disgusting server farm, and tipping off the police. He omitted his maniacal throttling of the pervert and his suspicious phone call to Syria. "You noted the FBI trucks this morning. That was my doing."

Nora picked apart his scanty narrative. "Did you receive a still or a video of the Golden Spike Resort and the room number?"

"Technically, the image is more of a three-dimensional moving picture than a video," Kenya answered. "I saw myself walking to the Golden Spike, pushing buttons on the elevator, and stepping off on the second level. Then, I slipped the paper under the door of room 264."

Nora cracked her knuckles. "Can I see?"

"I don't understand why you don't trust me."

Nora shouted, "Because you're not telling us everything!"

"The motion always ceases after I accomplish the job." He did not recall at what step in his after-midnight activities this image had frozen. *Hopefully not at the moment I was about to kill the guy.*

Nora held out her palm. Her no-nonsense expression left Kenya no wiggle room.

Sally demanded, "Give it to her. *All of them.*"

Watson dug in his trouser pocket. He sorted the five prints and handed her the one from Monday morning, the first day of their trip. This aerial photo showed him squeegeeing moths off the windshield.

Sally exclaimed, "That was at the gas station! I remember asking if you were looking at a UFO."

"Was there a drone?" Nora inquired.

"Not that I could see." While they studied the photograph, Kenya concealed Thursday morning's intimate snapshot of him and Sally dancing in the sheets under his thigh.

The next photo was from Tuesday, the night Watson crept through the sassafras trees onto the corn farm. This motion picture paused at the exact instant he jammed the road flare into the concrete storage bin's aluminum discharge chute. His face still smarted from the fire's fury. As Nora passed the print to her daughter, Kenya said, "I blew up a grain silo. When I was high-tailing it out of there, the farmer nailed me with a 12-gauge."

Sally asked, "Was that the night we—?"

"Yeah. The explosion woke you. I just finished washing off the blood." Watson glanced at Wednesday's image, grateful it only recorded him taking a sheet of letter-size paper from the shared printer at the Days Inn.

Sally questioned, "What does that say?" Her lips moved to make out the text.

"By the address for the Golden Spike Resort, there is a telephone number and a time. I dialed it—too early. No one answered."

"What was the area code?" Nora inquired.

"963."

Sally glared at him sideways. "That doesn't sound local."

"It's the country code for the Syrian Arab Republic."

"What? Were you calling the Assad Regime, the Kurdish rebels, or the Russians? Kenya, what in the Devil's name have you been doing?"

Her mother wagged her finger. "Cut the man a little slack. Try to appreciate what he is up against." She folded her hands and rested them on her lap. "Do you presume you must do whatever the Tandoori Box indicates? Did you ever disobey an instruction?"

Kenya's foggy memory had multiple holes, one being the night he slipped the Ritalin tablets into Nora's bottle of Lipitor. "I'd like to say yes, but I'm not sure. Maybe in the beginning. Half the time, I have no recollections of what I did." After he said this, he felt lousy—*guilty*.

"Who do you believe Theresa Johnson is?" Nora questioned. "Is she the true God or a cunning impostor?"

He stretched, depleted by his humiliating testimony. "I know I was relieved when Theresa told me I wasn't about to fall into a bottomless pit."

"Hell? The Prince of Darkness is a liar," Sally stated emphatically. "He is the father of lies."

Watson yawned. "Everyone's beat. Let's get some sleep. We'll talk more in the morning."

Sally held up a palm. "Not so fast, buster. I know how to add. What about Thursday? Show me the picture you're hiding."

Kenya winked. "Follow me, baby. We can review that one together."

Chapter Seventeen

THE CONCRETE TUNNEL, WET AND SLIPPERY, terminated at an energy-absorbing bumper for a narrow-gauge railway. Kenya spun the three-spoked wheel and lifted the hefty hatch. He lowered himself into the shaft, clinging to the slimy rungs bolted into the spider-cracked mortar. King, unhappy to be left behind, trotted around the open hatchway. Stale recirculated air whistled from a network of mold-clogged ducts. The reverberations of unbalanced electrical dynamos rattled the entire structure—the arrhythmic beats of a diseased heart. Flickering mercury-blackened fluorescent tubes cast funereal shadows on tilted racks of antiquated electronic apparatuses. A familiar tongue uttered his name. "Who's there?" Kenya asked, descending deeper underground. His feet landed upon a circular, metal-grated platform which ringed a twenty-foot-wide hole. "Hello?" he yelled past the rusted chain strung as a barrier. The faint plea, "Help me! Something is down here with me!" echoed out of the darkness. Radioactive gases hissed from safety valves plumbed into the enormous cylinder's plated walls. Geysers of luminous liquid shot through the steel grid, drenching his polished shoes and starched uniform. Kenya called, "Sally, is that you?" The Siren lured him nearer with her bewitching entreaty, "Throw me a line! I'm going under!" A red storage cabinet contained a white life preserver marked RMS TITANIC. He tied one end of the rope to a bulkhead and threw the cork ring over the side. Sally's voice warbled from a speaker box, "The demon mixes truth with lies to confuse us. Nobody's down there!" He squinted into the well, seeing Leviathan's scaly tail submerge into the glowing effluent. She questioned, "Did you bring the keys?" Kenya, startled to discover a pair of shrunken skeletons hanging below his throat, answered, "Yes, the bones are safe." A solenoid clicked, unlocking a massive vault door. Far above, King whined as his master withdrew down a corridor. Flashing emergency lights revolved on the low ceiling. Within a square bunker, a hooded figure stood before a blinking control panel. Edward, his long-dead brother, held out his hand and commanded, "Give me one of the keys, Kenya. We have momentous work to do."

Kenya smeared butter on his hot stack of "Hearty Griddlecakes" and reached for the genuine maple syrup. Sally and her mother had both ordered the caloric "Country Combo." They sat in a vinyl-covered booth at Clay's Country Kitchen, observing rubber-booted fishermen and camouflaged hunters claim their regular stools at the lunch counter. It was Friday morning, and the three journeyers were drowsy and grumpy.

"How did you guys sleep?" Sally inquired.

Kenya wasn't rested at all. The last vestiges of his sinister nightmare had trailed behind him throughout his morning routine (shit, shower, and shave) like the stank of a rancid fart. "Good," he mumbled.

"I, too, slept poorly," Nora responded, slicing a biscuit smothered with white gravy. "Your dog hogged the whole bed."

Not hungry, Sally picked at the hash browns. "The alarm beeped right when I was falling asleep. I kept reliving what took place last night." She surveyed the empty sky. "It feels as though somebody—*or something*—is watching us."

Nora summoned the waitress to refill her coffee cup. “Thank you, Nancy.” She smiled sympathetically at her daughter. “I understand your concern, but I think we are free from danger as long as we stick close to your boyfriend. To tell the truth, I’m excited.”

“Why is that?” Sally asked.

“I’m already writing my Nobel Prize speech,” Nora replied. “The boys in Stockholm may have to introduce a new category, such as a special award in paranormal research.”

Kenya, tolerating a phantasmagoric hangover, said, “You know we can’t share this with anyone.”

“I’m well aware of the limitations,” Nora said wistfully. “What’s the schedule for today, Mr. Watson? Search for your Forever Tree? Where do we start?”

Sally complained, “We sat in a car for four days. Can we take a break? Our mythological quest will wait a few hours. I need to ‘smell the roses’ before the men with the butterfly nets commit me to the booby hatch.”

“What do *you* want to do?” Kenya questioned. He pushed his empty plate aside and turned to monitor the cuckoo clock.

“Mono Lake?” Sally proposed. “The park’s brochure says the lake is ‘hauntingly beautiful.’ Mark Twain used to wash his dirty skivvies in the salty water.”

“I’m sure the lake is a tasty chemical brew to swim in,” her mom said. “Mono is one of the oldest lakes in North America. Let’s go there.”

Kenya gave in to their petitions. “Sure. Why not have a bit of fun?” He flagged Nancy for the bill.

After a ninety-minute picturesque drive through Inyo National Forest, the Lexus pulled into the Mono Basin Scenic Area Visitor Center. The modern museum housed various interactive exhibits. A theater featured a film on the region’s unique geography and the history of the original dwellers, the Kutzadika.

On the south side of Mono Lake, Nora, Kenya, Sally, and King strolled along the wide boardwalk among crowds of sunburned sightseers and a camera club enthusiastically setting up tripods. The Tufa Grove Trail hugged the rough shoreline, a pleasant hike on a clement, sunny day.

They were at a lookout reading an educational plaque and viewing the unusual limestone formations when Sally felt her iPhone vibrate. "I missed a call," she said, listening to the voicemail. "Delphic wants to rehire me!"

"What?" Kenya inquired in surprise.

"That was Vic Murray, the new director of Human Resources. He offered a raise *and* a signing bonus."

"Awesome!" he exclaimed, giving her a high-five. "Hurry, phone him back."

"They're three hours ahead of us. Vic told me he was driving home and to ping him in the morning." She smiled, tracking a flock of migrating birds with her dad's binoculars.

At a low point in the trail, Kenya asked in revulsion, "What's with all the bugs?" Swarms of alkali flies buzzed around puddles of creamy paste.

"They won't bite," Sally replied. "The Brewer's blackbirds and California gulls gobble them up like Fritos." Breathless, she focused on a long-billed brown-and-white bird wading in the water. "There's a Wilson's phalarope! Throngs of that species land here to pig out on flies and brine shrimp before attempting the three-thousand-mile nonstop flight to South America." Sally scrawled with a pencil in her birding notebook. She looked up to gather more characteristics and wavered. "Who's that?" An adorable girl of six to seven years of age walked slowly down the middle of the footpath. "Where is everybody? I don't see her parents."

"She ran away from them," Nora answered. "You know how kids are. I had to put a harness on you to keep you from running into traffic. These Tufa towers are exceptional. A couple of pillars are thirty feet high!" She took the digital single-lens reflex camera out of her haversack and zoomed in on the pale volcanic domes rising above Paoha Island. "We should have come earlier, at sunrise. Now the lighting is too flat."

At the next waypoint, Sally glanced rearward and sighed.

"What's up?" Kenya inquired, tapping her arm.

"The girl is wearing a school uniform with no shoes," Sally responded. "Something's not right. Where are her teacher and classmates? It isn't safe for someone that age to be out here on her own."

He shrugged and swatted at a swirling cloud of black insects.

"We'll keep an eye on her," Nora promised. She tramped the mushy beach and dipped her hand in the greenish liquid. "It's thick and slick with the consistency of mayonnaise. Try to picture this place before those thirsty Angelenos diverted water from the lake."

"That lost girl is still following us," Sally said. "It's odd how the kid stops when we do. I'm going to talk to her."

As King growled, Kenya tightened his control of the tether.

Nora gasped in stupefaction. "Her feet aren't touching the ground!" She elevated the camera's viewfinder to her eye and fired off a fusillade of shots. The scientist goggled at the playback screen. "What in the—"

Kenya, sensing danger, latched onto Sally's wrist.

She ducked from his grasp. "Let go! She's in trouble!" When Sally strode ahead, the child crouched and hissed.

The ensuing few seconds were chaotic. A mountain lion arising out of a mirage of shimmering light waves sprang onto Sally's back, dropping her to her knees. The tawny beast chomped her arm, heaving her body across the planked pathway into a ravine. The Rottweiler, foaming at the mouth, wrenched free from Watson's grip. Nora raked the thorny shrubs for improvised weapons as her daughter elbowed the cougar's snapping jaws away from her face. The snarling dog rocketed through the air, knocking the muscular cat off Sally's shoulders. Nora pelted the wrestling animals with stones and hollered. Kenya dragged Sally along the walkway to a bench. Her legs were chafed raw. Blood poured from puncture marks in her forearm. King howled in agony as the heavier predator's fangs locked onto the base of his skull.

"I'm fine," Sally said. "Go save King!"

Kenya reached underneath his T-shirt and tore the ball chain from his neck. He advanced toward the fighters, wielding one of the silver ID disks outward as if warding off a bloodthirsty vampire. The talisman burned red hot while these unbidden Latin words flooded from his lips: *"Vade retro Satana!"*

The panther reeled onto its haunches and, mewling in terror, bolted into the yellow rabbitbrush.

King lay in the dirt. Blood pumped out of his carotid artery. Cranial bone gleamed sickly white beneath the flayed flaps of skin. His eyes rolled to Kenya.

"Good boy," he comforted, applying pressure to the canine's throat. Watson tossed the car keys to Nora. "Get the box!"

Sally kneeled alongside them. "I'm sorry," she said. "I shouldn't have—"

"It's okay, Sal. The girl put one over on me, too." He stripped off his shirt and compressed the cloth to the dog's gaping wound. "How is your arm?"

Blood oozed from the teeth marks in her lower forearm. The surrounding tissue hemorrhaged an ugly purple. "It hurts," Sally said, sitting on the boardwalk.

King wheezed in shallow pants. Red fluid bubbled from his muzzle.

"Where is your mother?" Watson cried. He heard footsteps. A youthful couple pushing a baby carriage turned the corner.

The husband saw the bloodbath and halted. Wide-eyed, he asked, "What happened?"

"Mountain lion attack," Kenya replied. "It's gone now."

"So is the girl," Sally said quietly. "Was she an illusion?"

The wife, scanning the immediate vicinity, questioned, "What can we do to help?"

Nora rushed into view. "I've got it!" she huffed. "How does this thing work?"

"Give it to me," Kenya ordered. He unfastened the soaked rag from King's neck and pressed the Tandoori Box on the lacerations. The energized cube sent icy shivers up his wrists. Beneath the reddish-blue effulgence, the pulverized occipital bone and fractured vertebrae knitted themselves back together.

The mother stabbed digits into her cellphone. "I'm calling the park rangers."

"No, don't," Watson said. "We've got this under control."

"Your friend needs medical attention," the wife advised. "That wild cat could be rabid." She raised the phone to her ear. "Yes, I wish to report a—"

Nora snatched her cellphone and pitched it into the lake.

Sally pointed. "Look at King!"

The Rottie dashed down the embankment and dove into the salt water. His rump bobbed on the surface as he scoured the lake bottom for his new "toy." He fetched the phone and dropped it at the woman's sandaled feet. The dog waited for the speechless human to resume the game. She edged away in fear.

Kenya came to Sally's aid. When he lifted the block from the traumatized forearm, she touched the unblemished skin and grinned in wonder.

The father introduced his family. "My name is Nelson, and this is my wife, Gertrude. Our daughter, Grace, has a congenital heart defect. Several pediatricians diagnosed the condition as inoperable." Tears welled up in his eyes. "Are you a healer? Can you cure her? I swear we won't tell anybody about your wondrous skills."

Kenya hoisted Sally to her feet and squeezed her. He stooped over the baby buggy. The underweight infant gurgled weakly and waved puffy arms. Her porcelain epidermis had a bluish hue.

In a private huddle with his group, Watson questioned, "What should we do?"

"Why are you even asking?" Sally responded. "Treat her!"

"There may be serious consequences," Nora said. "You've seen the movie *The Butterfly Effect*? And if by accident, you induce cardiac arrest, you're facing a charge of involuntary manslaughter."

"I'm with you, Mrs. Green. We don't know what we're doing. She's only a baby. I couldn't live with myself if something bad happened." Kenya informed the family, "Sorry folks, but we can't help you."

Nelson, watching his daughter play with King's ears, said, "What I just witnessed was an honest-to-goodness miracle. Two minutes ago, I wanted to put your dog out of its misery. Now—*Lord have mercy*—he's fit as a fiddle!" Overwrought, the husband looked to his wife.

Hesitant, Gertrude bit her lip and gave her consent. "Mister, we'll give you everything we got. Gracie is our little ray of sunshine."

Nelson held forth a set of car keys. "Take the title to our Chevy Aveo. Darleen don't look like much, but she runs like a top."

Kenya walked to the muddy lakeshore and contemplated the paw prints emerging out of the lapping waves. *Is this why I'm here today, to save this girl?* Pensive, he juggled the box from palm to palm. A ragged clump of fur stuck to the "healing" side. Watson dunked the cube in the temperate brine and wiped the residual gore on his jeans. He appealed to the gods for enlightenment, receiving no response other than a painful gadfly bite on his ankle.

King waded into the lake and woofed twice. A white square—gray hair—would forever brand the side of his head. Kenya trudged past the teeming flies onto the boardwalk. He told the father, "Set Grace on a blanket in the shade." Watson showed the Tandoori Box to the couple. "To be clear, I can't guarantee success. In fact, I cannot say this machine will not harm, or even kill, your daughter."

Gertrude asked, "What is that? Did you make it?"

"No," Kenya replied. "Not me. I won this White Elephant gift at my company's holiday party. We recently learned of its healing properties."

Grace's lips puckered in delight as he placed the Tandoori Box upon the center of her chest. The girl's fingers trembled as the violet radiation spread up and down her sternum before swelling across her ribcage. A vermilion corona encapsulated Grace's heart, the long streamers of writhing plasma sizzling in the desert air. Excess static energy stood her chestnut locks on end.

"Why is she shaking?" Gertrude questioned. Nelson had to restrain his wife from getting in the way.

When the child's internal organs became visible to the naked eye, Nora croaked, "My god," into her fist. "See there? The blood leaking through a hole in her aortic arch?" She leaped in triumph. "Oh, good, the tear is mending!"

Grace wiggled her feet as her cheeks blossomed healthy pink. The celestial concept *"I AM GOD"* wormed its way into Kenya's brain. At that decisive moment, the Tandoori Box turned lifeless—cold and black.

Gertrude prostrated in supplication. "God bless you, sir!" she praised. "Please take my wedding ring. The stone is zirconia, but the band is real gold!"

Nelson jingled the Chevrolet's keys in his face.

Watson, spiritually drained rather than devoutly fulfilled, dismissed their offerings and bid them to go on their way. "I only ask for you to keep this between us. Nobody will believe you anyway."

"I fucked up," Kenya muttered. "Big time." He was driving back to the hotel.

"How so?" Sally inquired, rubbing her healed skin. "Apart from a cougar nearly eating us, I think our day went quite well."

He saw a stretch of broken yellow lines and took advantage of the brief opportunity to pass a caravan of recreational vehicles. "When I used the Tandoori Box to cure Grace, I felt—"

"Like God?" Nora questioned. She shoveled a handful of mixed nuts into her mouth and handed the bag forward.

Watson clutched the steering wheel. "For a minute there, I thought I had the power to move mountains or whole solar systems."

"I expect a god complex is a natural human reaction in a situation such as we experienced this morning," Nora commented. "Do you identify yourself as the Righteous One, the Prince of Life, He Who Quickeneth the Dead—or as my dad used to call him, the Big Kahuna?"

"No!" he answered forcefully. "For months, I convinced myself that I had become the Antichrist. Getting to wear a white cowboy hat for a change was incredibly liberating."

Nora combed her fingers through the silver fur on King's neck. "Kenya, are you contrite?"

"What do you mean? Am I sorry to have judged myself superior?"

She nodded, and he returned the nod.

"Then don't beat yourself up. Say ten Hail Marys, treat yourself to a Venti Iced Vanilla Latte at Starbucks, and move on. Everybody has egos, and everyone makes mistakes. On the other hand, I have formed an opinion that what you are doing is of paramount importance—and of great responsibility. I've mulled over why you were selected to receive the Tandoori Box."

"You think I was selected?" Watson asked. "I picked up that stupid gift in an idiotic office game—sheer luck."

Nora replied, "I doubt chance had anything to do with why we're here today. It takes a certain sort of individual—somebody with a strong backbone and quick wits—to withstand the hardships you are constantly subjected to."

"The previous box's owner wasn't able to handle the pressure," Kenya contradicted.

"What did he do?" Sally questioned.

"He hanged himself from a fire sprinkler pipe."

She punched him hard on the arm. "Why did you wait so long to tell us something so relevant?"

Watson disclosed Shashi Chatterjee's woeful story and the peculiar circumstances under which he'd adopted King. "I have no desire to learn the fate of those who came before him. After studying his collection of Tandoori Box pictures, I got the impression he barely lasted a year."

"When I first met King," Sally said, "I wondered if he was your personal guard dog. He appeared overly possessive." She reached across the seatback and petted the Rottweiler. "I'd be dead meat if he hadn't attacked that mountain lion."

"King frightened me when I brought him home," Kenya said. "Couldn't relax for a second—petrified the dog would rip me to pieces. We began to trust each other. Now, he's my best friend."

"What about me?" Sally asked. "Aren't *I* your best friend?"

He leaned across the center console and kissed her. "You're my best two-legged friend."

Nora inquired, "This is a rather personal question, but do you ever have thoughts of self-harm? I can hardly imagine the burden you must be carrying."

"The act has crossed my mind." Kenya addressed the rest of his response to Sally. "When you left me, I had bouts of severe depression. On one occasion, I snuck into a semiconductor factory and dumped a bag of human hair in the CFO's office. I felt so scuzzy afterward, I considered jumping off the Franklin Towers."

Sally frowned in dismay. "What kept you from stepping over the edge?"

"Although the Towers is the tallest building in Portland, it's only sixteen stories high. What if I landed in a bush and just broke my spine? I didn't want my girlfriend coming home to find me strapped in a wheelchair." She wasn't amused at his joke. "In actuality, I was too bummed to get out of bed and drive across town."

Nora asked, "You've heard the quote, 'Why do bad things happen to good people?'"

"That faith-killing paradox loops continually through my head," Kenya replied. "Evil and sin are the main themes of every Sunday morning sermon. If God is all-powerful and loving, why does he allow his chosen ones to suffer so much pain?"

Nora nodded. "Genocide and Ebola are prime examples of this philosophical conundrum. The Bible states no one is genuinely good except for God. I personally think that without divine intervention, more terrible things would occur."

Sally questioned, "Are you saying mankind's existential scales are tipped in our favor?"

"By a significant amount," her mother answered. "A mathematical formula could confirm my hypothesis."

"You figure you can establish the presence of a benevolent god?" Sally inquired.

"No, not me." Nora laughed. "Such a complicated supposition will require a luminary with the intellect of Albert Einstein or Stephen Hawking—legitimate geniuses—to calculate each variable. We are at an unprecedented time in human history when it might be feasible for statisticians to compile enough environmental data to demonstrate this corollary. For instance, you've heard the news reports on how many laptops catch fire or even explode?"

"My brother's hoverboard almost destroyed my parents' garage," Kenya responded. "Worthless piece of shit."

"Cheap knockoff batteries are a substantial problem," she said, not sure if he referred to the hoverboard or his brother. "Ten years ago, Dell recalled four million lithium-ion batteries manufactured by Sony. Plastic separators prevent the cathodes and anodes from contacting one another. To economize on space and weight, factories are fabricating these pieces smaller and thinner. If the lithium overcharges, the fragile separators melt, and the cells short-circuit. Ergo, you awake to the blare of a smoke alarm—*if* you're lucky."

"I read an article about e-cigarettes blowing up in people's faces," Sally said.

Watson chuckled. "Remember *Looney Tunes* with Bugs Bunny and the exploding cigars?"

"Kenya, the pictures weren't funny. One driver, blinded by the detonation, crashed her Land Rover head-on into a daycare shuttle. Everyone, apart from the vaper, burned alive."

"Misfortunes involving children are doubly disheartening," Nora acknowledged. "Why aren't higher percentages of rechargeable devices malfunctioning? Think of all the batteries in automobiles, power tools, mobile phones, cameras, and the billions of other portable electronic devices around the world. In reality, only a dozen laptop batteries caused damage or injury. Still, it cost Sony millions of dollars to replace them.

"To add to the lineup of perils you may encounter daily, what about the overheated power adapters piled underneath your desk at work? There are miles of electrical wiring threaded through the walls of the hotel you're sleeping in. Which general contractor hired the deadbeat who never bothered to ground the outlets in your room? Honda mailed you a recall notice concerning your defective airbags months ago. Why didn't you have those potential guillotines serviced before picking up Billy after school?" Nora flapped her arms. "On takeoff, a seagull is sucked into your plane's jet engine. Sorry, Mom, but I won't be home for Christmas this year. I'm at the bottom of the ocean, and I can't seem to unbuckle my seat belt. Let's not mention the escalating ISIS and Boko Haram suicide attacks. The checklist of the harmful or deadly is infinite."

"A terra cotta gargoyle could tumble off a church roof and crush my head," Sally remarked, putting her feet on the dashboard.

"We're all in agreement that human existence is wrought with hazards," Kenya said. "At any given moment, there's a probability that an asteroid will wipe out humankind. What's your point? Your 'one hundred and one ways to bite the big one' isn't doing much to dissuade me from taking a swan dive off the Franklin Towers."

"Sweet Jesus, Mother of Mary," Sally whispered. She raised a hand to her throat and shouted, "Holy shit!"

Watson, apprehensive that a brakeless cement truck was about to squash them, took his eyes off the road for a second. His girlfriend gaped at him. "Sal, what's that look for?"

"My mom spelled it out." Sally rapped her forehead with a knuckle. "Why didn't I make the connection? You're the missing variable in the empirical formula."

Kenya, checking the side and rear-view mirrors for vulnerabilities, stayed silent.

"You, Kenya Watson, are the X factor. Your actions tip the existential scales in humanity's favor! My boyfriend is a motherfuckin' angel's assistant!"

"Don't be absurd," he retorted. "I'm not superhuman. I bend over to tie my shoelaces just like the next guy."

Fired up, Sally waved her palms. "Each day, always on the dot, the Tandoori Box produces an image representative of the future. Frequently, the picture records your mundane activities:

eating ice cream, scratching your balls, whatever. At times, you execute a more intricate task. What is the outcome of these completed assignments? A life saved, a disaster avoided. Nelson and Gertrude's little girl, Gracie, could become a doctor *or the first female president.* Perhaps, even the trivial things you do—such as leaving the toilet seat up or down—can have a significant impact."

"Lorenz's chaos theory," Nora said. "Microscopic changes may result in large effects. The initial flapping of a butterfly's wings in Japan later precipitates a hurricane in Hawaii."

"I've done horrible deeds," Kenya confessed. "People died as direct repercussions of my actions. I'm not helping anyone!"

"There are always casualties in war," Nora said. "Remember when Theresa Johnson told us she was overworked and often had to multitask? I believe you and the Tandoori Box are merely tools in her belt. And I'll bet my bottom dollar, you're not the only one—*there's an army of assistant angels out there.*"

Chapter Eighteen

ON SATURDAY MORNING, BENEATH THE OWENS RIVER INN'S RED CEDAR ROOF, Nora, Sally, and Kenya hunched over the wet Tandoori Box photograph. King nosed a bowl of kibble across the kitchenette's floor.

"I dare say we're off on a hike," Sally said. "Did anyone pack bug spray?"

"There's a can in my suitcase," her mother answered, "along with sunscreen and bear repellent. The US Forest Service website stated that, due to the drought, there is an increase in bear activity. Wish I had the canister with me yesterday. I would have pepper-sprayed that panther."

"I've had enough wild animal encounters to last me a lifetime," Sally muttered, inspecting the scar on her forearm. "All I see in this picture is us on a dirt path winding through a bunch of pine trees."

Watson assessed the angle of the shadows in the photo and the prevailing cloud cover. He put away the magnifying goggles and massaged his temples.

"Look at your finger!" Sally exclaimed. The letters JOHNSON T. D. were branded into the pad of his thumb.

Kenya handled the remaining dog tag (the talisman he had used to fend off the mountain lion had disintegrated into dust after use). "The skies will clear by noon," he said. "Lace up your boots. We're taking a drive."

An hour later, the Lexus entered the parking area at Schulman Grove. A redwood bridge spanning a dry gulch led to the Ancient Bristlecone Pine Forest Visitor Center. Kenya attached the leash to King's collar and walked to a pair of chiseled signs. The Discovery Trail slanted up. The Methuselah Trail sloped down.

"Aren't we going inside?" Sally inquired. "The building is brand-new."

"I don't think there's time," Kenya responded. The dog pulled him downhill. "Hurry!"

Nora lifted the SUV's tailgate, grabbed bottles of spring water, and jogged after them.

Two-thousand-year-old limber pines dotted the sides of the rocky hills. Across a bald summit, the switchback track plunged below the timberline into isolated clusters of bristlecone pines. Shallow-rooted in dolomite soils, the stunted hardwoods had borne silent witness to humankind's accomplishments and missteps during the preceding five millennia. Bushy green needles sprouted from the tips of the twisted branches.

At an overlook, Kenya fretted. "I'm unable to spot it. Every tree resembles the Forever Tree, but none are anywhere near as impressive."

Nora, examining the prickles of a female pine cone, reassured, "Well, at least we're in the right ballpark." She returned the purple seeds to the ground.

In the distance, a low mist hung above Death Valley. Sally hooded her eyes and looked at the woodland. "There are thousands more out there."

The four-mile footpath traversed ridges and ravines before passing the world's second-oldest known living tree, the unmarked and therefore conserved forty-eight-hundred-year-old

Methuselah. At such a high altitude, the hikers begged for oxygen as they ascended the arduous incline to the visitor center. They sat at a picnic table, lunching on ham sandwiches and drinking grape Kool-Aid from plastic cups.

"These trees all look the same," Kenya grumbled. "We'll never find it."

"If you illustrated what we are seeking, we could better assist you," Nora recommended.

"Good idea," Sally agreed. She tugged a notepad out of her knapsack.

Watson opened the book and poised the pencil tip over a blank page. "My recollection is getting fuzzy."

Sally patted his hand. "Give it a try."

Kenya's jaw tensed as he sketched, erased, and sketched new lines. Satisfied, he held the drawing up for their appraisal.

Sally whistled. "Oh baby, that's. . .umm. . .good."

Defensive of his artwork, Watson said, "I can fix the shading." When the graphite point snapped, he balled the paper and threw it in the bear-proof garbage receptacle. "My artistic training is more Pollock than Rembrandt."

"Kenya," Nora asked, "would you care to take another gander inside the Tandoori Box? I understand what you saw previously disturbed you, but a fresh attempt may jog your memory."

Watson shrugged. "If we don't find anything on the Discovery Trail, I'll consider it. It's time to visit Uncle Charley." He headed to the pit toilet.

"What did he see?" Nora questioned. "Whatever it was certainly shook him up."

Sally loaded their supplies into the bag. "He won't tell me, Mom." She pouted. "Kenya keeps a lot to himself."

"Peter had secrets, too."

"Puh! Like what? Dad was an open book."

"To you perhaps," Nora answered. "Your father was seeing someone when he disappeared."

"Dad went to a shrink? He had a few issues. There's the deal with tight spaces and—"

"A lady at his advertising firm. A marketing executive."

Sally jerked her head. "Was not."

Nora raised her eyebrows.

"What! Why are you informing me of this now? I'm on my vacation!"

"I have no clue," her mother responded. "It just came out."

"Dropping the bomb that my father fucked around 'just came out'? That was twelve years ago!"

"Our audience with Theresa Johnson motivated me to do a little soul searching," Nora said. "Who knows how much time I have left before I hit the dirt."

"Deep mortal introspection doesn't mean *you* have to ruin *my* day!"

"Sorry, dear. It was not intentional."

"So, you're saying Dad skipped town with another woman? He wasn't murdered? Is my dad hiding in New York City?"

"I can't say if Pete is dead or alive," Nora replied. "In effect, he vanished while the coworker stayed put. The detectives questioned her and each person at the office. That bitch seemed genuinely upset. It just so happens she had a husband and three kids. Why do you believe he's in Manhattan?"

"The Big Rotten Apple is a fruit basket for cheaters. I should know. How did you hear of the relationship? Was there something in Dad's possessions? A telephone number?"

"The extramarital affair turned up in the police investigation. I felt such a fool."

Sally scowled. "Her husband must be involved. He learned of the hanky-panky and killed Dad."

"When I found out, I, too, wanted to murder your father. For months, I drove up and down the home-wrecker's street waiting for him to make an appearance. I brought a knife."

Kenya had returned to their table. "Everything okay?" He poured water from a bottle and scrubbed the microbial zoo from his palms.

"Everything's peachy keen," Sally responded. She stood and swabbed her face. "Let's get moving. We're burning daylight."

The Discovery Trail was an easy one-mile hike through a grove of aged trees that ended without success. In the NX, Sally sat behind the steering wheel. From the backseat, Nora and King watched Kenya lift the Tandoori Box out of the Woodward Supermarkets bag. He rotated the black block to the side where the photographs ejected.

"What do you need us to do?" Sally asked.

"Nothing you can do, except roll down my window as a safety measure." Watson used a pocketknife to pry up the miniature door. He braced the lid open with his thumb. "Last time, I blew chow all over my ottoman. Not a pretty picture."

Kenya squished his eyeball against the magnifying lens and peeped in the cube's slit.

The tree, already monstrous, had grown into a behemoth of aberrant proportions. Three-foot-long pine needles tipped branches sagging from an abundance of purple pine cones.

Sally, registering his astonished gulp, questioned, "What do you see?"

Kenya waved his arm for silence.

His concentration fixed upon the orange tail of a comet shooting over the horizon. *Something changed. Where is the cracked mud of the dry lakebed? The canoe and fishing nets are gone. What happened to the skeleton chiefs? How much time has passed? Thousands of years?* A coniferous tang reminiscent of the Pine-Sol detergent his mother used to clean the bathrooms tickled his nostrils. In the space between his ears, songbirds sang elaborate mating calls. The sentiment of well-being—wholesome and overpowering—flowed like warm honey through his veins and inflated the chambers of his softly pumping heart. The faraway sonic boom of the celestial object hushed the chirping birds. Polychromatic auras of scintillating dots amassed into the legless body of a reptile. Trepidation dominated his logical thinking as the yellow-bellied serpent slithered up the tree trunk.

"Kenya, are you all right?" Sally inquired. "Mom, he's—"

Watson's fists spasmodically clenched and relaxed. His fingers released the Tandoori Box onto the floor mat as his spine arched from the passenger's seat. Kenya's contracting muscles squeezed a sharp cry of distress out of his chest. During the epileptic episode's ictus stage, his limbs convulsed in unison. Then, his eyes rolled into his skull.

Nora shouted, "He's having a seizure! Quick, move him on his side so he doesn't choke!"

Kenya lay in the tall grass of a great prairie. The king cobra hung on the lowest bough, its cavernous mouth inches above his face. *This is not a water sprinkler,* he thought. *This snake is real.* Globules of venom dripped from its hypodermic fangs. He wriggled to the side. The tree's artificial shadow elongated as the fireball hurtled through the uppermost atmosphere. *The Four Horsemen are coming—and they're pissed.* Kenya rose and sprinted to a valley of glowing lights. Under the guise of a falling star, the olive green intercontinental ballistic missile thundered groundward. Kenya fell to his knees when a brilliance brighter than a thousand suns vaporized the bustling metropolis and the slumbering suburbs. At the speed of sound, the nuclear explosion's shock wave raced toward him, leveling all in its path. He flew backward as the blast tore off his shirt and sucked the wind from his lungs. Millions of homeless crows wheeled overhead as the Forever Tree burned to ash.

"Kenya, fight it!" Sally slapped his face, and, again, much harder with the back of her hand.

Watson gained consciousness, realizing he was in the Lexus. Nora held a paper bag over his mouth to ease his hyperventilation. He thrust her hand aside and blew lunch out the window.

Sally asked a second time, "What did you see?"

Kenya blotted his lips on his wrist and whispered, "Something very bad. *Something awful is about to happen.*"

At the visitor center's parking lot exit, Kenya told Sally to turn right.

She clicked off the car's left indicator. "We're not going to the hotel?"

"No," he answered curtly. His tongue hurt from the bite marks. "Not yet."

Sally scrutinized the clock in the dashboard. "It's late. Aren't you tired? You just had some kind of fit."

Watson pointed to the right.

They turned onto an unpaved lane heading north to White Mountain Peak. The undulating topography of granulated stone, punctuated by jagged boulders, reminded Kenya of the rover images transmitted from Mars *and* the weird landscape of his apocalyptic vision. As the grade elevated, the automobile rolled through more and fuller stands of limber pines.

At ten thousand feet in altitude, the vehicle jounced over the intersection for Silver Canyon Road. Across the snaking Owens River, the serrated edge of the Sierra Crest ridgeline cut into the washed-out sky. Loose gravel rattled within the wheel wells as the all-terrain treads adhered to the serpentine roadway. The automatic transmission shifted into second gear and surged ahead.

Nora leaned between the seats. "This is it. Am I right, Kenya? Time to put the pedal to the metal? Is the proverbial White Elephant shit about to hit the fan?"

King poked his snoot beneath her elbow as if he, too, wished to hear his reply.

"We're so close, I can sense it." He supported his aching head on the seatback and shut his bloodshot eyes. "I'm scared."

The woman laid a firm palm on his shoulder. "I reckon you are."

Watson felt the tires grasp air as Sally—*the coachman*—jockeyed the all-wheel-drive SUV—*stagecoach*—around a hairpin curve. *Faster, Jacob! Give the fiends a taste of the whip!* He remembered the Jesuit priest's words—*"Some of us may live tonight, but most of us shall surely perish"*—and gripped the door handle. His eyelids burst open. "I'm not ready. What if I don't have what it takes?"

Nora corrected. "What if *we* don't have what it takes? You're not alone."

"Yeah, you got us—the friggin' Mod Squad. You can be Linc, I'll be Julie, and my mom can be rich boy Pete." Sally whooped and gunned the engine. "This shit will be epic!"

King yowled approval and wagged his tail.

Beyond the dirty windshield, the scenery blurred by in shades of gray and green. Kenya sat higher in his seat, alert for bristlecone pines. *There's one! Too small. There's another one! Looks dead. There are two together!* While photogenic, none of the ancient, contorted trees came near to the stateliness of the Forever Tree. *Why in god's name can't I find it?*

The Lexus, still traveling at high velocity, arrived at the terminus of White Mountain Road—Patriarch Grove. Sally veered around the turnabout loop and stomped on the brakes. The front tires bounced against the logs placed as parking bumpers.

She switched off the ignition and, when he didn't move, questioned, "Well?"

Watson rubbed the Tandoori Box on his forehead. The dull headache, a symptom of dehydration and stress, drilled into his neck instead of diminishing. *Did this thing ever have power? What am I doing here? This is insane.*

Nora opened the door. King vaulted over her lap. She stepped onto the hardscrabble. The Rottie relieved himself on a Hummer's chromed wheel.

"Kenya!" Sally shouted in vexation. "Wake up! What do we do now?"

Watson answered in a monotone, "Quit yelling at me. I don't know." He jammed the cube into the knapsack along with the fork attachment Theresa Johnson had disconnected from her prosthetic arm.

The long-distance marathon's anticlimactic ending had sapped Sally. She laid her brow upon the steering wheel and gazed listlessly at the blank speedometer.

"Let's move out!" Kenya exclaimed with false bravado. "It's getting nippy. Bring a jacket." Behind the car, he swung up the tailgate and lifted the lid covering the spare tire. Watson removed Freejared's gun and tucked it in his waistband, covering it with his shirt. He leashed King and slung the canvas pack on his shoulders.

The sun sank below the mountain range the moment the travelers set foot on the Timberline Ancients Trail. Venerable sentinels from a bygone era stood guard as they approached the grandest tree of them all. Underneath the knotty branches, Kenya raised his arms and cried, "We found it! The Forever Tree is huge!"

At the head of a valley, steeped in the purplish splendor of sunset, the great Patriarch Tree dominated a strip of benchland. At four stories in height, the Pinus longaeva grew extraordinarily tall; however, it was the fluted main stem's mighty girth that thoroughly amazed.

Nora stroked the wavy fissures in the reddish-brown bark. "Multiple trunks have fused into one. This tree is remarkable, but I envisioned something more—"

"Magical," Sally finished. "I'm not receiving much of an 'it was worth driving across the whole country to see this half-dead tree' sorta vibe."

As night overshadowed twilight, Kenya fished a tactical penlight out of the knapsack and tilted the thin beam upward. "This tree isn't the Forever Tree. Although it's big, I thought—" He fell mum and cocked his head. "Do you hear that?"

"Your bag is buzzing," Sally responded. She consulted her wristwatch. "Eight-twenty. Way too early for the Tandoori Box to vadge it out."

Kenya dumped the sack's contents onto the hardpan. He put the black cube to his ear. "Hmm, it's not this." The humming redoubled as Watson unrolled the extra underpants he'd brought along in the inopportune event of an intestinal fiasco. He held up the artificial arm that Theresa Johnson had given him. The modulation changed in frequency when he turned the forked instrument in different directions.

"The steel prongs are acting as a tuning fork," Nora observed. "If I'm not mistaken, that note is an A."

Beneath the hoary Patriarch Tree, the white soil crunched underfoot as Kenya twirled in a halting circle. A full moon—red through the sultry haze—glinted on the pointed metal. The musical tones flattened or sharpened if he deviated from the natural note of A. Watson focused upon the sheer mountainside to the west and said, "It wants us to go that way."

"Kenya, it's too dark," Sally cautioned. "Let's come back tomorrow when we can see." She moved closer to King. "Are there snakes out here?"

He answered with no hesitation. "Pete the Pitiful Python is fast asleep in his den. We'll be careful and take it slow."

Nora distributed water and switched on her lamp. "Kenya, *you* go first."

The going was difficult. No maintained trail existed—simply the ruts worn by native animals weaving here and there on the dirt. Under the penlight's glare, Watson saw the erratic tracks of rodents. Now and again, he high-stepped above nuggets of desiccated spoor excreted from larger mammals. At a fork in the trace, he picked the skyward course. The bloody drag marks of something weightier signified that wild predators were on the hunt.

Numbing oscillations from the Y-shaped dowser spread to his wrist and up his forearm. Irritated nerves in his upper teeth shot hot and cold pangs into his sinus cavities' ethmoidal bones. To still the quivering, Kenya clinched his fingers around the prongs, only to receive jolts to his funny bone. He passed the device to Sally, hoping to give his fried neurons a time-out. The locator promptly turned off when it detected her hand. Theresa's arm piece was paired with him alone.

As the panting group crested the hilltop, swirling Santa Ana winds—hot, dry, and maddeningly itchy—blew them across to the cooler side. They rested on a granite lip, listening to the plaintive yelps of roaming coyotes.

Kenya swiveled the divining rod back and forth over the dim valley. His arc narrowed on a section in the seam of weathered bluffs.

"How do we get there?" Sally asked, evaluating the precipitous gradient below them. "It's too steep, and we can't see anything. We'll break our necks climbing down that." She glanced behind her. "We should find an easier route."

Watson's downgrade maneuvers started a small landslide. King accompanied his master but, voicing his disgruntlement, hastily stepped backward.

"Hold up!" Nora shouted. "There is another way." She pointed at metal stakes embedded in the rock.

"What is that?" Sally questioned as Kenya hauled himself back onto the shelf.

Her mother towed up the braided line. "It's a ladder." The homemade rope-and-wood contrivance descended into nothingness.

"Is this safe?" Sally inquired. "What about King? How is he supposed to get down there? Fly?" She kicked pebbles off the side, cupping her ear for much too long a time.

Kenya tested the rope threaded through the holes in the wooden slats. The nylon, sun-damaged and frayed, scratched his skin. "It's strong," he said. "I'll carry King." Watson considered lashing the one hundred and twenty pounds of muscle and teeth to his shoulders. *Preposterous. This dog isn't a baby in a papoose.*

As they argued their few alternatives, King, barking stridently, galloped into a cleft in the hillside.

On her stomach, Nora peeked down. "He's sitting on a ledge. That mountain goat somehow jumped almost fifty feet. The rope must end there."

"Swell. Now we *have* to use the ladder," Sally muttered. "There's no way he can climb back up here."

"I'll go," Kenya volunteered, sliding the buzzing tuning fork into his backpack. "If it's sketchy, I'll stop." His foot stretched past the edge, reaching for the first rung.

"You could fall!" Nora exclaimed. "Give me the car keys in case we need to get help."

Watson pushed the fob into her palm. "Don't worry. Providence left this ladder just for us." Again, his eyes swept the heavens for a sign. The single cloud—a white cotton ball—deliberately veiled the moon.

Hand under hand, Kenya hung on each dowel, warily lowering himself down the sheer cliff face. The ladder swayed fore and aft with every movement. The quartz wall scuffed his knuckles, and oak slivers pricked his sweaty palms. Halfway to the desert floor, Watson peered between his boots. King waited on the outcrop. His feet finally touched terra firma, and exhaling, he let go.

"You're next, baby!" Kenya called. "Piece of cake!" The temperature had plummeted into the fifties. He turned up his collar, glad he had suggested bringing the coats.

Sally gave him a mock salute. "On my way, Cap'n Crunch!"

Waves of doubt dashed through Watson as he beheld his beloved swinging over the brink. Up to this moment, their undertaking had felt like a game—a medieval knight's odyssey for the Holy Grail. Now, here in the cheerless darkness of no-man's-land, his insides knotted. Yet, as a commanding officer in any naval battle can attest, his anxiety changed to pride watching his first mate scurry down the rope ladder. "Mind the last step! It's a doozie!" Kenya teased as she neared the bottom.

Sally landed on the scree and skipped to him. "That was fun! I used to enjoy playing on the jungle gym at school."

"My little monkey girl," Kenya praised, pressing his cheek to her hair. He raised his arm at her mother. "You're up, Mrs. Green!"

Nora, more cautious in her methodology, clung to the inch-thick rundles as though her very life depended on each one.

"You're doing great, Mom!" her daughter encouraged. She aimed her flashlight into a tapered crevice in the mountain. "There's a path. We—"

Kenya, shocked by a shriek, spun to glimpse Nora hitting the ground. The woman's legs buckled upon impact. Her body pitched sideways, tumbled down an embankment, and smacked into a boulder.

They rushed to her.

Tears glistened in the corners of Nora's eyes as she clutched her ankle. "I-I think I broke my leg."

Watson stared at the lone strand of nylon dangling in the shifting air currents. Both the dowel *and* rope had snapped. She was lucky to have survived the fall.

Sally hunkered down beside her mother and laid a hand on her shoulder. "Can you move it?" She glowered at Kenya when he joined them in the dirt.

Nora pivoted her talus, grimacing in anguish. Both of her kneecaps were scraped, and a wine-colored bruise was centered on her forehead.

Sally took out her iPhone. She stood on her toes and raised the internal antenna high. "Fucking AT&T!"

Watson, a longtime Verizon customer, also had no signal bars. "I will fix this!" He extracted the Tandoori Box from his knapsack and forced a smile. "This always does the job." He held the hexahedron on Nora's inflamed limb, by now aware that it would not work. And, he was right, it didn't. When Kenya righteously proclaimed himself as God embodied in flesh, his Tandoori Box medical license was permanently revoked.

Anxious, Sally asked, "What's wrong? Turn it on!"

He shook the object. "Do you see any buttons?"

"Did you forget to leave it in the sun?" She pointed at him accusingly. "You said the batteries must be recharged daily."

Kenya flung the cube away. The useless block rebounded off the stone wall and bounced back to his feet. The mechanism hummed. Violet light—the deepest wavelength of a rainbow—lased from the slot in the front.

Sally sighed in relief. "There. Your damn box just needed a good whack."

Her mother pushed a dial on her wristwatch. "Dear, that's not what's happening. It's midnight."

"I don't feel well," Sally groaned, holding her abdomen.

"Me either," Watson moaned. In the downward-facing dog pose, he retched clear fluid onto the landing.

Sally replicated his actions, spewing purple Kool-Aid-stained chunks of Oscar Mayer ham and Nature's Own wheat bread across a hardy clump of bitterbrush. "Ugh! So gross."

Nora, graced with a cast-iron stomach, pressed her fist to her mouth and merely burped.

King, unaffected by the gizmo's salvo of alpha particles, sniffed the cooling runnels of vomit.

"We missed the birth," Nora said. She nodded at the now silent Tandoori Box. A photograph lay face up in a pool of lime-green jelly.

The sour, fishy odor made Sally gag once again. Glum, she inquired, "What is it now?"

Kenya got the picture and brushed off the filth.

Sally asked to look at the front.

"That *is* the front!" His teeth grinding, he shoved the print into her hands.

Sally inspected and returned the photo. "The thing really is busted." She wiped her fingers on her jeans as if done handling a steaming dog turd.

Bordered in white, the image reproduced the blackest of blacks.

Kenya put the Tandoori Box in his pack.

Nora, a lateral thinker, took the photograph. "Have you ever gotten a blank?"

Upright, he responded, "No. Never."

"Let's say the picture is accurate," she submitted. "Could it be your device recorded you in pitch-black conditions?" Nora held the print near the torch. "There's a red dot. . .no, two red dots."

"It doesn't matter, Mrs. Green." Watson squinted over the outcropping into the lowlands. "I'll make my way to the car and get the rangers."

Nora said bravely, "I can move my ankle. That proves the bone isn't fractured. It's just a bad ligament sprain." She placed weight upon the swollen joint and blanched.

"You stay with her," he told Sally. "I'll return as soon as possible."

Nora clamped his lower arm in a vise grip. "My leg feels like Sweeney Todd is hacking through the bone with a rusty saw, but I'll live. You guys continue on without me."

"No!" Sally hollered. "We're getting you out of here, Mom."

"Kenya, you know I'm right." Nora released him and wilted against the boulder. "If the photo is authentic, you're heading somewhere dark and probably treacherous." She faced her daughter. "He'll require your help."

"This is ridiculous," Sally objected, expecting Kenya to concur. When her boyfriend reached to hoist her up, she batted his hand away.

"There is something I didn't tell you," Nora said. "I'm not sure why I waited." Her dilated pupils reflected the constellations stippling the firmament. "Maybe I wanted to see how this all played out." The woman straightened to gaze at the wilderness to the west. "Out yonder. . .where those ravines unite? Kenya, that's where my class unearthed the Mayan drumhead you found so interesting."

"The tattoo on the dead man's back," he murmured. "A box."

"Go!" Nora implored. "Even now, you may be too late. Theresa forewarned that forces would try to stop us." She flexed her anklebone and winced. "It seems your friend wasn't kidding."

"The rope ladder broke—*that's it,*" Sally rebutted. Frazzled, she repeatedly checked her cellphone for coverage. "Supernatural beings had no involvement whatsoever."

"Your mom shall be okay," Kenya said. "We'll leave King to keep her company."

"No!" Nora exclaimed decisively. "King must go with you. He, too, has a duty to perform. My job is to remain here." She shook her can of bear repellent. "I'll be fine."

Watson yanked the Walther PPK from his belt and handed her the pistol.

"Adolf Hitler shot himself with this same model," Nora remarked, releasing the magazine into her palm to check for bullets. "Won't you be needing this for insurance?"

"Let's hope not," he answered, passing her the box of extra ammunition. "If we aren't back by daybreak, fire off three rounds every few minutes. Somebody will hear you."

As they prepared to depart, Nora said, "I nearly forgot to give this to you." She rummaged in her haversack and removed a shampoo bottle perforated with holes. Inside the plastic cage, an alien insect fluttered its wings.

Chapter Nineteen

WITH NO MORE WORDS OF DISSENT, SALLY TRAILED KENYA along the precarious rut leading to the foot of the hill. He took out the tuning fork and, detecting the distinct tone, zeroed in on the same distant mountain range where Nora had excavated the drumhead. King, unleashed and apparently possessing prior knowledge of their destination, led the way. They followed the domed ridge of a watershed, which gradually ramped up to the tree line. Every fifty yards, waist-high, conical stacks of igneous stones, each topped with a humanoid stick figure, marked the pathway. Whereas neither hiker speculated audibly on who had built the mysterious cairns or their purpose, Watson's thoughts dwelled upon an urban legend movie he'd seen as a teenager: a shaky, handheld documentary about a witch living in the forest. The young filmmakers had awoken to discover piles of rocks outside their tent. He remembered the ending—*sudden and unpleasant.*

For a taxing hour trapped in a brake of briers and brushwood, Sally and Kenya picked their way over a labyrinth of eroded snags. The humans, after receiving numerous nicks and bruises on their legs, gave up carving out their own route and tailed the Rottweiler through less jumbled sections. They emerged in a small clearing imbued with liquid moonglow.

Night bloomers swayed in the strengthening breezes. The air, redolent of jasmine, seemed foreign in this arid habitat.

King stiffened, growling deep in his chest.

"What do you hear, boy?" Kenya asked. He restrained the dog and combed down the raised hackles.

They listened to the rustle of feet on dry leaves and then the crisp snap of a twig.

"There's someone there," Sally murmured. She directed her flashlight into the heath's tangled confines. Two pairs of yellow-greenish eyes returned the bright glare. "What are they?"

"Just a couple of coyotes out for an evening stroll," he replied. "I assume these are the ones that were hooting and hollering when we were on the hill."

Four additional sets of shining retinas parted a cluster of deer grass.

King, lunging to get loose, pirouetted Watson to face backward. Fear expelled a gust of breath out of his mouth. "We're surrounded." He swept his light in an arc. "Where did they all come from?"

The closest, an abnormally large coywolf, tilted his grayed snout and bayed. Collectively, the other members of his band added their voices to the cacophony.

Her shoulders against his, Sally whispered, "There are too many for us to run. What do we do?"

While Kenya's hand fished fruitlessly in the seat of his pants for the gun, the Rottie, ready to rumble, broke free. Frantic, he watched his hound tear toward the pack, thinking, *All the Tandoori Boxes and all the Tandoori Boxes' men couldn't put King together again.* "Heel!"

"The medallion!" Sally shouted. "Show them the goddamned dog tag!"

Watson wrenched the loop from his chest and held the talisman forth. On this occasion, the sui generis words of banishment stuck in his vocal cords. The silver disk, like the Tandoori

Box, had lost its precious power to protect. He rasped, "No," as the wild animals charged forward.

At the moment the beasts mobbed the raging Rottweiler, the alpha male skidded to a standstill in a cloud of dust. The pack, castigated by his ireful keening, backed away, and, forming a ring on the fringes, cowered on their hindquarters. The subordinate members stared as their leader groveled up to King and, in a gesture of great respect, licked the white patch marking his throat. King, in turn, tongued the coywolf's head. Then, as quickly as they had congregated, the coyotes dispersed into the weald.

Sally took the chain from Kenya's fingers and hung T. D. Johnson's ID tag on King's neck.

Over and above the clearing, Kenya, Sally, and King climbed an incline composed of crushed rock. Here lay another obstacle, this one insurmountable. A boulder the size of a double-decker Greyhound bus blocked their path. Theresa's special arm attachment—its tips now throbbing hectic red—indicated that the Forever Tree, or whatever they were being inspired to find, was dead ahead.

The three scouted for a way around the impassable obstruction. Separate mounds of refuse, wood, and dirt barricaded access into the canyon.

"Which way, boy?" Kenya questioned King, who raised his leg and squirted a yellow stream on a brown cylinder. Happy with his business, the dog kicked up leaves, completely missing the pool of urine.

"It's a bucket," Sally reported, lifting the curved handle with a stick. She heaved a big hook from beneath a heap of shattered glass and soup cans. "What's this for?" With her foot, she tipped the triple pulleys encased in an oval wooden shell.

"That's a block and tackle," he answered. "They're used with a rope to hoist heavy objects."

"What were people doing out here?" Sally wondered. "Was this a town?"

Kenya exposed a square, concrete pad overrun with weeds. Rusty iron rods and a toppled frame of creosote-soaked timber were piled nearby. "This foundation is what's left of a stamp mill." He scanned the territory. "There's a mine here somewhere. Gold or silver. . .or uranium."

Sally poked her light into the pyramid of trash marked by King. "I see an opening in there!" She stripped off a green curtain of creepers. "Come look!"

They burrowed into the mess, removing lumber, metal, and miscellaneous debris meant to conceal the mine shaft. Sweaty and grimy, Kenya and Sally squirmed into a dilapidated shack built to shield the adit from the weather. A constant draft of cool air blew out of the hole.

"California Gold Rush," he said, rapping his knuckles upon the first blackened crossbar used to buttress the earthen roof. "This mine is probably a hundred and fifty years old."

"It looks dangerous," Sally warned, easing a ribbon of liverwort from the damp wall. She jerked backward when a clod of clay thumped to her feet.

The tuning fork sang the purest of musical timbres. Chills coursed up Watson's forearm and throughout his skeletal framework. The glowing tines tugged him onward. "It's safe. Stay close and watch your footing."

In the horizontal drift, they stuck to a narrow-gauge railroad track, at intervals tripping over uprooted gumwood ties or skinning their scalps on low-hanging hemlock rafters. Behind them, in the distance, the mine's moonlit ingress shrank to the diameter of a Liberty Head nickel.

Below the gallery's glittering dome of ore, they rested on a cart overflowing with tailings. A planked table held a mouse-nibbled accounting book and a tarnished brass safety lamp.

"How much further?" Sally inquired. By the penlight's pale glimmer, she appeared lost and frightened. "I'm getting worried about my mom."

Kenya veneered a smile onto his face. "We're practically there," he responded, handing her the water bottle and an energy bar. "Our cellphones will work once we're on the other side."

From whence they came, an ominous creaking resonated along the corridor. Grit rained to the floor as the material shoring the support posts crumbled.

"I don't like the sound of that," she whispered.

"It's the roof settling," he said flatly, peering into the passageway. "Let's keep going. This tunnel can't go on forever."

As they turned to proceed, a fungus-digested chock of pinewood used to level a joist decomposed into sawdust. The stout girder dropped an inch, knocking down a crucially placed screw jack. Corroded pinning bolts securing a ceiling crib constructed of equally rotted, rough-hewn logs failed. Their eye to the outside world winked out as eight tons of mountain caved into the tunnel with the boom of a thunderhead.

"Run!" Kenya yelled. A pother of pulverized minerals billowed past their shoulders as they flew pell-mell into the smother. He stumbled on the railroad tracks and landed hard on something soft.

Sally tumbled over his leg and fell onto his back. She rolled off, shook her light to restore electrical contact, and trained the intermittent rays down the entrance shaft—now a dead end.

"My penlight!" Kenya cried. He groped underneath the layer of gray powder.

"Where's King?" Sally questioned. She stood up and called, "King!"

Watson, realizing the doughy substance he had sprawled upon might be his dog, urged her to aim the light his way.

The missing torch sat on a soiled pair of coveralls stuffed with bones.

"Jesus!" he cried, scrambling past the hair-matted skull lodged in the battered miner's helmet.

Sally giggled hysterically. "Did you find my daddy?" Her emerald eyes looked as big as saucers.

Fresh oxygen originated from the direction in which they headed. Shortly, the particulate-laden air cleared. They hopped across the mummified cadaver and pressed on.

The scrapes of digging and the clatter of falling rocks resounded in the widening tunnel. They ducked beneath a splintered crosspiece, shouting King's name. Around a slight bend, the drift skewed upward.

Kenya squinted into the obscurity, certain he smelled vegetation.

At the beam's limit, King stared back at them, his eyes reflecting as two red dots. The Rottweiler's front paws, now raw from effort, bulldozed away the blockage to a ventilation shaft.

"Well, there's your Tandoori photograph," Sally said matter-of-factly. Cheek by jowl with the determined animal, she scrabbled out rubble with her bare hands.

Through the head-sized hole, Watson saw salvation.

Over hill and gully, Sally, Kenya, and King at long last faced the Forever Tree. The three pilgrims, plus the woman of science waiting under a swinging rope ladder for their return, had traveled many miles and had suffered many trials and tribulations to reach this sacred spot. In this place, no other *Homo sapiens* had ever set foot.

Safeguarded by the perpendicular walls of a box canyon, the bristlecone pine grew in a verdant glade dense with exotic species of flora and fauna, few of which would ever be seen on the *Discovery Channel*. Majestically soaring hundreds of feet higher than the tallest sequoia, the tree's bristly arms spread into the cyclopean sky. Although evolutionary biologists position conifers on the top branches of the phylogenetic tree diagram, the far-reaching roots of this singular Pinus longaeva abided a billion years before Earth's first land plants evolved from a green glob of algae. The prickly, purple pine cones held all the seeds necessary to create life.

The morning sun, a picture-perfect orange sphere of hot plasma, saturated the Forever Tree in diagonal blazes of precious gold. On high, the moon, now a reddish value not printed on any color chart, hung stationary, not unlike a wound-down clock pendulum.

A cynical observer on the far side of the dell might chuckle or, God forbid, make fun of the enthralled expressions adorning our intrepid explorers' uplifted faces. Kenya, his shirt ripped and covered with muck, stared in rapture at the spectacular prize he had only dreamed about. Sally, similarly enchanted, dipped her fingers into the torn pocket of her jeans. Without looking at her iPhone, she tapped a contact in its address book and pressed the minuscule speaker to her earlobe. Even though they were umpteen miles from any cellular towers, the digital connection transpired, and her mother answered. Nora did not hear her daughter speak, but a lucid vision of a tree more exquisite than anything she had ever known filled her mind with a peace that passed all understanding. She threw down the gun and wept into her folded hands. King, grinning, rolled on a spongy carpet of moss, waggling his healed paws in the sanative air.

Insomuch as time does not apply or even exist in this thin, harmonious portal betwixt worlds, on that Sunday morning, it is futile for us to establish or comprehend how long the wayfarers sheltered underneath the Forever Tree's green crown. Sally offered Kenya a pomegranate plucked from a grove of fruit trees.

His lips pink with juice, he uttered, *"ደኅና አደርኅ,"* the Amharic word for "good." She performed the ancient goddess dance upon a stage of sparkling gemstones. In a lush garden, King gnawed baby carrot shoots and lapped water from a sweet spring. After the frisky pup paddled in an emerald pool under towering waterfalls, he played a friendly game of hide-and-go-seek with a long-eared mammal whose sleek anatomy could be categorized as half feline, half rabbit. Sally and Kenya, their carnal pleasures satiated, slept dreamlessly on a soft bed of perfumed flowers. King, pooped from his romp, nestled in a basket formed by the tree's gnarled roots. A kaleidoscope of butterflies, resplendent in their brilliant colorations, flitted high over creation.

A rain shower pattering on palm fronds stirred Kenya. Propped on his elbows, the man sighed in complacency as the dazzling water drops washed away all of his sins. Sally, also naked, slept beside him. He clasped the woman's hand and lay back on the flowerbed. Directly overhead, in the blue vault of heaven, a ring of high-pressure atmosphere dispelled the cumulonimbus clouds to the four cardinal orientations. Feathered creatures splashier than any bird of paradise nested in the crooks of the giant tree. Downy, spotted fawns suckled their mother's milk in a sunlit meadow. *I could live here forever.*

Kenya gauged time by the sun's height. *Must be noon. Only a few hours have elapsed. It seems like years.* King, asleep beneath the Forever Tree's pine-needle canopy, moaned in terror as meat eaters chased him through a hellish dreamland. Kenya sat up and rubbed the lump tightening his chest. *If this place is Eden, why am I so edgy?*

Watson gathered his clothes, jacket, and backpack off the flat boulder they'd utilized as a tabletop. While he dressed, Kenya noticed a familiar noise originating from a bouquet of yellow poppies near the vale's entryway. In his euphoria to reach his transcendent goal, the tuning fork had slipped from his grasp. *We're here. If we've located what we came for, why is this thing still buzzing?* He picked up Theresa Johnson's arm accessory.

The perfect pitch drew Kenya straight to the tree's monumental trunk *and yonder.* On the opposite end of the canyon, a rugged footpath ascended up the side of the gorge. Something brushed his calf. He recoiled, relieved to see that it was just King.

Watson gazed past his shoulder. Already, the tranquil glen had disappeared around a curve in the trail. The adventurers had departed from their Garden of Eden without so much as a fare-thee-well. *Did the Forever Tree ever exist?* Kenya knocked his cranium, hoping to clarify his muddled cerebellum.

"What's troubling you?" Sally inquired. She looked ravishing with fuchsia orchids woven into her hair.

His girlfriend—*his betrothed*—changed outwardly as well as inwardly during the last several hours. If imaginable, this poised, intelligent, and capable woman emanated an even greater level of beauty and strength. *Have I changed?* He felt different. *But there is more to this, isn't there? I sense it in my bones.* "Were we—?"

Sally struggled to answer his question. "We found your tree. It was. . . ." She turned her vocabulary upside down, searching for an adequate word to describe the experience. "Lovely."

Kenya recalled a beguiling bed of flowers. "And did we—?"

Sally's bright smile dissolved into uncertainty. "I think we did." She frowned in puzzlement. "I'm afraid, before long, we won't keep any memories of what happened today."

He nodded in agreement. She turned to continue.

"Sal, wait a minute." Watson delved into his bag and gave her the shampoo bottle. "Here, you do it."

Sally unscrewed the lid. The odd, gilled insect crawled to the lip and flexed its stiff wings. "Goodbye, fly," she said as the bug buzzed back down the pathway.

"Where are we going now?" Kenya asked. He hadn't the vaguest idea.

She gawked at him in surprise. "Don't you know? Me and you? We're off to save the freakin' world."

Chapter Twenty

THEY HIKED UPHILL FOR AN HOUR. The land plateaued and unrolled into the hazy distance. A cyclone fence, garnished with razor wire, enclosed a flat field overrun with skeletonweed and sagebrush. The tuning fork, its tines now the color of blood, signaled that they were close.

Sally spotted a red WARNING sign and read the print aloud: RESTRICTED AREA. UNLAWFUL TO ENTER THIS AREA WITHOUT PERMISSION FROM THE INSTALLATION COMMAND. USE OF DEADLY FORCE AUTHORIZED. She saw the security cameras and stepped back. "Is this a prison?"

Even though his gut told him exactly where they were—*a very bad place*—Kenya shrugged. He identified a long, low, brown-and-tan edifice to the north. "That's the main gate. Let's check it out."

They continued along the fencing past fortified radio antennas and, perplexingly, a charred bingo tumbler. White sheep and black cows grazed on the green hillside. High in the troposphere, a parrot-hued Southwest Airlines jet painted a silver streak across the deepening sky.

A single-track country lane, originating from somewhere down in the valley, transitioned to macadam at the front gate. Inside the enclosure, the street ended at the ranch-style building.

At an intercom strapped to a zinc-coated pole, Sally pressed the push button. Static squawked from the speaker box. She leaned forward and whispered into the perforated grill, "Hello?" Sally tried again, this time louder. "Knock, knock! Who's there?" After hearing only the wind, she yelled, "Pick up the goddamned phone!" The white noise peaked before fading to an eerie silence.

Watson waved both of his arms at the closed-circuit camera. "This is a secure facility. Someone should see us out here." He added dancing up and down to his manic repertoire.

"Look around," Sally said, appraising the fractures in the pavement and the fence's corroded terminal posts. "This site hasn't been occupied for quite some time." She crouched in the road by a stagnant mud puddle. "No tread marks—coming or going."

In the hedge fronting the chain-link fencing, Kenya tugged free a fallen sign. The blue enameled emblem flaked on the edges, but he could distinguish the yellow *AGGRESSOR BEWARE* banner, eight white stars, and a neutron cloud whirling about a rocket's nose cone. "This used to be—"

King's urgent yapping interrupted his obvious deduction. The pacing animal had caught movement within the compound.

Sally, clinging to the mesh, shrilled, "Kenya!"

A young boy stood near the missile base's periphery, no more than twenty feet distant. Diminutive in stature, he wore blue jeans and a blue-and-black plaid shirt.

"Eddie," Kenya moaned. His fingers clawed the diamond links.

The boy beckoned for them to follow. Then, with a sly smile parting his lips, he turned aside. His red Converse Chuck Taylors skimmed the overgrowth without disturbing a single blade of grass.

"Eddie, come back!" Watson called in anguish. "Ed, I'm sorry!"

"Kenya, that is not your brother." She tried to draw him away. "Remember the little girl who was, in truth, a mountain lion? It's just another trap."

"No, it's not!" Watson catapulted his backpack over the fencing.

Sally, distraught by his angry-child countenance, questioned, "What are you doing?"

Kenya had already mounted the fence and was draping his jacket over the barbed spools. The sharp tips gashed both of his forearms as he swung past the obstacle and dropped to the other side.

"How do *we* get in?" Sally inquired, shaking the robust padlock. The U-shaped shackle snapped open, and the brass body fell to the roadway. "It wasn't even locked." When she gazed up, Kenya was gone. The wheels protested as Sally rolled the cumbersome gate wide enough to squeeze into the gap.

Sally and King pursued Kenya across the trampled landscape to the brown-and-tan building. Security lights and squeaking, wind-driven turbine vents were installed on the roof. She squinted through the windows, making out bunk beds, paper-cluttered workstations, a functional kitchen, and a rec room equipped with a big rear-projection TV, a videocassette recorder, and an extensive VHS tape library. Handmade quilts lay on worn couches. On a table in the austere dining room, five red-and-white dice rested upon a forfeited game of Parker Brothers *Risk*. Sally found the interior's forlorn atmosphere depressing.

Kenya tarried in front of a detached garage. The broad hood of a yellow school bus glistened through the sectional door's dirty windows. In a voice void of any emotion, he said, "Eddie wants me to go inside. He loves me. My brother is ready to forgive me." Watson tore himself from Sally's grasp and rushed into a side entrance.

The storage shed reeked of oil, bird shit, and cobwebs. CAMDEN COUNTY PUBLIC SCHOOLS lettered the sides of the long vehicle. Within the ghost bus, the phantom boy watched the flesh-and-blood man wiggle the double doors and then, frustrated, yank on the rear emergency exit. About to crack the glass with his own fists, Kenya glimpsed a lever on the dashboard. He raced to the driver's side, slid open the pane, and pulled the handle. The two doors parted with a baneful hiss. Watson climbed the three steps and stood before the thirteen rows of seats.

Halfway down the aisle, a shadow sat upon the same bench that once cushioned Edward Watson's decapitated torso. Lightheaded, Kenya used the seat backs to brace his jellified legs. He toddled down the constricted passageway. The student's hands cupped a teacher's present—mayhap a tortured frog or an apple stolen from her own desk.

"Eddie, I didn't mean for you to die," Kenya bawled. "It was only a stupid joke." As he inclined forward to better see his brother's unholy gift, his testicles' hyperstimulated nociceptors transmitted sickening waves of nausea to his central nervous system. Watson doubled over and fell down. On the rubber matting, Kenya felt a round object in his pocket. He extricated T. D. Johnson's bizarre gift—*"Kenya, the eyeball is what it is, an eyeball"*—from his trousers and mashed the ocular prosthesis to his right eye.

Through the visual distortion of a fisheye lens, the "boy on the bus" mirage evaporated, replaced by the solid metal bows of an M924 military transport's camouflaged canvas cover. A cream-colored snake, devilish horns raised above its callous eyes, emerged from underneath the troop benches, leaving J-marks on the dusty floor. When Kenya pushed up to look for Edward, the sidewinder bit his shin. He screeched in agony as the pit viper coiled to strike again. Watson crab-walked away from the rattlesnake until his spine thwacked the front panel.

Sally, hearing the ruckus, sprinted to the garage and twisted the doorknob—*locked.* She scavenged in the rubbish for anything hard.

The venomous serpent, shaking its rattles, slithered along the truck bed.

She swung a lead pipe at the chicken-wire glass that was fitted into the utility door. Sally reached beyond the window shards and turned the latch.

King darted into the shed, snout down, tracking his master's scent. The dog hurdled into the cargo vehicle's open back and ripped the sidewinder in half. His ears flopping wildly, the Rottweiler flung the tail onto the cement.

"Kenya!" Sally called, clambering across the transport's tailgate. She kicked the fanged head under the seat. "Were you bitten?"

"I thought I saw my brother."

"I saw him, too."

He grabbed a strap to stand upright. "Get me out of here. This truck gives me the creeps."

Outside the garage, the sun fell past the horizon. Beneath the soft, diffused light, the uninhabited missile base appeared haunted.

Sally detected his limp and had him sit on the sidewalk. "Let me see."

Kenya winced as he dragged up his pant cuff, but his mouth remained clamped shut. Blood trickled from two puncture marks located four inches above his ankle. The limb was swelling.

Sally poured water on the wounds. Her tremulous hands belied the placidity of her voice. "We need an ambulance." She took out her iPhone and, scowling in disgust, returned the brick to her pocket.

"We're here for a reason," Watson grunted. "Get the Tandoori Box."

Sally removed the black cube from his pack and held it to the injury. When the gadget refused to emit the hum of a gnat or the luminosity of a firefly, she asked, "Am I doing it right?"

"Let me try." No response. He unbuckled his belt. "Ah, it burns."

"A tourniquet will do more harm than good. We can still keep the venom below your heart." Sally got a plastic pail and sat him upon it. "Regulate your breathing and stay calm. Wait here. I'll be right back."

"Don't leave me," Kenya begged through shivering teeth. The epidermis surrounding the trauma had turned a ghastly shade of summer sausage.

Sally bundled her jacket around his shoulders and kissed his perspiring brow. She bobbed her head toward the building where the brass grommets of a threadbare American flag clinked against a flagpole. "The intercom had power. Maybe there's a working phone." Sally snatched the lead pipe and dashed between a pair of mushroom vents. Clammy air flowed out of the nearest duct.

Unable to gain entry at a set of brown French doors, Sally hammered with her fist. Not expecting an answer, she slashed the screen out of the window frame and used the rod to break the pane. Indoors, in a large room, a bikini-clad pinup girl grinned from a February 1992 RIDGID tools wall calendar. A mechanical device reverberated underneath her boots. Black binders and plastic-sleeved informational sheets covered the wraparound desk. The swivel chairs afforded a clear view of the front gate and fence through tinted bay windows. Radios, telephones, video monitors, fax machines, intercoms, computers, and a gun rack of M16 rifles packed the Security Control Center. An elevator was accessible by an orange door in the far wall. A dense film of dust masked everything. She lifted each of the telephones' handsets and twiddled tuners on the shortwave radios—all dead.

A long corridor divided the center of the building. Sally threw open every door in a vital search for medical supplies. Communication and maintenance equipment equipped the rooms. Opposite the kitchen, she saw a doorway marked INFIRMARY. A paper-wrapped examination table and a bulb-operated blood pressure sphygmomanometer equipped the office. Sally thrust aside a short stool and made a beeline to the glass medicine cabinet. Remedies lined the shelves. She jimmied the door. The long-gone doctor had thoughtfully adhered a strip of tape labeled RATTLESNAKE ANTIVENOM to a vial of crotalidae polyvalent. She nabbed a pack of disposable syringes and exited via the main security doors.

Sally hastened across the yard, shouting, "Take off your pants!" On the walkway, she guesstimated the proper dosage and, pulling the plunger, filled the syringe's barrel with antivenom. "Hold the flashlight steady."

"Christ, Sal!" Kenya groaned as she jabbed the hypodermic needle in his gluteus maximus. "What are you trying to do, kill me?"

"Stay still," she said softly. "You need hospital care. This stuff expired when I was busy learning my ABCs." Sally told him of what she had seen in the Launch Control Support Building.

He gripped her arm. "The elevator must descend to the level where they launch the missiles. We have to go there."

"We're not going anywhere until we get you medical aid. The military mothballed this missile range long ago." Sally stared at him. "What's the big rush?"

"Does this place feel decommissioned to you? To me, it *feels* deserted. Like somebody left and forgot to turn off the oven."

"How can this be? The government doesn't make clerical errors when it comes to our nuclear defense system."

Kenya inquired, "Ever heard of a 'broken arrow'?"

"The film starring John Travolta?"

"No, not the dopey movie," he responded. "I'm talkin' real nuclear weapon mishaps. There are recorded cases of B-52 airplanes colliding or dropping their atomic payloads by accident.

In 2007, cruise missiles were mistakenly loaded onto a bomber. The nuclear warheads weren't reported missing for two days."

Sally capped the syringe and stored it with the antivenom in the knapsack.

"FUBAR occurs more times than you'd believe in the armed services." Kenya stood and steadied himself on the garage. "You said air was blowing from that duct?" He hobbled to the rounded vent and stuck his hand beneath the galvanized hood. His fingers came away moist. At the other vent, Watson released a leaf. The strong vacuum sucked it up against the grill.

Sally helped him into the Launch Control Support Building and set him on one of Security's revolving seats. King lay upon the olive-and-white linoleum. "Hold on," she said. Her torch's yellow beam jiggled as she moved along the hallway. She returned with an aluminum crutch.

"Thanks. You didn't tell me about the vibrating floor."

"Sorry, I was in such a hurry to save your life, I may have neglected to mention it."

Kenya planted the crutch's rubber tip on the checkered tiles and pressed his ear to the underarm pad. "I hear heavy machinery. It could be the generator that powers the exhaust fans. Does the elevator work?"

Sally opened the orange door and pushed the control panel's singular button. A beefy direct-current motor in the attic spun into action. Shaken by the whirring, she quailed, terrified of what monsters might rise from the darkened shaft. The empty car clanked to a halt.

Kenya opened the collapsible doors: first, the gate that blocked people from falling to their deaths, then the actual elevator door. He bowed at the waist and drawled, "This way, m'lady."

King padded into the rectangular cab, turned around, and faced them.

"How are the generators still functioning after twenty-four years?" Sally asked. "The fuel would have run out or oxidized."

Watson treaded onto the nonskid plate. "We've witnessed odder oddities on this trip."

She stood firm. "If the shaft is flooded with water, we'll drown."

He wigwagged the crutch at the caged ladder anchored in the floor. "We can always climb down."

"Yeah, like that worked so well before. We're not leaving King up here by himself." Sally hopped aboard the industrial elevator. "Fuck it. Sometimes you just gotta have faith!" She hit the only button.

Kenya tilted his penlight upward as the lima-bean-green walls glided by. The motor's grinding ceased when the car bounced to a standstill. They were forty to sixty feet underground. He shoved the scissor gates open and stepped into a junction between two tunnels. The beam illuminated a fire extinguisher, a table, and stacks of chairs. A pallet of C-rations, water drums, and a stretcher were stowed behind the ladder. The dank area stank of diesel fuel, sweat, and mildew. Watson flipped the light switch on and off, cursing at the unrelenting gloom.

Sally had to amplify her voice to be heard over the din. "Where to?" Jittery, she peered into the duskiness. "The noise is coming from thataway!"

They came upon a massive blast door. Kenya pumped the long lever. After the greased locking pins yielded from their sockets, the balanced hatch popped open with a whoosh of pressurized air. The five-foot-thick steel slab pivoted easily on the giant hinge.

A breeze blew Sally's hair as they crossed a drawbridge into the Launch Control Equipment Building. The racket inside the gargantuan reinforced concrete dome deafened. She handed him the earmuffs that were hanging on a nail. Air-conditioning units, biological, chemical, and radiological filters, compressors, expansion tanks, electrical distribution panels, and the loudest culprit, a truck-size diesel generator, were bolted to a platform suspended by four twenty-foot-tall hydraulic shock isolators. Green and yellow status indicator lights glowed from various monitoring apparatuses.

Kenya fumbled his penlight as a klaxon horn blared a warning. The shattered lamp rolled over the floor's edge. "Go, go, go!" he yelled into her ear. They sped past spinning red emergency lights into the connecting tunnel.

The adjacent blast door, reduced in size yet weighing six tons, was just as sturdy. On the open hatchway's exterior, a cartoonist had inscribed the words *BEEP, BEEP!!!* above an illustration of the plucky Road Runner strapping his foe, Wile E. Coyote, to the "Fat Man" atom bomb. The sign affixed to the cement capsule's doorframe stated: NO-LONE ZONE. SAC TWO-MAN CONCEPT MANDATORY.

The man, woman, and dog passed through the eight-foot-thick shell onto another ramp. King-size shock absorbers also suspended the Launch Control Center.

The LCC was congruent in shape and volume to an eighteen-wheeler's cargo trailer. Harsh shadows shifted in unnerving patterns as Sally directed her flashlight about the space. When she turned on a wall switch, the room flooded with light.

A brown curtain provided privacy for the lavatory. Navy blue curtains screened a cot. Green racks of electronics crowded every wall. Bulky, black electrical cables snaked into the ceiling. Beige insulation dampened much of the clamor. There were two desk-like structures in the narrow room: the nearest on the right side and the farthest on the back wall. Both units twinkled with rows and columns of lights and switches. Heavily upholstered missileer's armchairs were positioned in front of the archaic consoles. The red chairs, outfitted with seat belts, resembled fighter jet ejection seats.

An open binder lay upon the deputy commander's station, a ballpoint pen atop one page. A black handset coiled above a 1950s-era rotary dial. Welded to a shelf of classified documents, a red safe stenciled with white paint advised: ENTRY RESTRICTED TO MCCC AND DMCCC ON DUTY. A pair of brass combination locks secured the steel box. Embedded in the LAUNCH ENABLE CONTROL GROUP panel, the six CODE INSERT thumbwheels were turned to sequences of numbers and letters. Beneath a hinged Plexiglas cover, the ENABLE switch was fixed to SET. Beside a keyhole, the arrow on the LAUNCH knob pointed to OFF.

Twelve feet away, at the commander's console, maroon guards shielded the toggles designated for arming the rockets. The ARMED light for one of ten missiles, LF2, glared bright yellow.

"I'm not likin' the looks of that," Sally said, signifying a digital clock fitted on the intimidating WEAPON SYSTEM CONTROLLER rack. The numbers displayed 01:10:08. While they viewed the seconds counting down, the TIME TO LIFTOFF changed to 01:09:59.

"We need to shut off the power!" Kenya cried. They hustled through the junction into the LCEB. He punched the red emergency button on the generator. The mammoth dynamo coughed, sputtered, and stalled. Thankfully, the annoying klaxon horn quit. The lights extinguished, then flickered back to life as a backup generator—this one, seemingly inaccessible—came online.

When they returned to the Launch Control Center, the yellow LF2 missile status light switched to red when the countdown clock ticked under the hour mark.

"This isn't happening," Kenya stammered. He staggered along the computer racks, withdrawing a magnetic floppy disk from a vintage IBM drive. The eight-inch diskette slipped from his fingers and fell to the floor. "This crap is primeval!"

"The launch knob is set to off!" Sally exclaimed.

Kenya looked for a way to open the control panel. "Something is bypassing the switch. A circuit board may have shorted out. Or a rat chewed on the wires. We've got to escape!"

Sally gripped Kenya's arm. "If there is a liftoff, and there is a retaliation, this bunker is engineered to take a direct hit by whatever the Russians or Chinese stock in their arsenals. There's no place on Earth safer than right here, right now. Plus, we have no idea where the rocket is located. Or if this," she jutted her chin out at the clock, "is even legitimate. What if we're experiencing a test sequence?"

Kenya dug his thumbs into his eyes until he saw the rings of Saturn. "Does this *feel* like a test to you?"

"It *feels* like the end of the world," Sally answered. She shook his shoulders. "You can make it stop."

"How?"

"You're a programmer." Sally pretended to type in the air with her clickety-clacking fingers. "Do your thing—write the most bitchin' code of all time."

Watson circled the room, examining everything closely. The software engineer moved the deputy commander's missileer chair to the MONITOR AND ALARM rack. He slid out the heavy-duty keyboard. After ritualistically cracking his neck and blowing on his fingertips, Kenya flicked on the CRT monitor. A command prompt and a blinking cursor appeared upon the smudged monochrome screen. When he typed DIR, a list of files and directories scrolled downward. With his left hand, Watson indicated the shelf above the console. "Find books that might help."

Sally dumped the three-ring binders into a pile. She sat alongside King and leafed through the tabbed dividers. Sally held a book underneath the CODE INSERT thumbwheels. "USSR," she read. "The Pentagon aimed our fuckin' missile at the fuckin' Kremlin."

"Moscow. Figures. Is there a default code?" Kenya questioned. "A target that won't initiate World War III? Some unpopulated island in the middle of nowhere?"

"P7," Sally answered.

"What's P7?"

"God knows, but the entry doesn't list a city next to it."

He thumbed the CODE INSERT dials to P7.

She compared the liftoff clock and her wristwatch. "We only have thirty minutes."

"There are millions of lines of code. There's no way I can keep it from firing." He whammed the keyboard back into the frame.

Sally surveyed the expanse. "What about these electronics racks? Let's destroy the motherboard!"

"Which one?" Kenya inquired, prying on the metal panels. "These security fasteners require a special screwdriver."

As though hearing a dog whistle, King jumped to his paws and yowled.

"What is it, boy?" Watson asked.

The Rottie yelped three more times before loping over the drawbridge and through the blast door.

Kenya held a palm out to Sally and said, "Give me your flashlight. I'll see what's bothering him."

The animal waited in the elevator. Kenya shut the gates and used the crutch to press the button.

As the car inched up, Sally questioned between the bars, "Kenya, where are you going?"

"You'll be okay down here if there's a problem."

Sally, her mouth letting loose a volley of unladylike language, started to scale the ladder.

The cab stopped on the ground level. Kenya opened the gates and hollered, "I love you!" down the shaft. His passionate declaration echoed hollowly as he slammed the orange door and slid a small file cabinet in front of it. *It'll take a while, but she'll eventually break free.*

Watson saw the M16s in the gun rack. *I may need one of these.* He seized the carrying handle and slung the rifle onto his back. With the crutch jammed under his armpit, Kenya limped out the doorway. His leg no longer burned like the dickens, but the limb moved as stiffly as a stove-length of firewood.

The wind had picked up. Far ahead, by a volleyball court's drooping net, Johnson's ID tag reflected from King's collar. *My dog knows where to go. He always knows where to go.* A furtive shadow passed in front of him. *Eddie?*

Kenya ignored King's agitated yips and focused the torch's ray across the field of whipping grasses. Still as a corpse, a boy sat upon a white, conical contraption. *Eddie!* When he approached the child, he discerned—nothing much surprised him now—that his brother hovered twelve inches above a UHF antenna.

"Say something!" Watson begged, reaching out with both arms to the translucent form. "Please tell me you forgive me!"

The specter—its vacuous eyes as Stygian as the pits of Hades—motioned for him to come close. Mentally and physically exhausted, Kenya keeled over on a clump of weeping lovegrass. He reclined on the delicate tuffs and stared wonderingly into his own private universe. *There are so many other worlds to discover.*

Kenya felt no pain. The hefty weapon was a comfort. *My punishment, my redemption.* He ran his fingers along the smooth stock and ridged cartridge clip. His ribs rose as he inhaled the sweet fragrance of gun oil. The muzzle smelled of a Fourth of July celebration on the Delaware River—the final time his parents took him and Edward to watch the fireworks extravaganza.

As the demon nodded approval, Kenya depressed the release, pulled the rifle's charging handle to the rear, and let go. With a rewarding snap, the bolt loaded a round into the chamber.

The M16 was a long gun. By stretching his arm and extending his throat, Watson managed to wedge the barrel into the soft pocket beneath his jaw. Lastly, he flicked the selector lever from safe to full-auto and hooked his thumb around the trigger. *Soon, every one of my questions shall be answered.* The man who had been through so much slowly exhaled and shut his eyes. *Ed-ddwaaaard. . . .*

"Pickles," a voice said gently. "Get up, Pickles. There is work for you to do."

He heard the safety click on and sensed the gun sliding from his grip. *Eddie is the only person who called me by that nickname.* Kenya's eyes flew open. The imp had vanished. His younger brother, still ten, and shrouded in the same new clothes he had died in, tossed the machine gun into a ditch. This boy, unlike the malignant spirit, appeared substantial. His hair moved in the wind, and his feet were firmly set upon the ground.

"Come with me," Edward ordered. He offered Kenya his hand. "There's not a moment to spare."

The man on the crutch and the boy holding him up leaned into the gale.

Kenya was overjoyed to be with his brother, yet he was skeptical. "Are you real?"

"It's all real," Edward responded in a youthful tone, "and it's all an illusion." He called attention to a tall motion detector on the property's boundary. "That, big brother, is as real as life gets."

"What is? Where are you taking me?"

"Must you ask? Your assignment, Pickles, is to forestall Earth's ultimate battle between good and evil—*Armageddon.*" Edward spread his arms and frowned in discontent. "At least until Zion sorts out who's in charge." The boy scooped up a length of rebar and gave it to him. "Don't waste time attempting to prevent the rocket from launching. That window of opportunity has expired. Concentrate on defusing the warheads."

Kenya felt overwhelmed. His brain hurt. "How will I do that?"

Eddie giggled, an innocent sound that moved the heavens. "If I knew how to do it, do you think I would be here talking to you? I never got to finish the fifth grade!"

They neared a depression in the terrain. A block of concrete, with contours similar to a steam locomotive's cowcatcher, sat on three rusty rails.

"I've got lots of questions. Are you—" Kenya realized his brother's hand had slipped from his embrace. He groped at the wind. *Edward had disappeared.*

Recessed in the cement, two round, hinged hatches abutted the missile silo's indestructible Launcher Closure Door. The bigger, human-sized hatchway had no latches. Watson used the iron rod to unbind and bend the five lugs securing the smaller port. He raised the blue weather cover. Blowing sand sifted onto a combination lock. He heaved on the pit vault's handles. *Locked.* Kenya stood and wailed out his brother's name. The howling gales muffled his desperate pleas. *Numbers. Digits. I saw six digits somewhere. Portland? It was when I went to find Sally in New York City.* He opened his wallet and shuffled the assorted cards: library card, driver's license, outdated Blockbuster Video card, and a deck of credit and debit cards. Watson sailed each rectangular piece of plastic into the whirlwind, almost giving up before holding high the singed World Trade Center ID badge. He kissed Meredith Wong's picture and flipped over the card.

On his knees, Kenya entered Meredith's ID number: 071504. He spun the combination dial three times to the right, stopping on 7. Next, left one full turn past 7, pause on 15. He mopped sweat out of the corners of his eyes and turned the knob to 4. Watson bit his lip and tugged the handles. The A-plug's lubricated O-rings freed from the pit with a satisfying pop. He disengaged the locking bolt and activated the hydraulic pump. The Personnel Access Hatch eased up on two brass cylinders. Kenya jumped into the shaft, leaving his crutch and King behind.

The ladder dropped to the first level. There on a cylindrical barricade, Kenya entered the same digits into a combination lock inset in the top. *Nothing.* He started from scratch. *Gimme a break, Johnson.* As kids, Kenya and Eddie had played "I Spy" together. They'd used a simple "letter to number" cipher to hide encrypted notes around the yard for each other to find. When unencrypted, 071504 spelled "god." Kenya pictured King, reversed the letters, entered 041507, and prayed. A motorized jackscrew retracted the ponderous B-plug down the tube. After a considerable delay, he expanded the ten rungs and descended into the silo's NO-LONE ZONE.

Fortunately, the lights in this hot and humid bunker worked. Banks of fluorescent fixtures brightened the ringed configuration of the Upper Equipment Room. Standby generators whined, and lead-acid batteries hummed underneath his feet in the Lower Equipment Room. Kenya's shoulder rubbed the curved launch tube as he jostled past husky electronics racks. The floor, comparable to the layout of the Launch Control Center and Launch Control Equipment Building, was framed with pneumatic isolators. Synced to the timer in the LCC with a thick copper cable, this TIME TO LIFTOFF clock exhibited: 00:15:34. He hunted for a way to shut it all off. Dozens of fat connector plugs fed into the D-BOX. Instructions glued to this distribution cabinet assured the missile could be "Safed" from explosion by using the "Safing Key" to remove the "Locking Pin" from the "Safing Receptacle." The SAFE-ARM status bulb was unlit. Watson explored his pockets for a key, only feeling T. D. Johnson's linty prosthetic eyeball.

Kenya opened the barn doors hinged into the launch tube. Practically within reach, the glossy side of the seventy-one-foot-long and eight-feet-in-diameter LGM-118 Peacekeeper intercontinental ballistic missile mirrored his pallid visage. He used a hand crank to lower a ramp. On the edge of the scaffold, Watson lay his cheek upon the fourth stage—the deployment module, which accommodated the ten reentry vehicles. None of LF2's cone-shaped hundred-kiloton nuclear warheads contained scoops of vanilla ice cream. The Kevlar skin felt warm—*alive.* Kenya, remembering how he had nearly blown his own brains out with the M16 rifle, impelled himself away.

Close, but out of touch, an access panel centered the four-foot-high final stage. A two-person work cage fitted with spotlights dangled from an electric winch. Tool belts hung on the safety railing. The rig ran on a circular track encompassing the cap of the pitch-dark silo. Watson dove into the cage, turned on the lights, and pressed the right arrow push button. Bit by bit, the work cage traveled in the correct direction. At a standstill, he used a tethered Torx driver to extract the dozen screws from the convex hatch, finally able to untighten the twelfth one, which fell to the bottom of the silo. Kenya set the small doorway aside.

Fuel and oxidizer tanks, axial and attitude control engines, lithium-ion batteries, communications systems, and guidance computers crammed the compartment.

Kenya had avoided accepting his inexcusable role in Edward's awful demise by immersing himself in his favorite hobby—electronics studies. The long days and solitary nights spent locked in his childhood bedroom, tearing apart electrical appliances, enabled him to locate and disconnect the umbilical cord linking the ordinance battery to the multiple independently targetable reentry vehicles. This small act—popping a thirty-nine-cent purple plug—rendered the MIRVs harmless and, therefore, staved off an all-out nuclear war.

The exalted Forever Tree survived extinction, and thus, the human race lived to see one more day.

Our hero smiled in relief. *Child's play.*

An earsplitting siren ruined his moment of triumph. Rotating beacons radiated ill harbingers across the entire facility. At the base of the missile's canister, a rocket motor fired into a water reservoir tank. Wisps of scalding steam crept up the smooth casing of the rumbling first stage. The metal basket jangled against the wall.

Time to scram, Sam. Watson stabbed the left arrow push button, bounded over the railing, and sprang through the barn doors before the work cage bumped the scaffolding. Lights pulsed as electronics in the Upper Equipment Room awakened. The liftoff timer flashed: 00:04:58. In panic, he clung to the ladder's side rails and hoisted himself to the surface three rungs at a time.

"Let's go, boy!" Kenya shouted at King. He disregarded the crutch and fled to the Launch Control Support Building.

Sally met them halfway there and leaped into his arms. "Did you stop it?"

"No!" Watson glanced at the launch site. From a pole-mounted speaker, a mangled tape recording blared a garbled warning. "There's no time. Get to the bunker!"

In the Lower Equipment Room, explosive cartridges pressurized the huge piston assembly attached to the four-foot-thick Launcher Closure Door. With a bang, the one-hundred-ton lid flew off the missile silo, smashed the perimeter fencing, and, plowing an ugly furrow through a farmer's field, missed a grazing heifer by a tail's length.

"Get down!" Kenya bellowed. He collared King and threw himself on top of Sally.

The ballistic gas generator ejected a burst of steam powerful enough to cold launch the two-hundred-thousand-pound Peacekeeper ICBM two hundred feet in the air. A shower of Teflon-coated urethane pads peeled from the weapon's sides as it shot out of the steel canister. The igniting solid propellant blasted an enormous flame from the first stage's single engine.

A tremendous roar trembled the earth. Acrid, white smoke enveloped the compound. At an altitude of one mile, the rocket yawed due west soon to be swallowed up by clouds.

Sally, uncovering her ears, sobbed. "We're doomed!"

King's fevered barking turned their heads. The overgrown pasture was on fire. A fierce tempest drove the inferno toward them.

"Come on!" Sally yelled, uprooting Kenya from the firenado's path.

The conflagration chased them into the ranch house. As the tiny elevator lowered into the depths, the windows in the Security Control Center blew out of their frames. Protected within the concrete egg, the survivors listened to the overhead structure crash to the ground and burn to cinders. At last, all was quiet.

"Will the Russians retaliate?" Sally asked anxiously. "Should we stay in the bunker? There's plenty of food and water."

Kenya drew her close and grinned. "Let's linger in the pits of Hell for a little while longer."

On what remained of a forgotten missile range, the man and woman stood arm in arm, appreciating the scenery. A large dog sat by them, scratching its head with a hind leg. The devil winds (Santanas were unusual for this time of year) had lulled, allowing the Big Pine Volunteer Fire Department to swiftly put out the wildfire. To the east, past the black swath shaved across the bucolic countryside, our solar system's fiery ball rose over the regal White Mountains. This Monday morning, except for some smog on the horizon and a weather forecast of patchy rain, turned out to be a glorious day indeed.

Epilogue

TODAY, ON THIS MOST CRITICAL MORNING, Kenya overslept. The alarm was set for midnight. He hadn't heard the radio turn on, and evidently, neither had Sally. As Watson tossed aside the comforter, Omega meowed in irritation and leaped off the bed. At the windowsill, Kenya opened the green Woodward Supermarkets bag and reviewed the newest Tandoori Box image. In dismay and then sudden horror, Kenya realized what his eyes were seeing. He jerked Sally awake.

Sally's golden locks fell in swirls onto the pillow. "What's going on?" she asked groggily.

"Look!" Kenya thundered in her face. He paced the bedroom, shaking the photo in the air. "We are so, so fucked!"

The last four months passed quickly for Kenya Watson, Sally Green, and her mother, Nora Green. Before long, the specific—*and most peculiar*—details of their journey to the West faded from memory. By and by, the fresh travel photographs of the Ancient Bristlecone Pine Forest overwrote the dreamy mental image of the Forever Tree. For example, one day at breakfast, while Sally spilled the pulpy seeds from a ripe pomegranate into a bowl, she questioned, "Kenya, do you remember where we bought the delicious pomegranates? Those seeds were sweet and juicy. These sour things taste like cardboard." Kenya, also not remembering the Edenic grove of fruit-bearing trees, stared at the bright red pomegranate as if she held a red onion.

Their active lives returned to a semblance of normalcy. Sally was rehired at Delphic Industrial Sciences as a senior business analyst. Kenya still worked with her at DIS; however, he had interviewed at several businesses, the most recent of which—a pharmaceutical company developing chewable medications for pets—appeared promising.

Nora resumed teaching archeology at the university. Thus far, she has not found the correlation between the black box on her Mayan drumhead and the shiny men in her nightmares, but on her frequent archeological digs, whenever she rests with a shovel in hand, she takes a moment to gaze into the great unknown. Professor Green will never abandon her hopes of exhuming the link bridging primitive humans with extraterrestrials.

The Greens' world-famous cabinet of curiosities now housed four new items of real significance: a blue glass medical eyeball, a fork attachment fitted for a prosthetic arm, a melted plastic ID badge salvaged from the World Trade Center, and a slightly radioactive thirty-nine-cent purple plug once used to arm ten multiple independently targetable reentry vehicles. T. D. Johnson's identification tag still hung from King's neck.

And how did the psychic Rottweiler fare? If King was not at home under the tender care of *his* adopted family, the heroic dog volunteered as a therapy animal at a children's center. There, he bathed in unbridled love and attention.

Omega, when not keeping her furry canine friend in line, catnaps.

And on the subject of love—*true love*—Kenya and Sally became engaged. On a balmy night after work in early September, as they ferried to their house on Peaks Island, he dropped to a knee and proposed to her before a group of commuters on the raked prow of the *Bay Mist*. The ring wasn't fancy (there were to be no more winning lottery tickets); nevertheless, she flung her arms around him and avowed, "Yes, I will! Forever!" A week later, Sally learned that she was one month pregnant. The Native American obstetrician, consulting his Viagra calendar and *The Old Farmer's Almanac*, informed his queasy patient with a conspiratorial wink, "By my calculations, I estimate this conception occurred during the Red Moon—a very good omen!" Kenya, thrilled upon hearing the wonderful news, grinned the biggest grin of his life.

Once again discussing the capacity to love—in this instance, *love withered on the vine*—on a brisk afternoon in October, as the autumn winds tore the marcescent leaves from the beech trees, Nora answered a tentative knock on her front door. The handsome, youthful man she'd blissfully married after graduating from college stood on the rubber HOME SWEET HOME doormat. An embarrassed smile stuck on Peter Green's greatly aged face. Sally's father hadn't been butchered by the advertising executive's jealous husband after all (on many a lonely evening, Nora had entertained this homicidal fantasy whilst sipping a glass of red wine), nor had probe-wielding space aliens abducted the graphic artist (chugging a bottle of her finest Cabernet Sauvignon made this remote possibility seem entirely plausible).

Disarmed by his unexpected arrival, Nora invited the man she had shared her bed with for seventeen years inside for a cup of fresh-brewed Colombian coffee.

Pete, munching on a stale almond biscotti, told his side of the story. "I had a typical midlife crisis." He peeked up and smirked. "You may have heard some things about me and a gal at the firm." Nora's spouse went to the fireplace and touched the framed family portrait. "One day, when I was walking down Madison Avenue, I decided to throw my design portfolio in the trash and get the hell out of Dodge. It all had become too much.

I yearned to be reborn." On the sordid streets of New York City, Pete had traded a six-pack of Stegmaier ale for a homeless man's ID cards. Under his new identity, "Carlos" hitchhiked across the good old U. S. of A., paying his way by toiling as a field hand in strawberry patches. Two years in the scorching sun burned his skin to a crisp. His back ached from constant bending. Pete had used forged papers to enlist as an able-bodied seaman on a Liberian-registered cargo vessel. After a decade upon the high seas—free-spirited and unattached—while docked at the infamous "port of death" (now Brazil's industrious Port of Santos), the sailor had fallen extremely ill from an Aedes mosquito bite. Bedded in a rundown hospital on the outskirts of São Paulo, as a class of Portuguese-speaking medical interns had taken turns diagnosing his worsening condition, the penitent deserter had resolved that, if he recovered, he would return home and make amends to those whom he had forsaken.

Nora—not trusting a single word the douchebag sitting before her uttered—opened a kitchen drawer and pulled out Adolf Hitler's long-lost Walther PPK. Sally's mother waved the brain-stained gun while issuing this unveiled threat: "If you ever attempt to contact my daughter or me again, I swear to God, I'll murder you myself. No jury on Earth shall convict me for slaying a dead man." At the kitchen sink window, Nora watched Pete zoom away in his cherry 1965 Ford Mustang. She washed out the coffee cups, saucers, and the tray used to serve the hard-as-rocks Italian biscuits. Nora twisted the wedding band over her ring finger's knuckle and threw the fourteen-karat anchor down the drain. She switched on the garbage disposal and laughed as the blades ground her marriage into chips. To this day, Sally still believes her father is buried beneath a sidewalk in Midtown Manhattan.

On the Columbus Day weekend, Sally and Kenya endured the long drive to Cherry Hill to announce their engagement to his parents. Both clans welcomed her and forgave him with open arms.

Earl treated everyone to platters of grilled lobster and sizzling shrimp at his restaurant of choice, Red Lobster. Kenya, feeling mentally sanguine and physically fit, expressed sincere interest in most of Kevin's college sports stories and wholeheartedly congratulated Jordan on his crowning achievement: a spot in next year's Rubik's Cube World Championship. On the few occurrences when Sally perceived her fiancé tensing at one of Melinda's snide remarks, she gave him a good kick in the shin.

At Dorothy and Donald's house, Kenya and Sally joined the family in the dining room. Cardboard replicas of the Niña, Pinta, and Santa Maria centered the table. Dot's physician had adjusted her psychotropic medications, and she did reasonably well at restraining her evangelical outbursts during Don's political rants. Maggie, attending Narcotics Anonymous meetings, had gained a healthy amount of weight, and her pupils no longer measured the diameter of LSD microdots. "Aunt Flo and her cousin, Red, came to town," she whispered to Sally, her new closest friend. "First visit in three years!" Shelly—the most responsible member of the bunch—had reserved an unoccupied chair, complete with table settings, for little Meg. Over dessert, Kenya made a mental note to find his missing stepsister.

When Sally and Kenya returned to Portland from their "Wild West Adventure," she clipped all the articles referencing the "giant meteorite" or "blazing comet" that thousands of people had spotted splashing into the Pacific Ocean. She pasted everything in a HOW I SPENT MY SUMMER VACATION scrapbook. Conspiracy groups scrutinizing the dozens of uploaded YouTube videos theorized that Washington had inadvertently launched a nuclear missile. World leaders—especially Vladimir Putin and Kim Jong-un—were up in arms. Anti-war activists staged demonstrations outside the White House. The United States Federal

Government denied all these allegations. How could the Pentagon admit to misplacing one of its own ICBM silos?

The piece Sally adored the most, and the page she framed and hung on the living room wall, pertained to her mother's rescue from the high desert. The *Inyo Register* posted this blurb on their webpage:

> *Law Enforcement Rescues Woman*
>
> Staff Writer - Monday, August 29, 2016
>
> BISHOP, CA Today, at approximately 11 a.m. local time, the Mono County Sheriff's Office received a call from the Ancient Bristlecone Pine Forest Visitor Center. Campers near Patriarch Grove reported gunshots. "They were regular as clockwork," Jason Honeywell of Murrieta, age 22, told reporters. "Every fifteen minutes, we heard three bangs. Me and my friends knew someone was in trouble, so we told a ranger." With the aid of a loaned California Highway Patrol helicopter, mounted rangers located Nora Green, age 52, and administered medical assistance for a sprained ankle. After her horseback ride to the parking area, Green declined an ambulance transfer to Northern Inyo Hospital.
>
> "I'm such a klutz," said Green, a resident of Portland, Maine. "Every Girl Scout knows, only a fool goes hiking alone. It was so beautiful, I thought I might get a nice photograph of the Patriarch Grove from up on the ridge. While eating my sandwich, I noticed a rope ladder hanging off the side of a cliff." The professor of archeology at the University of Southern Maine tapped the inflatable ankle brace and chuckled. "I think you can imagine what happened next."

> Questioned whether she had seen any strange lights in the sky as described by locals, Professor Green said dolefully, "Well, when I bumped my noggin in the fall, I probably saw some stars."
>
> The Sheriff's Office did not recover a pistol or rifle in the vicinity. Professor Green denies owning any firearms. "I don't believe in them," she insisted. "Those kids must have been hearing things."
>
> Many thanks to our partner agencies for their assistance in the search.

Each morning, at the stroke of midnight, the Tandoori Box delivered a new photograph. To Kenya, these daily snapshots of his future actions became second nature, akin to eating a big bowl of Froot Loops and afterward brushing the granulated sugar from his food color-stained teeth. Most days, not much of note transpired (or so the itty-bitty cog in the cosmic machine presumed). Sally jumped in when Kenya needed a lookout or an extra set of hands. In addition, Nora, her ankle fully healed, helped Kenya and Sally carry out any missions required to prevent the world from toppling off its axis.

Watson no longer endured the low self-esteem of guilt or the profound regret of remorse for any of the tasks he performed for the Tandoori Box's benefit. In a way, as Sally had implied, he did feel a little bit like a "motherfuckin' angel's assistant." Whether Kenya seeded USB drives loaded with malicious Chinese viruses onto the parking lot of a prestigious law office or hurled a brick labeled *IF YOU DON'T SIGN THE DIVORCE PAPERS TONIGHT, THE NEXT ONE WILL BE A MOLOTOV COCKTAIL* through a bail bondsman's plate-glass window, he rarely gave these transgressions an afterthought.

Kenya prayed for a reunion with T. D. Johnson. In his dreams, his protector assumed diverse personas, the most common character being a middle-aged, one-legged veteran. Watson, walking Portland's busy streets, often stopped to stare at a man's uneven gait or the dissimilar shades of a woman's eyes. While his guardian spirit periodically watched over him from on high, so far, they had not reached out.

And alas—but maybe for the best—Kenya never saw his younger brother, Edward, again.

On Friday, the sixteenth of December, Kenya exited the elevator on the second level of Delphic Industrial Sciences' central office. He experienced a powerful sense of déjà vu as he strolled along the industrial-carpeted hallway. A year had passed, to the day, since the previous holiday party.

This morning, Joyce Benning was not there to greet him. After her termination, Ted, her husband, filed for a legal separation. On probation, the bankrupt human resources director presently resides in her parents' basement.

The two detectives who arrested Joyce had not fared well either. Carter Savage had wrecked his pickup truck while driving home after drinking numerous boilermakers with his partner, Anita Ortega. Early the following day, an angler's propeller had struck a metallic object lying just underneath the misty surface of Long Creek. The Police Department winched a Toyota Tacoma from the water. Savage was strapped into the custom leather seat. Surprisingly, and leading to departmental rumors of suicide, air still filled the Limited's cabin. Detective Ortega had fallen into a deep, fingernail-chewing depression. The chief put his number-one investigator on medical leave. For years, she had harbored a serious crush on her boyish partner, always feeling too weird to articulate her fondness. Anita, during sessions with a notable past-life regression therapist, had determined that in the 1960s, her previous incarnation, "Valentina," had married Julian Savage, the regional sheriff. The first name of the couple's only son? Carter.

Watson omitted a side trip to the breakroom to nuke a frozen entrée in the filthy microwave. He didn't need to. Sally had cooked their potluck dish, a tureen of her mom's delectable Hungarian goulash.

Kenya *was* carrying *something*—a White Elephant. Today, the reusable bag under his elbow did not conceal a plastic, farting ass bank or any other laughable novelty gift. This time, the green sack cradled the Tandoori Box.

Watson entered the meeting room. Most of the employees were sitting in rows of folding chairs. He noticed the brightly striped bowl of goulash on the table. Sally chatted with Frank Walker and Susan Thorpe—by the looks of it, a conspicuously pregnant Suzy Thorpe. Sally caught his eye and shot him a worried glance. Kenya moved closer, curious to hear their conversation. At fifteen weeks into the gestation period, despite Sally's complaints of tight clothes, her baby bump barely showed. Apart from their immediate families and friends, they hadn't divulged their engagement or pregnancy to anybody at the office. *Perhaps tomorrow we'll—*

A meaty palm pounded him on the arm.

"Hey, Doctor Watson!" Russell Fisher nodded at the bag. "What did you bring this time? A coin-operated dildo?"

"You'll just have to wait and see," Kenya replied, placing his submission atop the red-and-green tablecloth. He noted that Russ was empty-handed. "Where's your entry?"

"This season, White Elephant gifts aren't high on my shopping list," Fisher griped. "Valeska and I split up. She cleaned out our bank accounts and flew the girls back to Belarus. I'm rooming with the bums at the YMCA."

"Glad to hear your wife finally sized up what an asshole you are." Kenya shouldered past his wide-eyed "friend" to sit with Sally.

Pamela Cousins, dressed in leopard print and matching pumps, raised her hands and hollered, "Okay, everybody. Let's simmer down!" This year, the administrative assistant experienced emotional and spiritual breakthroughs by attending a series of motivational seminars hosted by guru Toby Rollins. After she had accomplished the highly acclaimed coal-walking activity, as the sympathetic paramedic had bandaged her roasted feet, Pamela had excitedly blurted Rollins' slogan to the gawking onlookers, "If you're not in pain, baby, you ain't livin'!"

A gray-haired man decked in an Italian suit and a Jerry Garcia silk tie sauntered into the conference room. Pamela turned and led the round of applause.

David Hutchings addressed his workers: "Welcome, my friends, to the Delphic Industrial Sciences Christmas party!" Apparently, the Chief Information Officer missed the Human Resources Department's edict directing management to deemphasize religion at company-hosted events. "Thank you all for coming." He wiped a speck of white powder from his nostril. "What a fabulous year we've had! Praise God!"

With his palms clasped together, the silver-tongued devil droned on about increasing overseas sales and his plans to defeat the competition. "With the Almighty's blessings, *and your continuing devotion,* David—*that's me*—will strike down Goliath."

The software engineer tuned out the static. He patted his pants pocket, distinguishing the outline of the latest—*and please God, let it be the last*—Tandoori Box photograph. This morning, as Sally slept, Kenya had gone berserk when he recognized what the stinking image portrayed. Although he hated himself for screaming at his fiancée, he suspected that under the current circumstances, his distress was understandable and forgivable. In the print, Sally had held her prize at Delphic's luncheon party—*a small, black cube.*

Hutchings bestowed December's Pinnacle Award upon his nubile executive assistant, the bubbly Sunshine Meadows. He wished each person a "Happy and Productive New Year!" and bid them farewell. His private jet waited on the runway, ready to fly Sunshine and him to the Caribbean island of Aruba.

Pamela, bravely stamping out the embers of envy and resentment smoldering in her embittered heart, focused on how delightful she had felt as Toby Rollins' medical staff had applied cooling aloe to the rising blisters on her raw feet. Ready for combat, the admin strutted to the midpoint of the space.

Watson's stomach cramped. *The game is about to begin.*

A few months earlier, around the time Kenya had learned of Sally's pregnancy, he and Nora had settled on a solution to rid themselves of the Tandoori Box. Even if his efforts were for altruistic motives, the daddy-to-be was bone-tired and burned-out from the daily grind of serving as Heaven's fix-it man. Watson had no intentions of chucking the boomerang-block in a vat of sulfuric acid or pancaking it in a car crusher. At this year's holiday party, he planned to give the cube away as a White Elephant present. *How ironic.*

Naturally, Kenya doubted their risky idea would succeed. *Why should it?* Last December, what had prompted Shashi Chatterjee to sneak into DIS's conference room and place the Tandoori Box with the other gifts? *Had it been a photograph? Who'd helped him? What had Chatterjee called it—the Best Buy Box?* And the thing that really gave Watson the heebie-jeebies? *If the restaurant owner had also functioned as a do-gooder underneath the auspices of Zion's Maintenance Department, why had he killed himself?* If he ever ran into T. D. Johnson again, he'd be sure to get that sticky question answered. But for now, *right this minute,* he had to change Sally's fate.

Pamela rolled the silver bingo cage to the front. She had reused most of the existing ping-pong balls, only adding three for new personnel and deducting four for those who had quit or had been terminated.

The long parade of wrapped White Elephants plodded along the tabletop. Unpacked bags heaped the floor—all except for Kenya's entry inside the Woodward Supermarkets tote.

"Everybody listen up!" Pamela commanded. "Same as last year, we will play the White Elephant game." She rushed through the rules.

Harvey Grubman, whose zitty complexion had improved during a strict regimen of Proactiv treatments, pointed at the green satchel. "Why is that one still in the bag?"

"It came that way," Pamela responded impatiently. No matter how hard she tried to protect her "happy zone," Grubman always wriggled under her skin. "Any more questions?"

Susan Thorpe, rubbing her distended abdomen, requested to go to the ladies' room.

Pamela, about to turn away, wavered. "Of course, dear. We'll start without you."

Suzy hurried down the hall.

The bingo cage clattered as the administrative assistant cranked the shaft. One after another, the dipper scooped up each employee-labeled ping-pong ball and plunked it onto the metal ramp. "Milton Mumford!" she shouted.

Milt homed in on the gift he desired. He ripped off the paper, revealing Sally's contribution, a Costco-size can of stewed tomatoes. "Oh. . .I get it," Mumford muttered, glaring suspiciously at his coworkers.

Pamela summoned Frank Walker next. In that he had no enthusiasm for taking Milt's lifetime supply of preserved vegetables, Suzy's boyfriend unwrapped a packet of six donut-shaped Weener Cleaner Novelty Soaps.

Gregory Barnes claimed these useful personal hygiene items, and Walker opened a fresh prize, a Boob Beanie.

The fun persisted. Suzy Thorpe returned from the bathroom to win a Honeymoon Survival Kit. Lady-killer Jack Gantz wound up with a Blowjob Bib. Kenya's boss, Marisa Lanka, a yellow chip recovering alcoholic, won a Tequila Shot Gun. The contest went on and on until there were just two items left upon the countertop. As Murphy's law—*anything that can go wrong, will go wrong*—would have it, three players remained: Russ, Kenya, and Sally.

"Kenya Watson!" Pamela sounded off, waving him forward. She was ready for this nonsense to end.

Kenya approached the bench and stood between the Woodward sack and a soft article wrapped in brown paper. He peered at Sally. White as a ghost, she closed her eyes and shook her head in resignation. Kenya untied the brown package. It contained a life-size, anatomically correct, green Alien Blowup Doll.

As Watson paced to his chair, Pamela called Sally's name. In a daze, she took the Woodward tote and clutched the final gift, the Tandoori Box, to her chest.

"Girl, let's see what you won!" the politically incorrect but eminently perceptive Deiter Steuben yelled from the cheap seats. "I'm guessin' it's a bun in the oven!"

Everyone snickered when Sally refused to show her prize. The table was empty. The game was over.

Pamela raised the concluding ping-pong ball high. "One of you didn't bring a gift," she accused. "Don't fret, I had a premonition this might happen." The grinning admin held forth a pair of strikingly repugnant Cat Poop Earrings. "Here you go, Russ. We're out of time."

The portly hardware engineer chortled. "Uh-uh. I get to swap the nothing I got with whatever she's got. Them's the rules. Sorry, babe."

Russell Fisher slipped his pudgy fingers in the handle of the green jute Woodward Supermarkets shopping bag. As kismet deemed fit and proper, the last White Elephant was now his.

TAH, THE ODD, MAGENTA-GILLED CREATURE Professor Green discovered in the shower at the Best Western in Gary, Indiana, twitched her segmented tail in elation and anticipation. The tympanal organs in Tah's legs had picked up the frenetic ultrasonic clicking of Cazz, her lifelong mate. Due to a freak windstorm (and his mumbled miscommunication about where to rendezvous in the event of an emergency), the last surviving individuals of their kind had been separated for months. *I am home,* Tah thought. Her gorgeous iridescent wings shimmered as she soared on a warm updraft into the highest branches of the Forever Tree.

www.ingramcontent.com/pod-product-compliance
Lightning Source LLC
Chambersburg PA
CBHW020256030826
48979CB00026B/1267/J

* 9 7 8 0 9 9 1 4 2 4 8 9 4 *